T0361661

The SEARCH COMMITTEE

José Skinner

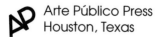
Arte Público Press
Houston, Texas

For Melynda, *por supuesto*

The Search Committee is funded in part by a grant from the Texas Commission on the Arts. We are thankful for its support.

Recovering the past, creating the future

Arte Público Press
University of Houston
4902 Gulf Fwy, Bldg 19, Rm 100
Houston, Texas 77204-2004

Cover design by Ryan Hoston
Cover photo by Tails Kubi / Shutterstock.com

Library of Congress Control Number: 2025930185

Chapter One

The job candidate's flight was due to arrive at 11:33 a.m. and Assistant Professor William Quigley, who didn't teach until evenings on Wednesdays, volunteered to pick her up. The airport, which was surrounded on three sides by sugar cane fields and had ratty bougainvilleas spilling from chipped terracotta pots on its observation deck, looked like something out of a Graham Greene novel. Quigley called the aesthetic "tropical ramshackle," and he intended to use both the allusion to Greene as well as this clever coinage to charm the candidate if the chance arose.

Lest the airport itself be insufficient to convince her she had landed in the tropics, or at least the semi-tropics, lest it escape her that it was March and already 90 degrees and those were real royal palms lining the medians in the parking lot, he had dressed in his best tierra caliente outfit: cream-colored guayabera, bone-toned linen pants, Panama hat and the huaraches he'd bought across the border in Mexico, eight miles to the south. He'd been keen from the beginning to sell the South Texas setting to the applicants, trying to work palm trees and the beaches of Padre Island into the Modern Languages Association ad before conceding to the other members of the faculty search committee that those probably did make it sound too much like they were advertising a vacation resort rather than a tenure-track position in the Department of Languages and Literatures at Bravo University.

He'd written her name in the best block letters he could make, MINERVA MONDRAGÓN, on a flap he'd ripped from a box of copy paper. He felt simultaneously foolish and important as the arriving passengers eyed him and his placard with curiosity. It was unusual for someone flying into Providencia, Texas, to be met by a stranger. But the sign was necessary because the committee had not interviewed her in person at the MLA convention, only later by phone, so no one on the committee knew what she looked like. There was no image of her on the website of the school where she was finishing up her graduate work, or anywhere else on the Internet that he could find. There were several Minerva Mondragóns on Facebook, but none of them could have been her, except for the handful with blank silhouettes instead of pictures. He dared not message any of those because the Equal Employment Opportunity Commission representative had warned the members of the search committee not to contact any candidate through social media.

The stream of arriving passengers slowed to a trickle, petered out. No Minerva Mondragón. How could she have missed him? As he descended the escalator to baggage claim, a slender young woman in a black suit and a pointy-collared white blouse rose toward him on the adjacent steps. (Later he'd learn that the suit, fitted so nicely at the hips and flared at the bottoms, was fashioned after the one Pam Grier wore in the film *Jackie Brown*. A bit of cosplay, perhaps; her CV listed two conference papers on blaxploitation films.) He inched the placard up so she could see it, and when she passed him, she took notice and burst into laughter.

"Yes, yes!" she said, and reached out as if to grab him, although by then they were well separated.

She came back down the escalator to where he stood, sign at his side, feeling his face flush, which deepened the flushing in idiotic circularity.

Her fingers were as small and slender as the pencils he gave his students for filling in the bubbles on their faculty evaluations, but the strength of her grip conveyed a self-confidence that put him paradoxically on alert and at ease. His own hands were disproportionately meaty and shaking a small woman's hand in his mitt always felt awkward. Certain Latina colleagues in Languages and Literatures greeted each other, and sometimes other men as well, with cheek kisses, and that seemed to him a much more appropriate way of greeting a woman than seizing her hand. He believed the kissers were all Mexicans or Mexican Americans or other sorts of Latinx. He couldn't tell the difference. He'd been living on the border and teaching at Bravo almost three years now and he still had a hard time solving for the X. Among themselves, they could distinguish Puerto Ricans from Cubans, say, and even Monterrey Mexicans from Mexico City ones, based, he supposed, on accents and lexicon. He'd heard New Mexicans like Ms. Mondragón were a breed (though he'd never use such a word!) unto themselves: tough mountain people as opposed to the gentler, more pastoral Tejanos. But what did he know?

"You don't have any other luggage?" he asked, eyeing the leather bag slung over her shoulder.

"No. I was just down here looking for you."

He supposed it made sense for her to have gone to baggage claim to look for him; indeed, that's where he'd headed when he realized he'd missed her coming through the arrival gate. But he felt it somehow put him at a disadvantage for her to have been actively looking for him instead of staying upstairs, bewildered, waiting to be found.

"Is that sugar cane out there?" she asked as they walked to his car.

"That's right!" he said, sounding a bit too surprised, he supposed, but most visitors had no idea what that monstrous grass was.

He told her about the conflict between the sugar baron and the airport people over burning the fields at the end of the year. "They have to burn at night when the airport's closed.

Even so, the airport people are always lodging complaints with the FAA over the soot."

"Sugar baron? Sounds like a powerful man." She had mobile lips poised to say wry things, and she seemed to find the idea of a sugar baron amusing.

"That he is."

He was tempted to add that every so often Mexican immigrants hiding in the fields got burned alive in the fires. The sugar people insisted they gave fair warning by announcing the impending burns on megaphones from all corners of the fields, and that they couldn't help it if the immigrants mistook this for the Border Patrol trying to frighten and flush them out.

But Quigley didn't mention this macabre detail. One didn't want to distress a candidate with such stories.

"It's like a Graham Greene novel down here sometimes," he said. He stopped, turned, spread his arms. "Just look at that terminal—tropical ramshackle. Total Greeneland!"

"Greeneland" had become a literary term for a Third World place where nobody knows whom to trust; but he didn't go on about it, for fear of appearing pedantic.

The plan was to take her to lunch and then to her committee interview. After the interview, he'd drive her to her hotel so she could rest. Another committee member would pick her up at seven and take her to dinner, to which everyone in the department was invited. Quigley was disappointed that no faculty member had responded to his invitation to join them for lunch, but ever since the dean's office stopped picking up the tab, attendance at these meals had dropped off drastically. He could only hope a few would show up for the dinner. He couldn't since he taught on Wednesday nights.

"Where would you like to go to lunch?" he asked. "We have a lot of good Mexican places around here."

"Mexican? What a surprise."

How to evaluate her wryness? As a sign of easy collegiality, or as a potentially troublesome sarcastic streak? Again, he wished one of the more experienced committee members had deigned to join them. Personally, he believed he liked her attitude. Wasn't her response better than a fake and overeager "That sounds great!"?

"Well, more like Tex-Mex," he amended. "The real thing's across the border. Margaritas made with fresh limes. Seven kinds of mole."

"Let's go there."

"To Mexico?"

"Sure, why not? Is it too far?"

"No, no, it's not far. Eight miles."

He surprised himself by hanging a left on Alamo Avenue and heading south to La Reina, the city on the Mexican side. It was as if her suggestion were a challenge he couldn't refuse.

"There's a great place right on the plaza down there called Las Brasas," he said. "They make the guacamole right at your table with the biggest, butteriest avocados."

The thought of the guacamole didn't entirely melt the tension that had dropped into his stomach like an ice cube as soon as he had accepted her challenge, because how could she not know about all the trouble in Mexico with the drug cartels? Yet it had been months since he'd heard anything about shootouts in La Reina, so he supposed things were relatively calm at the moment. At any rate, he would refrain from mentioning the situation, just like he'd refrained from telling the hideous story of the "wetbacks" (as many locals, Hispanic and Anglo alike, blithely persisted in calling immigrants from the south) burned alive in the sugar fields. She was the third candidate they'd interviewed for the position, and if she turned it down as the first two had, the provost would likely not authorize a new search and perhaps eliminate the faculty line altogether, and Quigley's committee would be seen by the whole department as having failed.

"A plaza in Mexico," she said, almost dreamily. "That sounds nice."

She settled into her seat with a sensuousness that sharpened his caution. He was single and available, but as the EEOC rep had twice reminded the search committee, it was forbidden to inquire into a candidate's marital or relationship status. If he was to learn about her own availability, he'd have to wait for her to reveal it. Meanwhile, he hoped she realized that the seats were leather—a Bravo academic's salary wasn't great, but how bad could it be if a young assistant professor could afford a new, fully loaded Camry with leather—okay, leatherette—seats?

"We'll park on this side and walk across the bridge. The plaza's only two blocks from the river."

"This is better than driving across?"

It is if you like to see the hubcaps still on your car and your job candidate's bag in the trunk when you come out of the restaurant, Quigley thought.

"It's faster," he said, which was also true.

Quigley had recently learned that "plaza" didn't just mean a town square. It was also the drug cartels' word for "turf." This new knowledge had darkened his image of the La Reina plaza proper, which he had known as a sunny place filled with balloon-men, shrieking children, strolling lovers and old guys getting their shoes shined. Now he pictured it empty, with machine-gun-toting narcos circling it in their black SUVs, though surely this was an exaggeration. What did he know? He hadn't been to La Reina in over a year.

"Actually, maybe we don't have enough time," he said, slowing, looking for a place to turn around.

"That's too bad," she said, sounding genuinely disappointed. "That must be one of the attractions of working here? The proximity to Mexico?"

"Well, for me it was. Is. What the hell, let's go." He sped up.

She laughed the same merry laugh she'd laughed on the airport escalator. He felt himself blush again.

"The situation doesn't frighten you?" she asked.

"The situation?" he said, the ice cube recrystallizing.

"The narco situation. The 'exceptional situation,' as some politico from down here put it."

Okay, then, she'd brought it up, not he. "Oh, you have to keep your eyes open. But that's a good idea wherever you are, right?"

Quigley didn't want the "situation" to frighten him. If he became frightened, it would keep him away from Mexico altogether and indeed rob him of one of the main perks of working at Bravo. Ms. Mondragón was right, it was a definite benefit to be able to pop over to Mexico on weekends or after work, maybe even get a cool summer place in the mountains around Monterrey or Saltillo. True, he hadn't been to Mexico in months, but not, he told himself, because he was scared to go. He'd just been awfully busy this semester with service work—search committee work, for example. Heck, even the seasonal Texans, old retirees from Iowa and Minnesota who came south every winter, still ventured there, though in much reduced numbers from previous years. Rumor had it that the State Department might soon issue a travel warning for all of northern Mexico, but that hadn't happened yet. The job candidate wanted to visit Mexico, and it was his job to show her around, get her interested in the area. So, yes… Let's go.

Chapter Two

As befit a candidate for a position in Border Studies, she peered intently at the currency-exchange houses, the bulk clothing warehouses, the used car lots—all those border enterprises that thickened on either side of the road as they approached the bridge. He refrained from sharing with her his thought that any number of them might be involved in laundering drug money.

"A lot of blood banks," she observed. "Quick cash for the migrant journey north."

A moment of silence as Quigley considered this. Then he pointed to a sign in front of a doublewide trailer: ¡Bienvenidos, Hermanos Transmigrantes!

"Is that some kind of migrant welcoming station? Pretty bold, if so. What might the Border Patrol think?"

"No, no, that's for people heading south," she said. "See those cars in the lot? The ones with the chains? They're being towed all the way down to Central America, and these transmigrante places are where they get the manifests for transport through Mexico."

Her actual writing involved borders not in any geopolitical sense but as "sites of cultural liminalities," as he recalled from her dissertation abstract, whose title, if he remembered correctly, was *Red Oni, Blue Oni: Transposing Tropes of Domestic Power in La Familia Burrón*. She'd included the first couple of chapters of the dissertation in her application, but he hadn't read much beyond the abstract; he took its promise to show how "nomadic and hybridized forms of critique could provide a transdisciplinary gaze at transcultural worlds" as a warning to back off. Culture studies wasn't his field, and he didn't want to wade into a bog of jargon. (As committee member Charles DeWitt had quipped, trying as always to live up to his surname, the poppier the subject, the boggier the analysis.) The actual subject matter seemed entertaining enough, though. *La Familia Burrón* was a popular Mexican comic book about a lower middle-class family in Mexico City, and oni referred to certain Japanese mythological figures featured in manga and other Japanese pop culture. The mother in the Burrón family was a perfect personification of red oni—impetuous, defiant, full of wild schemes—while the diminutive father was quintessentially blue—level-headed, serene and often caught off-guard by his wife's antics. Truth be told, the only question he or anyone else on the committee would have about the dissertation was whether it would be finished by the time she'd be hired in the fall. She'd completed her coursework and passed her comps at the University of New Mexico's Department of Comparative Cultural Studies, but the dissertation was still a work in progress, so she was therefore abd, all but dissertation.

The very word "liminalities," along with the fact that *La Familia Burrón* was a comic book, was bound to set off a few in the Languages and Literatures old guard at Bravo, who grumbled that these new fields—Border Studies, Culture Studies, Gender Studies, Queer Studies, Masculinity Studies, Fat Studies—didn't belong in their department, or in any other for that matter. But since the position had been the idea of the chair and the dean—two men, both named Garza, of one mind in so many matters that faculty often referred to them collectively as the "chean"—there was nothing the old guys (and they were all guys) could do about it. It hadn't helped that Quigley, in a discussion about the new position at a department meeting, had spoken of "border" as a "floating signifier," because then they must have imagined the new hire floating around on her signifier ready to land on their toes with any number of new courses of her concoction. What if she proposed, say, a course on the border between Romantic and Modernist literature? That would make neither the Romanticists nor the Modernists happy. No, when the old guys thought of the word "border," it was best for them to think it meant *this* border, the border near whose bridge Dr. Quigley and Ms. Mondragón were now parking, the border that imperceptibly flowed rather than floated: the Rio Grande.

Quigley inhaled the smoky smell of Mexico. Not a fragrant smoke—more like burning tires. Whenever he heard some oil-patch Texas politician rail against government regulation, he felt like inviting them to smell the unregulated odors of Mexico, eat the frankenfish from the polluted Rio Grande, visit the not-exactly-built-to-code slums on the hillsides of La Reina and otherwise enjoy the many delights of a country operating under what he understood to be a minimally functioning government.

"If we're gonna walk across, I'd better change shoes," she said.

He opened the trunk for her, and she bent over to change from heels to flats. She grabbed his arm for balance. That strong grip again.

They followed a ramp onto the bridge. Scads of people were crossing on both sides, the American authorities inspecting the vehicles coming in.

She paused on the bridge to contemplate the river. "The water's so green," she said. "And clear."

"Looks refreshing, doesn't it?" Quigley said, sweat prickling his scalp. "But I wouldn't drink it."

"Of course not."

What a silly thing to say, Quigley thought. "Don't drink the water!"—that tired old cliché about the Third World. (Come to think of it, wasn't "Third World" politically incorrect now? Or just geopolitically obsolete? "Underdeveloped" or "developing" sounded so paternalistic. "Emerging," down-right larval. You could just say, bluntly, "poor countries," but poor for whom? Forbes' second-richest man in the world that year was a Mexican, the telecommunications mogul Carlos Slim.)

"By the way, you might want to put your phone on roaming," he said. "Or turn it off. As soon as we cross that marker, the calls are international."

"The satellites are that accurate, huh?"

"Yeah. Well, not quite. There's a Dreamer who got deported and dumped down here—one of those kids whose parents brought him to America illegally, you know, undocumented, when he was little—and sometimes you can see him pressed up against the fence here on the Mexican side, that corner right there, talking on his cell to his friends and family in the US. He can get reception right in that spot. The US is the only place where he has friends and family, poor guy. I had him in one of my comp classes, before they deported him. He doesn't even speak Spanish."

He felt a clutching at the cuff of his pants and jerked his foot back.

"What is it?" she said. "Oh! Children!"

Three tiny, stained hands mushroomed their way through the gaps in the bridge deck and opened, palms up. He had forgotten about the child beggars who somehow managed to crawl along the bridge's trestle. Though you couldn't see their faces, you could hear their high-pitched supplication. As always, Quigley didn't know whether to acknowledge the oppressiveness of charity by not giving—and risk appearing callous—or give and risk being seen as naïve and self-congratulatory. Minerva delved into her shoulder bag; taking his cue, he searched his pockets for change, making sure to hold back quarters for the turnstiles, their only barrier before entering Mexico.

They pressed coins into the little palms and watched the hands clamp shut and withdraw.

The guardhouse at the end of the bridge on the Mexican side stood empty.

"Nobody to check our papers, ey?" she said.

"Nope, no I.D. needed to walk south across the bridge," he said, feeling, as he always did when crossing like this into Mexico, a kind of giddy elation at the freedom of it. No documents—that was the upside of no regulation. Just waltz right in.

"Crossing back into the US, that's different," he added.

"Oh, goddammit."

"What?"

"You didn't bring your passport, did you?"

"No."

"Neither did I, but I think you're supposed to have a passport now to re-enter the States."

"I think you're right. It used to be so easy. Say 'American' and they waved you in."

It was a post-9/11 thing, this passport deal. He'd overheard a colleague outside his office door recounting to another professor how he'd forgotten his, and the border agents, in trying to decide whether to let him back in, had peppered him with questions about his place of birth, Fairbanks, Alaska. "They wanted to know what kind of birds were native to the area. I said, 'penguins!' and that did it. Penguins are a southern hemisphere thing and there's not a penguin within 10,000 miles of Fairbanks, but I knew that was what they wanted to hear."

"No offense, but you *are* a US citizen, aren't you?" Quigley asked her.

"Of course."

Problem was, Quigley thought unhappily, she looked plenty Mexican enough to hold them up on the way back. How long of an interrogation would the CBP officers subject her to? Would they now be able to get lunch, through US immigration and to the meeting with the search committee on time? Dammit, he hadn't had time to think this little jaunt through and here they were.

"They'll ask you where you were born. Then they'll ask you what birds you have there."

"Birds?"

"Native to your area. This is a big birding area down here, and it's expected that visitors know their birds. What can I say?"

"Birds. I was born in New Mexico, so let's see. We have a lot of hummingbirds. I used to know some of the names. Rufous. Plain-capped star-throat."

"Plain-capped star-throat hummingbird. That's pretty impressive."

"What's your bird?"

"I'm from Minnesota, so I'm going to say bald eagle."

"You have bald eagles in Minnesota?"

"Sure. Around the lakes."

"Well, you can't get more American than a bald eagle, I guess."

As was typical these days, a small tank sat at the foot of the bridge on the Mexican side, a black-masked soldier manning a machine-gun in its turret.

"That guy is supposed to reassure you," Quigley said. "He belongs to the Marina, the Navy. That's the only branch of law enforcement the federal government down here trusts."

"Navy guy in a tank? That's odd. And why the mask?"

"It's so the bad guys can't identify him."

"That's not very reassuring, when the soldiers are afraid of the bad guys," she said with a little laugh.

"I'm not actually that up to date on the narco wars, I'll admit it," she added. "I'm based mostly in Mexico City, which has been mostly spared the violence."

"Mexico City, home of... what's your comic book family?"

"*La Familia Burrón.*"

A fat taxi driver with grease on his chin flung open the back door of his cab and gestured for them to enter. Quigley shook his head. The only cabs you were supposed to take in La Reina were those your hotel or restaurant called for you. Other cabbies could rob or kidnap you. The taxis without license plates were especially suspect—those were "pirate" taxis, his students had told him. And all cabbies, without exception, should be suspected of being (speaking of birds) "falcons" for the narcos. The falcons kept the gangsters apprised of comings and goings of interest. Naturally, he wasn't about to tell the candidate all that.

"It's close enough to walk to," he told her, peering over the people in front of him, hoping the towering palms ahead marked the central plaza.

The sight of a middle-aged winter Texan couple in bright shorts waddling into a pharmacy advertising a "Viagra special!" put him at ease. Under a palapa across the street, another gringo sucked on a gigantic goblet of neon-green drink.

"The plaza's right up here," he said.

He was wrong. There was nothing in sight but a seemingly endless string of pharmacies and dentists' offices.

He turned to two boys in identical red T-shirts sitting on a cinderblock wall. "*Por favor, ¿el restaurante Las Brasas?*"

"*A la vuelta*," one of them said, with a languid sweep of his arm.

Sure enough, there it stood, around the corner, the kitschy faux castle he remembered from his previous visit.

"Those kids are probably no-nos," he said. He'd heard about them from his students.

"You mean, *ni-nis*? As in *ni trabajan ni estudian*," Ms. Mondragón corrected, "they neither work nor study?"

"Oh, right, yeah."

So that she'd realize he did in fact know something about them even though he'd goofed the name, he added, "Their ranks have swollen since people stopped coming across from the US to shop. Notice how empty the pharmacies and souvenir stores are. And the maquila factories prefer to hire women. There's no work for these guys, and for whatever reason they don't go to school. Oh, jeez, you just said you know the term, I guess I'm mansplaining."

"No, not at all."

He might have added that they were easy recruits for the narcos, and that the larger the narco presence the more the violence and the fewer the shoppers, in a vicious circle, but he reminded himself again to keep things positive.

"A great thing about Bravo is that it offers in-state tuition to Mexican students from the three border states of Tamaulipas, Nuevo León and Coahuila," he said.

"How did that happen?"

"The Texas legislature approved it years ago, before all the anti-immigrant hysteria. That was also around the same time that it approved the name Bravo for the university. We used to be Rio Grande Junior College, you know, before Austin decided they needed a System school with a lot of Hispanics to pump up diversity stats and bought the campus. Since the Mexicans call the river the Bravo, it was seen as a friendly gesture. Also, you must admit it sounds kind of peppy."

"Bravo U! And you!"

"Bravo, you passed! Bravo, you're a college graduate!"

As they approached the dark entrance to the restaurant, she said, "Well, I don't think kids like the ones back there can afford tuition, in-state or out."

She was probably right about that unless they were already on the narco payroll. If they were, it was unlikely that they had in mind a college career. What was that narco motto he'd heard from his students? *"Mejor cinco como rey que cincuenta como buey."* Better to live five years like a king than fifty as an ox. It had become a running joke in one of his freshman classes, the students warning him if he piled too much work on them, they might just have to abandon their ox-like student lives for the kingly ones of drug dealers.

And speaking of kings, the restaurant's staff made them feel like royalty, holding open both massive doors and ushering them to an enormous, round table from where they could watch the cooks tending to whole goat carcasses splayed on spits above open fires. A great deer-antler chandelier hung above their table, casting a shattered amber light on the fancy-faceted glassware. A group of portly, cigar-smoking businessmen sat at another table, guffawing, the remnants of their feast crumbing and staining the thick white tablecloth. It all seemed quite normal. Still, his testicles clenched unpleasantly as he recalled his students telling him of the local narco boss, Tony Tormenta, visiting restaurants like this one. First, an emissary would precede the big man to announce to everyone his imminent arrival and kindly ask them to stay, but to hand over their cell phones. (Of course, they *had* to stay; Tony didn't want anyone leaving and blabbing about where he was dining.) Then the narco would arrive and feast with his henchmen at his leisure, the outside of the restaurant surrounded discreetly by two rings of policemen in his pay, the inner ring consisting of state police and the outer one of more expendable municipal cops who would bear the brunt of any attack by rival gangs or the Marina. As soon as he left, the phones were returned to their owners and everyone was free to leave—their checks taken care of, naturally, because the narco was a gentleman. Well, that would be one way of not having to pay for the candidate's lunch, not to mention a good excuse for arriving late for the committee meeting. The levity of the thought relaxed his balls a little.

A dignified old waiter with a napkin draped over his forearm approached. *"¿Qué les servimos de tomar?"*

Ms. Mondragón ordered a margarita. Now what was he supposed to do, he wondered, tell her it wasn't good form for a job candidate to order an alcoholic beverage, especially at lunch and before her interview with the search committee? Warn her that they made the drinks super-strong here because they'd learned that gringos come to Mexico expressly to get smashed? Or... join her? Okay, meet her halfway. He ordered a beer. They had two hours before they were expected on campus. She was enjoying herself, and that was a good sign, was it not? He'd been to two candidate lunches at the Casa del Tamal near campus, both for positions in rhet/comp, where the candidates' cool regard of the velvety décor, zero interest in knowing what *tlacoyos* or *chalupas* were, and general inattentiveness to the conversation practically screamed, "No, señor, I'm really not the right fit for this Taco Tech! I'm gonna take that position they offered me up at U of X." And he'd been right: they both withdrew their names from consideration after having wasted everybody's time by going ahead with their remaining interviews and teaching demonstrations.

And then there was the medievalist and the long-eighteenth-century guy, who after accepting positions at Bravo had promptly put their courses online (always encouraged by the administration) and peeled off to Austin and New York, respectively, craftily maintaining mailing addresses in Providencia and showing up at convocation or the occasional department meeting to give the illusion they still lived in the area, which they were nominally required to. Minerva did not strike him as that sort, not just because she was a woman and Hispanic (though, let's face it, weren't women on the whole more responsible than men, and wouldn't a Hispanic woman feel a special responsibility toward her people?) but because, unlike those two sour grifters, she simply seemed like the kind of charismatic teacher who'd want to engage students face-to-face at Bravo.

"I've never walked into Mexico," she said. "Only driven or flown. That felt weird."

"Weird?"

"Like you just stroll into this whole other country, and nobody knows."

"Now you see why after people commit a crime, they immediately think of disappearing into Mexico."

"And some of them do, right?"

"Oh, sure. But it's not that easy. There's always Interpol and that sort of thing."

"Interpol. Those guys only go after major criminals, don't they?"

"I guess so. Maybe."

Actually, he knew nothing about Interpol. On the news, whenever an American fugitive was caught in Mexico, Mexican authorities handed him over to their American counterparts on the bridge. Quigley always assumed the Mexicans must have had some kind of outside help—Interpol?—because when did they catch anybody on their own? Impunity was the word in this country. He had recently seen a headline on a Mexican paper in a Providencia convenience store, *"¡Impunidad de juniors!"* and had gathered that the article described how the children of the privileged—"juniors"—were immune from punishment for their crimes. He'd mentioned this to some of his students, and they had concurred with his interpretation as well as with the sentiment of the article, agreeing that the privileged in Mexico were indeed so immune, because they enjoyed *prepotencia,* the arrogance of power. Another slang term for them was in fact *"prepos,"* his students said, and he wondered if the echo with the American "preppy" was more than a coincidence.

But now he'd gone and done it, brought up the subject of crime himself. There was a compulsion to do so whenever Mexico was mentioned these days.

"Some people like the grilled cabrito kidney," he said, returning to the menu.

He himself was repulsed by its urinous tang, but organ meats were always a good subject-changer. Everybody liked to talk about tongue and tripe and the time they accidentally ordered offal at an exotic restaurant.

She placed the menu at the table's edge. "I'm going to be boring and go with the chicken enchiladas."

"Good choice."

She touched her tongue to the salt on the lip of her glass, took a sip. "You could really disappear down here if nobody was looking for you."

"If nobody's looking for you, why would you need to disappear?"

She laughed her trilling laugh again, wagged a finger at him, took another sip. She was down to the ice. And if she ordered another? Would he make it his business to intervene? "You who seem like you know your movies, did you ever see *A Winter Tan?* Actually no, never mind." Maybe it was *he* who shouldn't be drinking this early.

"What's it about?"

"Oh, just this comp lit professor who disappeared into Mexico. A student of Paul DeMan's, incidentally. The deconstructionist?"

"Yes, I know who Paul DeMan is."

A little eyeroll tone in her response, he thought, which she then tried to mitigate with a bright, "Any good? The movie."

"No, not really."

"What happened to her?"

"The professor? She disappeared."

"Why'd she come down here?"

Ms. Mondragón now seemed to be having fun not letting it lie, so he might as well bludgeon it down bluntly. "She was a second-wave feminist who decided to commit her life to sexual adventure and fucking as many Latin lovers as possible."

"Oh. I see."

She poked her lime with her straw, while Quigley, surprised at himself, studied his own lime quarter and tried desperately to think of a new direction for the conversation.

"Well, excuse me as I also disappear for a minute."

She got up with the help of three steadying fingers to the table, hoisted her bag over her shoulder and headed, presumably, to the ladies' room.

Chapter Three

This is what she remembered: the old waiter saying, *"Por acá, señorita,"* and gesturing toward a hallway tiled floor-to-ceiling in blue tiles, an aqueous passageway that made her woozy—woozy, what a great word. Now she placed her steadying fingertips against the cool wall. Strong margarita back there. Bad girl. She was making young Professor Quigley nervous. But what a doofus! That goofy Panama hat with its way-wide brim, the polished huaraches. The doofus from Duluth, Minnes*oo*ta. His accent and anxious demeanor reminded her of William Macy in *Fargo,* though from his name alone she'd inevitably pictured Tom Selleck in that forgettable Australian western *Quigley Down Under.* She shouldn't have egged him on about *A Winter Tan,* and she hadn't actually been offended by the way he described it, or about his supposing she didn't know who Paul DeMan was, not really. Still, he probably did need to be more careful about how he spoke in front of job candidates.

As she searched for the lady's room, an idea for a paper popped into her mind: a semiotic analysis of the various designations for women's and men's rooms. In establishments like this, the signifiers must surely be *"Damas"* and *"Caballeros."* *Damas* with perhaps a lady in a hoop skirt carved on the door, *Caballeros* featuring a nobleman on a horse. The restrooms in the biology building at her school were—of course—designated simply ♀ and ♂. Back in Providencia, Texas, there must be a hunters' bar with Pointers and Setters.

No *Damas* here, or *Caballeros*, either, that she could see, so she pushed on an unmarked door, which flew open so easily she would later wonder if the two boys on the other side hadn't pulled it open. Were the boys waiting for her, or did they just happen to be there? Had the old waiter set her up? Was the whole thing premeditated or a crime of opportunity? These were questions she would soon be turning over and over in her mind, in the darkness of her abduction. What was certain was that she found herself in a delivery area of some sort that opened into the alley, face-to-face with the two boys that Quigley had asked for directions.

The one closest to her, a ruddy, wide-faced kid with hair like dry sisal rope, yanked on the door, but it had latched shut behind her.

"Ah!" he said. Mock surprise, or real? The boy behind him, fox-faced and darker, held a dirty rag to his nose; his eyes were glassy.

She pounded on the door, but no one opened. The boys hung back, the rag's sharp odor of epoxy cutting though the greasy smells from the dumpster. Fox-face ogled her shoulder bag as he sniffed his cloth.

She headed purposefully to the alley. Hyper-aware now of her surroundings, she sensed them behind her. Any closer and she'd be forced to spin and engage, before they had a chance to grab her. A green taxi came lurching down the cratered alley, and she hailed it. The driver, hunched turtlelike to regard the boys, seemed to understand her predicament. She went around and got in behind him.

What was he waiting for? "*¡Vamos, ya!*" she said.

And then she was fumbling for the inside door handle to get out, but there was no handle, and the boys were sliding in beside her, crushing her against the door. She jammed an elbow into the ribs of the one next to her, and then she saw it, a nasty-looking little tarnished pistol, waving in her face.

The ruddy boy forced her to the floor with simian strength while the one with the gun shouted at the driver, "*¡Vámonos, cabrón, métele, métele!*" The taxi took off with a leap. They kept her down, elbows and knees digging into her, a hand stinking of solvent grinding the side of her face into the grimy floor. They showed her the pistol again, pressed it to her cheek, said "*¿Eh? ¿eh?*"

She remembered what her martial arts teacher, her sensei, had said about cats: they might be small, but just try holding one when it doesn't want to be held. But a cat didn't understand what a gun was, and this was the kind of ratty gun that looked like it could go off all too readily in the unsteady hand that held it.

So okay, okay, I won't move, you little shits, you fucking little shits, and she stayed down there, immobile, staring at their white Nikes, the adrenaline compelling her to memorize every detail: the eight eyelets, Velcro upper straps and, curiously, the laces on their left shoes untied, probably a gang sign. A rusted-out gouge in the floorboard showed pavement speeding below them, and from the steadiness of its blur, she guessed they were on a highway, headed out of La Reina.

Chapter Four

Quigley watched clouds of smoke rise from the griddles and regretted having brought up *A Winter Tan,* not to mention describing it so crassly. (Good lord, at least he hadn't added that the woman in the book/movie was killed in the end in a Mexico City hotel by a jealous lover.) He was beginning to regret this whole jaunt to Mexico, really. When it became clear that no one else was going to join them for lunch, why hadn't he just taken her to the student union for a taco and then fobbed her off on a grad student who would tour her around the campus until it was time for the interview? This was all way beyond the call of duty. He wasn't the search committee chair. Heck, he was the most junior of all its members.

Well, at least she was relaxed and seemed to be having a good time. Probably her first visit to a campus as a job candidate. She wouldn't be so cavalier if she'd been on the market for as long as he had back in the day, applying for dozens of tenure-track positions over three years while toiling away on various campuses as an adjunct. His Bravo interview had been his sixth campus interview, and by then he knew the ropes. One thing you learned was not to keep your hosts waiting, and she was sure taking her time. Then again, she'd been traveling all morning, and it was none of his business what she was doing in the *Damas* room.

He ordered the enchiladas suizas for Dr. Mondragón and the cabrito stew for himself and waited for her to return. *Ms.*

Mondragón—she was abd, he reminded himself, and until she finished that document, she was not yet a Doctor of Philosophy. Now it occurred to him that it would probably be a good idea for someone on the search committee to call her dissertation chair to confirm that she would have the dissertation finished and her Ph.D. in hand by Bravo's hiring date, as the regs specified. Any doubt about her ability to do so wouldn't bode well for her candidacy if someone really wished to press the point.

He eyed the melting rocks in her glass and recalled her unsteadiness as she had gotten up. Was it possible she didn't need this job, having already gotten an offer from another school, but had decided to take advantage of the free trip and drinks? That sort of thing was rumored to happen. He'd always suspected it was a story concocted by guilty-minded search committees who sometimes did the opposite: invited applicants for campus visits while already knowing they were going to hire an inside candidate.

Or, having gotten a glimpse of the area, maybe she'd decided she didn't want the gig and believed she might as well kick back? His gaze penetrated the smoke and came to rest on the art deco façade of the Capri Hotel across the plaza. He envisioned a drunken afternoon with her, ending up at that hotel. Career ruined—his career. Insane.

A younger waiter trundled a cart to their table and started preparing the guacamole, cleaving the avocados in two with one rounded motion of his knife, flicking the pits out and scooping the flesh with an equally smooth movement, then chopping the onions and cilantro into the yellow-green mound. He wished she were there to admire the dexterity of it all. Had she gone outside to smoke, maybe?

By the time the old waiter arrived with the food, he was frankly worried. He didn't have the Spanish to fluently ask the waiter to send a woman into the ladies' room to see if she was okay, but he tried. The waiter agreed, *sí, sí,* but as Quigley watched his goat stew get cold and the old waiter attend other tables, he realized the man must have misunderstood or blown him off.

He strode down the blue-tiled hall to the restrooms, knocked on the *Damas*, called her name. No response. Called again, louder. Nothing. He looked around, saw nobody, so he cracked the door and called, "Dr. Mondragón. Ms. Mondragón. Minerva!" Silence.

He couldn't phone her, even assuming she got reception in Mexico, because he'd accidentally left his cell phone in his car, perhaps unconsciously fearing pickpockets. If he had her number, he could maybe call her from the restaurant's land line, but he'd entered it on his cell and couldn't remember it beyond the 505 area code. To get the damned number, he'd either have to go back across the bridge to his car, or call Esmeralda, the department's administrative assistant, from the Las Brasas phone and explain what was happening.

There was something hellish-looking about the restaurant now—its dark, heavy furniture, the naked, splayed kid goats on spits dripping grease onto hissing embers, the smoke, the ghoulish old waiter to whom he had no other choice but to speak again: "*¡La señorita! ¿Dónde?*"

A couple of other waiters heard him; amused scorn crossed their faces. It was plain to them that the young woman had walked out on him, and that the best thing for him to do was to quietly acknowledge the fact and proceed alone with his lunch with as much dignity as he could muster. Or, what the hell, let him make a scene and embarrass himself further—the customer is always right. Their faces returned to serious.

The old waiter touched the dark bag under his eye and tilted his head to the front door, signaling them to go out and look around the street. He turned back to Quigley and held his thumb and forefinger an inch apart—"*un minuto.*" Quigley took his seat and watched the waiter go into the kitchen and return with a short, dark woman who undid her apron as she proceeded down the blue-tiled hall. Quigley got up and followed them.

The woman came out of *Damas* and shook her head. *"No hay nadie."*

"¿Dónde? ¿Dónde?" Quigley knuckled his head.

A man in a suit came out of the men's room, and Quigley accosted him. *"Señorita, chiquita. ¿Usted ver?"*

The man regarded him with shiny, skeptical eyes, and brushed by. *Otro gringo borracho.*

The old waiter's eyes cut to an unmarked door. Quigley pushed it open. A delivery area opening onto an alley and the street.

"You're saying she came out here?" he said in English. "Is that what you're saying?" He started out to the alley. "Just walked away? Disappeared, like she said she was going to do? That's crazy. That's fucking crazy."

"La cuenta," called the waiter.

He stabbed the *"un minuto"* sign at the waiter and went on. The hot, fetid alley was empty, the side street it led to nearly so. Just one taxi, whose driver held his hands out in a "where to?" gesture. But he remembered again his students' warning that the taxistas were all "falcons," spies for the narcos. Better not even ask the guy if he'd seen her. Quigley circled around to the plaza, which was also nearly abandoned. He asked a pair of shoeshine boys sitting in the dense shade of an ebony tree if they'd seen an *"americana, chicana,"* and they gaped at him and shook their heads.

The old waiter had followed him and now stood in front of the restaurant with his arms crossed. Next to him stood a solid-looking man with a goatee and a shaved head. The solid man approached Quigley.

"The check, sir," he said with a silver-edged smile.

"The check, the damned check. Well, how much do I owe? I'm looking for someone. A woman, this tall, slender, dark hair. Dressed in black. I *can't* have lost her. She's the candidate!"

"The candidate?"

"Yes, the candidate, the candidate! She's been kidnapped, or something. She's gone!"

The solid man's brow wrinkled. "I shouldn't make too much scandal, sir."

"You shouldn't? *I* should. The police. The police need to look for her. And who the hell are *you*?"

"Police? No. No, no. The police would be a mistake."

"Why? You're trying to protect the restaurant, aren't you?"

"They'll take you to the delegation for questions. They'll arrest you."

"Arrest *me*?"

Something told him the man might be right. Quigley had gotten the idea from his students that the Mexican police were to be avoided at all costs.

"They'll detain you. Sir, you should come back inside."

"And do what? She's not there, we've already looked for her."

A police car nosed its way into the plaza by the side of Las Brasas. The man's eyes darted from Quigley to the patrol car and back to Quigley.

"We'll look for her. You must go home. Where you park?"

"On the US side of the bridge. We walked across. Now you're saying I should just *leave?*"

The patrol car purred up next to them and stopped. The solid man made a click of disappointment with his tongue. The cop at the wheel stared at them with oily, porcine malevolence. The old waiter slipped back into Las Brasas.

Quigley had taught a section of sophomore literature the year before, a special topics course of his own devising, English Writing in Mexico. It had covered works by Greene, Porter, Lawrence, Lowry, Kerouac, Burroughs, McCarthy and other English and American writers with novels set in Mexico. "A sinister place" was how Burroughs described the country, and hell-in-paradise was Lowry's formulation. The main character in Lawrence's *The Plumed Serpent* opined that "Mexico had an underlying ugliness, a sort of squalid evil," and a Mexican jailbird in McCarthy's *All the Pretty Horses* summed up McCarthy's own jaundiced view of Mexico as a place where "evil is a true thing." Quigley's students neither objected to nor endorsed these condemnations, and of course these opinions did nothing to discourage the kids from coming down here with some frequency, to visit relatives or to shop or to party. It was difficult to get them to generalize about the country. They knew that the police couldn't be trusted, that corruption was rampant, the poverty depressing. But he couldn't see them calling it an evil hell.

Well, good for them. But right now? In that semi-deserted plaza hammered by the sun, its newspaper kiosk blaring bloody headlines about the violence (*Six Decapitated Bodies in Monterrey!*), the oily policeman watching him with his piggish eyes while this other man was warning him to leave the country following the disappearance of an innocent young woman he had made the mistake of bringing here? Oh, Quigley felt the evil, yes, he did.

The solidly built man beckoned to a taxi, but it veered away from them. He whistled, and a second, apparently braver, one pulled up. The cop watched. The man opened the door for Quigley and told the driver, "*Al puente.*"

Chapter Five

As though he could no longer trust his eyes, Quigley turned to scrutinize every woman they passed, even those too heavyset or colorfully dressed to be Minerva. He wouldn't have trusted the solid man's urgency, either, if not for the fact that the man had hustled him off without asking him again to pay the check.

"Go home," the man had insisted as soon as the police appeared. "We'll look for her."

It was cowardly to leave. He should tell the taxi driver to circle around, he should keep looking for her. Hell, he should tell him to drive straight back to the plaza and he should tell the cops, "Look, assholes, there's a woman missing, *una americana*, and I don't care who you really work for or what your deal is, I want you to find her," but he didn't know how to say all that in Spanish, and even in English the words sounded laughable. He imagined the cops asking him to come to the station to file a report, but the last thing you wanted to do, according to his students, was get in a Mexican cop car, much less go down to the station with them. Likely as not, they'd turn the tables on him and then he'd be one of these gringos you occasionally read about in the papers, locked up for weeks and even months in a Mexican jail without a hearing. Then what good would he be in finding her?

Besides, the driver's instructions were to take him to the bridge, and Quigley sensed the driver was going to obey the

man who gave them. The taxi drove up to the bridge turnstiles and the driver, still looking stolidly ahead, asked for six
dollars. Quigley gave him a five and four quarters, and the
driver returned to him one of the quarters and pointed to the
turnstiles. The day a cabbie gives you fare money back to
make sure you get where you're going, now that's a guy who
wants you to get there. On the other side of the bridge, a gigantic American flag billowed in the breeze, and Quigley
thought, *There. Over there I can get help.*

He weaved his way between the pedestrians trudging
over the bridge, cut in front of the customs line, and in his
haste to get to the CBP agent stepped over the yellow Wait
Here/*Espere Aquí* line before the agent had finished interro-
gating the woman in front of him.

"Step back, sir," the agent, a beefy woman, barked.

Quigley retreated two steps, bumping into the som-
breroed man behind him, who glared at the gringo in a panic
to get back to his country.

The agent lifted a latexed finger. "Now come forward."

"The person I was with, she got lost. She—"

"Citizenship."

"Hers? American. US. She was with me and then—"

"No, sir. Yours."

"American. US."

"Passport."

"I didn't bring it."

The CBP agent regarded him heavy-lidded. The line behind him lengthened.

"Sir, how do you expect to cross international borders
without a passport?"

"Just go ahead ask me about the birds in my hometown.
That would be Duluth, Minnesota."

"Birds?"

"Whatever you ask people to prove they're from where
they say they're from. Look, I have a driver's license. Won't
that do?"

"Where do you work, sir?"

"Okay, that's good. I'm a professor at Bravo. Assistant professor. I was with another professor in La Reina. A student, actually, a graduate student. I lost track of her. I think she's still down there. I mean, I know she is, unless, for some—"

"A professor and his student, down in La Reina."

"She's not my student. She's from another school, interviewing for a professorship with us."

"You were having the interview in Mexico?"

"The lunch before the interview. What does it matter? There's a woman missing!"

She looked him up and down, and he realized how ridiculous his tierra caliente outfit—the vanilla ice-cream linen pants, Panama hat, sandals—must look to her. This wasn't Acapulco, this was south Texas ranch country. Here, even professors wore jeans and boots. A nutty professor he was, then. At any rate, a guy who taught all of nine hours a week and the rest of the time did... what? Go to Mexico to have lunch with students, female ones? While she, a hard-working CBP agent, was helping secure the border against the hordes. On the wall behind her hung a poster describing the penalties for smuggling aliens, and another warning that it was a crime to lie to a federal agent.

"Where'd you have this lunch?"

"Las Brasas."

"Good margaritas."

"She got up to go to the restroom, I thought. She never came back."

"How long ago?"

"An hour? Hour and a half?"

He realized his story did not impress her and that he would have to plead. "Look, can't you do anything about it? Something's wrong, I know it."

"Us do anything about it? Such as?"

"Help look for her!"

"Sir, you do realize Mexico's another country."

He tensed his jaw against the condescension. "Yes, of course."

"With its own laws and law enforcement."

He waited for her to finish her lecture to the clueless professor.

"Not that they work!" She lifted a pudgy hand. "I'm not saying that! But when you go over there, you're subject to their laws and jurisprudence."

"You're on your own."

"It's their country."

"Yes, you said that."

"The United States does not have jurisdiction."

He hung his head. "Okay. I got it. But when an American citizen goes missing down there, what does one do?"

"One could report it to the consulate. But one might wait for more than an hour before one sounds the alarm."

"Okay."

"Good luck, sir."

And just like that, she was done with him and summoning the next in line. She hadn't taken information from his driver's license or even asked his name. He supposed that was a demonstration of her power. At the other end of the scale, she could have ordered him strip-searched in one of the windowless rooms he was now walking by. Her decision. *Prepotencia.*

He located his car amid the bashed-up hulks—the lot doubled as a municipal boneyard—the light from the chrome and glass cutting his eyes even through his sunglasses. He felt in his satchel for his phone.

Son of a bitch. He hadn't entered Minerva's phone number, goddamn it. He'd have to call Esmeralda at the department office to get it. Yeah, sure. And when he confessed, Esmeralda would raise holy hell, order him back to campus, call the chair and the dean and take it all out of his hands. End of his involvement. End of him.

No. He'd race back to campus, quietly get Minerva's number from her CV, and call her in private from his cell to try to find out what had happened. It was past 2:00 already, and by the time he got to school, the search committee would have gathered around the conference table, waiting for him and Ms. Mondragón. Diosdado Duarte, the committee chair, would have Minerva's CV spread out in front of him, or be passing it around to the others so they could refresh their memories.

He glanced at his heat-shimmery dashboard for the parking stub, and then remembered the attendant hadn't given him one; he had paid his two dollars on entry. He took a deep breath. He had left no paper trail of his visit to Mexico—no credit card payment at the restaurant, no stamp in his passport. True, there were cameras on the bridge, but those seemed to be trained on traffic coming into the US, not pedestrians going the other way. There was the customs agent he'd argued with, but that bitch had likely forgotten all about it. Now he would exit this parking lot with no one noticing and be freely on his way. He rolled his window down, and the air seemed to have a hard clarity to it despite the smoke from a cane-field burn-off. What at first had seemed to him an act of stupidity—his failure to give the Las Brasas man his number or any way of contacting him with news of Minerva—now seemed to him part of a fortuitous pattern of erasures of the trip to Mexico. It was as if that visit hadn't happened at all.

Of course, there was a record of her having boarded the plane from Albuquerque to Providencia. And pictures on security cameras of the two of them meeting at the airport. But wait. Most footage would be of him waiting in vain for her with his sign before he'd turned and gone down to baggage claim. He'd seen her on the up escalator as he was going down, and she'd laughed and reached out to him in her merry way before getting to the top and coming back down. They shook hands at the bottom of the escalator and walked straight out to the car. Had any cameras recorded that brief interaction? Had it taken place in a blind spot? Impossible to know. Maybe he should swing by the airport and check it out. No, no, idiot, no returning to the scene of the crime. But what crime? Why was he even thinking like this?

What crime? Why, the crime he was going to commit when he walked into the meeting and announce that she hadn't shown. That he hadn't met with her. Hadn't even seen her.

Chapter Six

They tied her hands and feet with a coarse yellowish rope and gagged her with a rag stinking of epoxy. She now sat slumped against the stained wall of the bare room they had hustled her into some twenty minutes away from where they'd snatched her. She had tried to stay calm and calculate the time traveled as well as the speed of the car. She still felt a throbbing where they'd pressed their heels and knees into her back during the drive.

The two boys dumped her things from her leather shoulder bag and squatted on the floor and went through them. She watched them warily, her tongue jammed against her tonsils by the gag. Yes, these two kidnappers were definitely the "*ninis*" Quigley had asked for directions in La Reina. Just a couple of kids in bagged-out jeans and red Ferrari T-shirts, rampant black horse against a yellow shield, no doubt their gang colors. Each still had one Nike untied, the left one.

They stared at the screen of her cell phone.

"*Es del otro lado,*" one said.

"*¿Ya ves, pendejo? Es gringa.*"

Of course she was a gringa. Hadn't they heard her speaking English to Quigley and understood that they were visitors from across the river? Or, high on dope, had they sensed an opportunity and snatched her without considering the implications of having an American on their hands?

Her phone screen glowed silver in the dim room. An identical light spurted along the edges of the foil-covered windows. She glimpsed figures moving about in a curtained room across the hall—women, she believed. She could not imagine who they were.

"We are going to lose you," one of the boys said in English. "Do not scream, or is bad."

Lose her. For an exhilarated moment, she imagined this meant release her. Because weren't they blaming each other for having nabbed a gringa? She understood their Spanish perfectly, but she needed to play dumb, a dumb *pocha* who didn't understand what they wanted, who was more trouble than she was worth, whom, yes, they needed to lose, pronto. Lose her, let her go, let her go back to her country. *No vale la pena*, she yearned to tell them, you guys are absolutely right. It's not worth it to abduct a gringa, too complicated, *mucha lata*. But no, no Spanish, she reminded herself. Play dumb, play dumb.

They undid the nylon rope from her wrists, plucked out the saliva-heavy gag. Her tongue sprang forward, and she tasted bitterness. She rubbed the ruts in her wrists and lifted the back of her numb hand to wipe spit from her chin. She pushed herself up higher against the wall, leaned her head back and breathed deeply.

They left her feet tied. So, they weren't going to release her, not just yet. She stifled an urge to strike out at them, to shout for help to the people in the next room. But who were those people? What was this place? No, don't do anything rash, she thought, not without an escape plan. Just keep playing dumb.

"Who is the guy?" they asked.

The guy?

"The guy with you. Who is the guy?"

The guy she was with when they grabbed her? The guy at the restaurant? She had to dig him out of what seemed now a remote past. Oh, that guy, that was the guy who was going to send, had already sent, the cavalry after them. They needed to understand that. They had to save themselves by releasing her now.

"Is he your husband?"

"No. He..." She needed to tell them something impressive. Something to frighten them. He was an FBI agent. DEA agent. *Es de la D-E-A.*

No, no, what was she thinking, that would be the worst thing to say, it would panic them. She wasn't thinking right. Her head wasn't clear enough yet for strategic lies.

"A professor."

She rubbed her wrists, and feeling needled back into her numb hands. Professor—that was just powerful enough. Professors could find things out. They did research. *Investigación.* They would investigate and discover where she was. She wondered if her phone had GPS. Didn't all cell phones have it?

The fox-faced one with the phone stared at it while the other one gazed into space. They didn't bother to press her finger on the touch ID to unlock the device. They clearly had no game plan for the likes of her. They probably didn't even know how to say "ransom" in English. So, lose her, kids, lose her. She wasn't the right victim for them.

"You are professor too?"

"A student." And emphasized: "American."

She recalled an outburst she'd seen recently on Univisión, a video of an upper-class Mexican woman berating a pair of lowly Mexican traffic cops, *pinches indios nacos muertos de hambre,* an outrageous, racist outburst, but it had worked, it had cowed the cops and they backed off. Maybe something like that would do the trick. Whatever worked, however ugly.

She watched them. The wheels turning in their ni-ni minds, however sticky the gears might be with the glue they'd inhaled. A *gabacho* professor having drinks with his female student at a fancy restaurant in Mexico.... Maybe they were thinking they could just blackmail him. Make her write him a love letter mentioning their little lunchtime getaway to Mexico, then threaten to send it to his wife and his boss. Blackmail was much easier than an international kidnapping, no? But that was ridiculous. How could she prove to them he even had a wife? (Did he? He hadn't worn a ring.) Or convince them that it was a big no-no for American professors to go out with their students?

The wheels spinning in her own mind were greased; she willed that they slow down. Remember, they're kids, just kids, younger even than the freshmen she taught as a grad student T.A., and just as confused and unsure of what they were doing. She could maybe talk sense into them.

"You need to untie my feet," she said, reaching for the cord herself.

The ruddy one with the sun-bleached hair bent down to help her. He was fair-skinned enough to give a certain kind of parochial gringo pause ("that kid's a Mexican?"). A "*güero de rancho*" as they said in Mexico, a country blondie. As he loosened the rope, she felt her thigh muscles tense as she visualized a front kick to his red face and a sweep kick to knock fox-face off his feet and then run to the people in the other room. But who were those people? All the voices sounded like women's. How could they not know she was a captive? Were they complicit?

"Where's the bathroom?" she demanded. "*¿Baño?*" Her bladder ached, but she was absurdly proud that she hadn't wet herself during the ordeal.

Fox-face made the same gesture he'd made when Quigley had asked them the way to Las Brasas: a backhanded motion that told her to go down the hall in the direction opposite of the room with the people.

The stench hit her before she opened the door. The toilet bowl brimmed with turds and overflowed on the floor around it. In a corner stood dozens of plastic beverage bottles full of yellow liquid, some cloudy, some clear and jewel-like in the sun angling in through a small window. She swallowed hard and held her breath to keep from gagging, squatted and gushed on the floor. She fled the vile room still dribbling and stopped in the hall to bury her nose in the crook of her elbow.

The ni-nis emerged from the room they'd held her in, regarded her for a moment almost shame-facedly, and exited through a metal door. She heard the drawing of a bolt and the click of a heavy padlock.

She strode down the hall to the room with the voices. A dozen or more women of all ages gazed at her blankly.

"Who *are* you?" she said, in English. More blankness.

It was time to drop the pretense of not knowing Spanish. "*¿Quiénes son?*"

"*Igual que tú,*" one said.

Same as you. For a second, she heard this as *you're no better than us,* a reprise of the perennial tension between Mexicans and what they now must take her to be, from her accent, a Mexican American, a pocha, each side believing the other thought itself superior. But the middle-aged woman who had spoken looked more defeated than defiant. She wasn't challenging her; she was inviting her into a shared misery. And there was misery here to go around. A girl in a corner sat weeping into her knees, while another nibbled furtively at a piece of tortilla, her eyes wary. A group of three lay in fetal positions on thin mattresses, presumably asleep. It stank of unwashed bodies long confined, pungently sour.

"*¿Qué es esto? ¿Cómo se llama este lugar?*" Minerva asked. She needed to put a name to the place, the situation.

The woman gave a little shrug, as though the answers were obvious. "*Un secuestradero.*"

"*Secuestradero.*" Minerva repeated the word slowly. A mouthful. She knew the verb "*secuestrar,*" to kidnap, but she'd never heard this derivative noun. She tried to think of the equivalent in English. Kidnappery? Safe house, she supposed, though that was odd in its own way. Safe for whom?

A car rumbled by on the street. So, they were in a city or a town. Minerva bent the foil covering the window and peeked out, and the woman slapped her hand. *"No haga eso."* In her glimpse, Minerva had seen that the house was right on the street and that the window, surprising for a first-story window in Mexico, had no bars. Whoever was holding them must be very confident that they wouldn't escape. Perhaps the street was guarded, but she hadn't spotted anybody, any sentinel, out there.

A phone rang, and the girl who had been weeping lifted her face from her knees and clutched at it.

"Sí, Mami," she said. *"Sí. Pero, ¿no puedes hablar con Jorge otra vez? ¡Mami, sáquenme de aquí!"*

This was the strangest kind of kidnappery. No bars on windows. No one tied up, no guards apparent. A victim with the use of a phone, talking to her mother about, it would seem, her ransom.

She asked the woman who had slapped her hand, *"¿No hay policía?"*

"Sí, hay policía. Mucha."

Okay, she got it. There were plenty of police out there, but in Mexico one didn't call the police to get the bad guys. The police *were* the bad guys, or so Minerva had always heard. There was no point in calling them or trying to get their attention. The idea was to avoid getting them involved, or further involved.

"¿Cuántas somos?" Minerva asked the woman.

The woman said there were fifteen women being held. Sixteen that morning, but one had been released midday. There were some men being held in another part of the building. How many, she didn't know.

Minerva said they could scream. All together, screaming out the window. One voice, *a grito pelado*. The street was right there. Someone would have to hear. Even if the police didn't respond, maybe someone else would. A group of citizen vigilantes maybe? The army, or what had Quigley called those soldiers? The *Marina*.

The woman looked at her as if she were crazy or stupid or both. Minerva didn't have the strength to argue. A thick fatigue had wrapped her like a scratchy blanket. She sought a place on the grimy floor and lay down.

Chapter Seven

The three other members of the search committee, plus the Equal Employment Opportunity Commission rep, were already assembled around the conference room table when Quigley walked in, sans candidate. Professor DeWitt, a full professor, and the most senior member of the committee, raised his bushy eyebrows. The word supercilious had been coined specifically for him. Quigley had never known anyone with such pelts above the eyes, much less the ability to arch them so disdainfully high. Quigley had to wonder if to increase the effect the man didn't comb the fur upwards as part of what he'd once heard him refer to as his "morning toilet." DeWitt was the department's Victorianist, and he used those kinds of expressions in ironic homage to his field.

Dr. DeWitt kept the brows raised high through Quigley's shrug and his, "Well, I just kept waiting." Quigley's heart flopped with his lies, but it was okay if his distress showed, at least to a point. His colleagues' voices came to him as if from a chorus:

"Maybe she missed her connection."

"Did she call the department to let us know?"

"Somebody ask Esmeralda."

Diosdado Duarte, the committee chair, up for tenure that year and therefore a department workhorse, propelled himself from his seat and strode to Esmerelda's office. At Bravo, being a good team player like Duarte won you more points toward tenure than the tenure and promotion guidelines, despite what their emphasis on research would have you believe.

Duarte's voice came to them in a mumble, with Esmeralda's words piercing through. "You think I wouldn't have told you professors? *Ay, sí,* like they call and say they missed their flight and you professors are sitting there waiting for them and I don't say nothing. *Ay, no,* please."

It was the Department of Languages and Literatures, but no one had ever dared correct Esmeralda's English, not even Professor DeWitt.

"Well, let's call *her,* then," DeWitt said in the sing-song voice he used when he was truly annoyed. What with the first two candidates for the position having withdrawn — one because she felt her husband would never get a decent job on the economically depressed border and the other after getting an offer from another school — DeWitt's patience, short to begin with, was coming to an end.

The enormous relief Quigley would feel if Minerva answered her phone was tempered by his certainty that she would let the cat out of the bag and tell them that Quigley had taken her to Mexico, where they'd somehow gotten separated. But, God, yes, let her answer, let her have a mobile and let her service work in Mexico and let her be safe.

"Where are you going now?" DeWitt asked Duarte.

"To get Esmeralda to call?"

"That phone works," DeWitt said dryly, nodding at a beige contraption stuck on the end of a fax machine.

Duarte, shy to begin with, had a phone phobia, and DeWitt knew it. His affliction had become apparent to all the committee members during his thick-tongued performance at the initial phone interviews with the candidates. (He confessed afterwards that he found it "unnerving" to converse with a person without being able to see that person's facial expressions and body language and thereby "take the full measure of their intentions.") Cindy Wheeler, the fourth member of the search committee, exchanged a glance with

Quigley at DeWitt's meanness. As Duarte stumbled to the phone, it occurred to Quigley to heroically reach for it first and ask Duarte to read him the number. If she answered, and please, please let her answer, he would ask her where she was, and, with a feigned surprise he hoped would be convincing enough to mask the nearly hysterical relief he'd feel, exclaim, "Mexico! How did you wind up there? Never mind, I'll come get you now!" But Duarte was already punching in the numbers, his jaw muscles bulging.

Quigley pivoted in his chair and watched, electrified. Duarte, receiver at his ear, squeezed his eyes shut and monotoned, "Dr. Mondragón, this is Diosdado Duarte at the Bravo University English Department? Give us a call at your earliest convenience, please? Thank you."

DeWitt gave a little snort. Earliest convenience, right.

"Maybe we should call the airline," Cindy suggested.

"Oh, they don't give passenger information," Quigley said quickly. "It's a confidentiality thing."

"Remember that poet who got sidetracked coming down from San Antone?" Duarte said, energized by his success over the phone. "The one with the visiting position? Before your time, William. Some rancher over in Zapata County found him hunkered down with the cattle, barfing up the peyote buttons he'd dug up out there. Kind of thing that really helps the university's reputation."

"This Mondragón's a poet, too," said DeWitt.

"Oh yeah?"

"You didn't read her CV? Down here, under Other Publications. A poem in *Kumquat Meringue* and another in something called *The Coffin Factory*."

"Guess I missed that. Well, a couple of poems don't make her a poet, but point well taken," said Duarte, who had a good rhet/comp man's indifference to the form. Contempt, even. "Intelligent gibberish," he'd once called it.

Quigley wondered if it was the same in all schools in Bravo's tier, with composition getting the big bucks because it taught something "practical," literature considered snooty because it upheld high culture and the "canon" and creative writing dwelling at the bottom because its practitioners, even among their own, were suspected of being frauds.

"Let's not speculate as to her state of mind," warned the EEOC rep, a snowy-haired gent from electrical engineering. As of last year, every search committee had to have an EEOC rep from another college sitting in on interviews and formal deliberations, thanks to a lawsuit by a white male candidate for an ethnic studies position who had charged that a question about his ability to understand discrimination was an act of discrimination itself. The judge had dismissed the complaint, snarkily ruling that the plaintiff was begging the question ("How does he know what discrimination is? Because he's suing for it!"). And in an aside that further riled the plaintiff and guaranteed a whole string of appeals and ongoing headaches for Bravo, the judge had said the man had gone to court "out of a sense of privilege." Now the university placed one of these reps on each search committee to nip any possible discrimination in the bud or at least show it was making good faith efforts to do so.

"I don't think poetry writing is a constitutionally protected disability, or is it?" said DeWitt, sharing a guffaw with Duarte.

"Not protected like the members of the Church of the Thousand Peyote Gods," he added, and they laughed again.

Quigley stared hard at the tabletop, listening to this prattle while trying to swallow his heart back down. So Duarte'd been able to leave a message. That meant she had mobile phone service in Mexico, right? Presumably? And presumably she carried a cell in her shoulder bag? Though he couldn't remember her checking it.

Now the important thing was for him to call her cell as soon as he could from his own phone and implore her to call *him* first, not the department. What a great, great thing if she answered him. So sorry, she'd say, but she'd gone outside the restaurant to walk around the block and clear her head and got disoriented, but not to worry, she was in a cab and almost to the campus, and no, of course she wouldn't mention anything about their having been across the border. See you in a minute!

"Could I look at her file?" Quigley asked, unable to still the trembling in his hands as he took the pages.

Only Wheeler and the EEOC rep would have noticed his agitation. Duarte was still too pleased with himself and his phoning success to notice. DeWitt, to whom it hadn't occurred that Minerva's nonappearance might be a consequence of force majeure and not her fault, leaned back in his chair, stewing in his disgust.

Memorizing her cell phone number calmed Quigley. Distracted him. That's all he had to do now, focus on it, and repeat it over and over in his mind until he could get to his office and punch it in. As he left the conference room, trying not to move his lips, he vaguely registered Wheeler's bemused expression.

Quigley's office window looked down upon the university gallery where they were now mounting yet another student exhibit of Frida Kahlo-inspired paintings of tormented bodies and disembodied hearts. He was not a praying man, but the soft deliberateness with which he entered Minerva's number was a pious pleading to unknown forces that they might assist her in answering. As the phone rang, he watched a pair of students hang a painting of a green-complexioned woman lying on a bed of monstrous white lilies, her guts spilling out of her body. When he heard Minerva's chipper "Hi!" his own chest exploded in relief, "Oh, hey, hi!" And just as immediately it imploded back to black-hole heaviness as she continued to instruct the caller to leave a message.

He kept it short and grave. Very, very sorry that they had gotten separated. Please call him as soon as she got this message. This number, please, not the department number. He recited his cell number slowly and carefully.

He slid the phone into the lower pocket of his guayabera. It would hang there heavily, and he'd want to remove it, but that was why it was a good place to carry it, so he'd be conscious of having it with him at all times.

What, oh what, was going on? Maybe her being something of a poet did explain a lot. He recalled a dinner at an MLA conference where the director of a creative writing program somewhere out west said they had to keep hiring poets, because their existing faculty poets kept "wandering off." Quigley had wondered what that meant, exactly—just literally wandered off into the sunsets or mountains or streetscapes they described in their poems? Is that what Minerva had done, followed her poet's nose into the streets of La Reina, attentive only to the directions of her muse? Gone to hunt for peyote, like Duarte's poet? This now seemed plausible. Indeed, she'd hinted at it herself. He recalled her words as she got to the bottom of her margarita: *You could really disappear down here*....

Chapter Eight

The light of the setting sun flared golden around the edges of the foil-covered window. Since her fellow captives weren't going to let her peel away the foil to study the lay of the land, she was going to have to wring what information she could from them, taciturn as they were.

What little the women did know was that they were in a town a few kilometers west of La Reina and south of the Río Bravo, in a border area called Frontera Chica. When she asked what the layout of the secuestradero was, if the kidnapped men were close by or in some remote part of the building, if there was another bathroom besides that awful one, the woman to whom she had first spoken murmured, "*Es todo un secuestradero.*"

"*Pero, ¿qué tan grande es?*"

"*Todo, todo,*" the woman said, making a circular motion with her finger.

Okay, yes, she got it. The whole place was a kidnappery, the whole building, or compound, or whatever it was. And yet, again, the street and freedom were right there! How could you keep a bunch of people like this captive in the middle of a town?

"*Todo, todo,*" the woman repeated, and several others nodded.

It was as if they were dogs outfitted with obedience collars that gave them an electrical jolt whenever they stepped over an invisible boundary. Perhaps one of them had tried to escape and been brought back, and this was all the shock they needed to stop probing the perimeter. But had they tried to escape en masse? Had they tried ramming this gutted sofa through the flimsy window and spilling out into the street? Because, as with the screaming she'd suggested earlier, the whole town would then be alerted to what was going on. Wasn't it worth a try? It was outrageous, insane, that a bunch, perhaps dozens, of people could be held against their will in an ordinary house in the middle of a town. Where were the guards, even?

A key rattled in the metal door and the ni-nis reappeared, carrying two steaming metal buckets of—the fragrance was unmistakable—tamales. Were these two kids it, then? The only overseers? Unbelievable! Why, they could just over-power them then and there!

The sound of her phone diverted her attention. She'd made the dramatic opening notes from Beethoven's Fifth Symphony her ringtone the day she'd begun waiting to hear from Bravo University, following her phone interview with the search committee. It sounded ridiculously ironic now.

The fox-faced ni-ni dug in his pocket and brought it out, and he and the other one stared at the screen. The ringtone died at the third ta-ta-ta-taa, and the phone went to messages. The ni-nis listened to the message and then played it for her, holding it up to her ear.

"Is the guy?"

She nodded. Yes, it was the guy. The professor she was with when they grabbed her, if that's what they meant.

"*Que lo llame pa' trás*," ruddy face said to fox-face.

"*No, cabrón, ¿y si la hace de pedo?*"

"*No más pa' decirle—*"

"*¿Decirle qué, güey? Chale...*"

So ruddy face wanted her to return the call. But to tell him what, the fox-faced one wanted to know. Clearly, they were at a loss as to how to handle her, an American hostage.

There must be someone above them they hadn't told about her yet, some adult—maybe they were afraid to?

She held her hand out for the phone. Give it up, kids, you're over your heads.

Fox-face slipped it back in his jeans pocket.

The other women peeled their tamales and ate them with their fingers, indifferent to her and the ni-nis' dilemma. Minerva, realizing how hungry she was, did the same, pinching chunks of pork from the masa. The ni-nis passed around a black trash bag into which the women dropped their empty husks before returning to their usual places, resignedly, zombified. The ni-nis dragged another thin, filthy mattress into the room, and ruddy face indicated with his chin that this was to be Minerva's.

She already knew what she had to do. She eyed the transom window above the door the ni-nis came in and out of. Narrow, but she judged that she might, just might, be able to squeeze through. To reach it, she had only to fold the mattress in two, or thirds, and hoist herself up. And she had to do it that very night, while the ni-nis were still unsure of what to do with her. She'd make it easy for them and escape. The US border was just a few miles north, or so the women said. It was not inconceivable that she could be at the university by mid-morning and—miracle of miracles—summon the strength to give her teaching demo, as scheduled. Maybe!

Chapter Nine

After leaving the message on Minerva's phone imploring her to call him, Quigley decided to stay on campus until his evening Rhetoric and Composition class. Normally, before meeting his class, he would take the freeway overpass to Doña Tota's for an agua fresca and a pork gordita, but he clung to the hope that Minerva would at any minute return his call to say she was on her way to campus. "So sorry," she'd say, "I'll explain when I get there," or maybe she'd just show up without calling, having lost her phone or whatever. Either way, he needed to intercept her to beg her to not say anything about their jaunt to Mexico. He'd gotten only two bites of Las Brasas guacamole and left the goat stew untouched and coagulating as he went to search for Minerva. His appetite hadn't returned. He grabbed a black coffee in C-Building and took a picnic bench by the freshman dorms, from where he could monitor the turnaround in front of the humanities building. Any taxi or Uber bringing her to campus would drop her off there, surely.

His Camry sat shimmering in the sun, parked nose-in to the hedge of bougainvilleas that divided student parking from the faculty slots. He kept every window cracked, in the hope that it might mitigate the incredible heat that built up in cars, even in March. There was no need to fear thieves—crime was low on campus, as it was in Providencia as a whole and along most of the Texas side of the border. Street crimes—assaults, muggings, robberies—were all remarkably low. Yes, a huge amount of drugs and people were smuggled across that border, but the smuggling took place largely under the radar. If you didn't read in the papers the estimates of how many tons of drugs and how many people were trafficked over the river yearly, you wouldn't know it was happening. Busts of safe houses hiding drugs or people happened regularly, but hardly ever violently, and often without arrests, the smugglers having been tipped off and fled. The local police seized the buildings and any abandoned vehicles, and the smugglers wrote off the losses as a cost of doing business. As long as the smugglers got to move a reasonable amount of product and the authorities were able to replenish their coffers with a reasonable number of forfeitures, everybody was reasonably happy.

One candidate the committee had interviewed had asked, during the obligatory now-what-questions-do-you-have-for-us finale, about the crime situation. DeWitt told her it was perfectly safe for anyone to walk around downtown Providencia at any time of the day or night. She may or may not have believed him or thought this was the macho-man in him talking, but it was true. "Two murders last year, total," DeWitt said, citing FBI statistics. "A comparable-sized city in other parts of the US would have about twenty." He didn't add that the comparably-sized La Reina, over in Mexico, had had at least two hundred. Quigley had once remarked to his Mexican-American students that an excellent argument against racism was the fact that they, who were so little prone to violence, were genotypically (not to say phenotypically) indistinguishable from their violent cousins on the other side of the river. Clearly, then, the differences in behavior were cultural, not genetic. The argument had been received with more suspicion than acclaim, so he kept it to himself after that. There was no reason for him, a white guy English teacher from the opposite end of the country, to wade into the choppy waters of eugenics and race.

There were lots of kidnappings of Mexicans on the Mexican side, although statistics were harder to come by, since most of them went unreported. The families preferred to deal directly with the kidnappers, and the Mexican authorities maintained that most of the victims were people who owed the narcos money or were otherwise tied to "irregular" activities. But the disappearance of an American in Mexico would get reported in the US media, and the fact that you seldom heard such stories meant that it didn't happen often.

The coffee burned in his stomach and sped up his thoughts. Crazy as she may be, would Minerva truly have pulled a disappearing stunt just then? "You could really disappear down here," she'd said, and then added, "if nobody was looking for you." Of course someone would be looking for her—though not him. She would understand perfectly well that he wouldn't want to put his job and career at risk in a futile attempt to track down a disappeared person—a person he was supposed to take care of—in Mexico. Wouldn't she?

If that was the case, if she'd left on purpose and they were in on her disappearance together, why didn't she at least have the decency to answer her goddamned phone and let him know she was okay? Then it occurred to him, a spike to his heart, that she might not have her phone with her at all. Crossing the bridge, they had talked about reception, or lack of it, down in Mexico, but he hadn't actually seen her cell, had he? Might she have left it in her carry-on, where it had been ringing, a muffled cry in the trunk of his car?

He tore across the parking lot and flung open the trunk, heat billowing into his face. He glanced over his shoulder like a thief, then unzipped her carry-on. He rummaged around, feeling satiny things and feeling creepy about it. No phone. Her laptop yes, its metal warm.

Would she really leave all her stuff? Every change of clothes? Her *laptop?* Was there any academic in the world unhinged enough to abandon their laptop? On the other hand, your computer might be the first thing you'd abandon if you

wanted out of the academic life. Not to say she wasn't scholarly, but she hadn't struck him as much of a research grind.
More of a teacher, outgoing and charismatic. Which meant
she'd be a good fit here, since Bravo, despite its official designation as a Research II school, was focused primarily on
teaching, not scholarship. The admins begrudged having to
pay for travel to conferences. If you got a Fulbright, say, you
were expected to somehow continue teaching even if you
were headed to New Guinea to live with jungle tribes. Teach-
ing-intensive research institution, the school called itself, trying to have it both ways.

Great fit she was, yeah right. Too crazy to even make it
to the interview. How hadn't he seen right off that she was a
headache? Full of that "red oni" impulsiveness she'd written
about in her dissertation? A more experienced faculty colleague would have had her pegged right off the bat, and not
let her lure him into Mexico. Why, oh why, had they even put
him on a search committee?

He removed her laptop. Better take it into the building;
the heat in the trunk might damage it. In the unlikely event it
wasn't password protected, he might find some clues about
her on it. As for the rest of her stuff, it was troubling to have
to leave it in his car—it was *evidence*—but what else was he
supposed to do with it?

He bounded up the rear steps of the humanities building,
the computer tucked under his arm. The door to the Department of Languages and Literatures was shut tight, blackness
behind its narrow window. Good. Nobody to take her call
there. She would be forced to call him.

A voice came to him from behind. "You're a Mac guy
now, William?"

"A what?"

"Macintosh?" Duarte nodded at the laptop.

"This? Oh, no, it's..." Good God almighty, he almost said
it—the candidate's. "I'm borrowing it."

"Looks like Esme's locked up," Duarte said, cupping his hands around his eyes as he peered into the window. "And the candidate hasn't called yet."

"Don't worry about it. She has my number, so she'll call me."

Duarte seemed more relieved than curious, but Quigley felt a need to clarify. "I emailed it to her earlier in the week, when we decided I would be the one to pick her up, in case she had trouble with her flight."

"That was smart."

It also wasn't true, but it was plausible. It would have been weird to admit to what he'd done—copied it from her CV and called her after Duarte already had, leaving her his cell number. Because why would he do that? Just to save telephobic Duarte the agony of having to speak on the phone? What a terribly thoughtful colleague!

As Duarte turned to leave, Quigley said, "You don't think that for some reason she might have gone straight to her hotel, do you?"

"We don't tell them where we're going to put them up before they get here," said Duarte. "Don't want to scare them off. The Super 8 on Business 83? They'd google it, and that could kill the deal." He gave a hearty ho-ho-ho, more pained than mirthful.

Quigley's own laugh caught in his throat.

"Don't worry, man!" said Duarte, clapping him on the shoulder. "It's not your fault she's a poet!"

There it was again, the poet thing. That was what the narrative was shaping up to be: the scholar-cum-poet, off in her own world, failed to appear for her job interview. Another story to entertain fellow academics with, like the one about the peyote-eating poet from San Antone. This narrative would conspire with their wounded pride at having been snubbed by yet another job candidate.

Even if Duarte asked Esmeralda to track her down, Esmeralda would refuse to. Quigley could already hear her words: *Ya se chingó*, she's fucked herself. And DeWitt, the de facto committee chair, wouldn't make her do it. Quigley could hear him as well: To hell with the search. We tried. Let the dean close the search, let's be done with it. And that would be that.

Unless Minerva had planned her disappearance, unless her vanishing act hadn't been as spontaneous as Quigley liked to imagine it, wouldn't she have told someone where she was going to be interviewed—a mentor, a friend, a family member? And wouldn't they remember the place, some school way down in Texas, on the border with Mexico, an interesting name, Bravo, yes, that's it.

Soon enough, they'd begin to call, inquire about her. Flight records would be sought. Airport videotapes examined. His car searched. Even if he got rid of her stuff, they'd find one of her goddamned hairs or something and it would all be over.

What was he thinking, get rid of her stuff? As if he were guilty of having done something to her! This was intolerable. His hand trembled so violently his key kept missing the groove in his office door lock. He collapsed into his swivel chair. He lifted her laptop's lid and her login screen lit up with Aztec calendar wallpaper, but everything behind that stony disc was password protected, naturally. He had to go to the campus police right now and let the chips fall. Cancel class and go straight to them.

But the campus police hadn't even been able to track down the graffiti artist who had repeatedly tagged their own building. What could they do about a disappeared person in Mexico? Not a damned thing, probably, like the CBP agent at the border had said. Maybe the campus cops knew somebody who could go to Las Brasas and try to find something out, discover whether anybody had seen anything, knew anything? The CBP agent had said something about contacting the consulate. Maybe he should do that and forget the cops. But which consulate, the American consulate in Mexico or the Mexican consulate here? How was he supposed to know these things?

Okay, okay, it was decided: go to the police. He supposed it was true what the agent had implied, namely, that the authorities wouldn't act on a missing person report until that person had been gone, what—twenty-four hours, forty-eight? Regardless, it didn't absolve him of the duty to report it right away.

First, he needed a few moments to assess how much trouble he personally would be getting into. He began by scanning his email to see if he'd received any kind of memo from the university regarding travel to Mexico. It didn't take long for two messages to pop up, messages that he'd previously ignored, one from the campus police warning students to exercise due caution when traveling to Mexico over spring break, and one from something called the Office of Risk Management stating that although the Department of State had not issued any new travel warnings for Mexico, the university was requesting that all its employees "defer non-essential travel to Tamaulipas state."

Was La Reina in the state of Tamaulipas? Another quick search revealed that it most certainly was. How could he not know that? (Or: How was he supposed to know that?) And was he, a professor, really an "employee"? Weren't the employees the secretaries, the maintenance guys, the administrators? (Of course he was, idiot.) How could he know that the travel ban hadn't been lifted? (Any further message saying that it had? No.) Was it not "essential" that the Border Studies candidate visit La Reina? (In what way was it essential, sir?)

His goose was cooked. *Soy chingado, estoy chingado,* or however Esmeralda would say it. Whatever the verb form used to mean he was permanently, irrevocably, fucked. The worst thing, the most damning, was the coverup, the lying he had done to the committee, the failure to report the disappearance right away.

Goddammit, how would he ever find another academic job after this? It was the only kind of job he had prepared for.

And how could he have allowed this candidate to put his career on the line? He thought back on her cavalier attitude, of the margarita she ordered, of the fact that she had been the one to insist (had she not insisted, in a way?) that they go to Mexico in the first place.

But what kind of thinking was this? Blaming the victim was obscene. Was he through with this obscenity? Got it out of his system yet? Good. Time to go to the cops and spill the beans.

Chapter Ten

Assistant Professor Quigley, ready to face the music and go to the campus police with his story, took out, for the second time that day, his black Sharpie and wrote on a sheet of paper, as steadily as his trembling fingers would allow, "PROFESSOR QUIGLEY'S CLASS CANCELED." As he formed the block letters, the "D" scrunched to fit, he remembered folding his Minerva Mondragón sign and stuffing it into the airport trash receptacle. It was an act that now seemed fraught with dire significance. The fumes from the marker, so pungently exciting that morning over the prospect of the job candidate's visit, now carried the odor of doom. He remembered the two boys sitting on the wall, the two ninis he'd asked directions to Las Brasas, exuding a similar chemical stench.

A knock made him jump. A tiny voice said from the hall, "Professor, are we having class today?"

Quigley opened the door. A wee girl with enormous, innocent eyes stood before him.

"Why wouldn't we have class today?" he said crossly.

He didn't have the slightest idea what her name was. With four classes per semester and thirty students a class, he'd given up on trying to remember names. He couldn't recall her face either, and suspected she was one of the steady twenty percent who missed class regularly.

"No, I'm just saying! But I can't come. Are we doing anything important?"

"Oh, no, we're just going to play tiddlywinks for three hours," he said.

It was plain from her continued expression of innocence that she was unfamiliar with both sarcasm and tiddlywinks. He wasn't sure what tiddlywinks were himself and regretted the sarcasm.

"Why can't you come? You're already on campus. What was your name again?"

"Marisol, sir. I told my sister I'd babysit her kids." She produced her iPhone and prepared her thumbs. "How do you spell? Tiddly..." Then, either his annoyance finally dawned on her, or she read some game-changing message on her device, because she blurted, "That's okay, Professor, I can come," and bolted.

Now Quigley felt committed to meeting the class, at least for a while. He could always let them out early to work on their research papers, whose topics he'd already approved. (In his first semester, he'd made the rookie mistake of not screening topics, and the papers came back overwhelmingly in four areas: Jesus' truth, Hitler's evil, serial killers and teen pregnancy.) "Library days," these periods were called, but he could bet not a one would actually go to the library.

He checked once again to see if he had his phone on its loudest ring volume—*please call, please*—and trudged downstairs to meet his class.

As usual, the front-row students beamed at him while those in the back looked down, hoping not to call attention to themselves. One in the middle said, "You look worried, sir!"

"No, no. No worries," he said worriedly.

An instructor from a previous class had slashed an X through the word "your" on the whiteboard and written "YOU'RE!!" beside it. Quigley tried to wipe it off, but that chemical smell so redolent of new emotional complexity told him it had been applied with a Sharpie rather than a whiteboard marker, and the eraser passed over it without effect. The students laughed.

"I can understand exasperation over a homonym error," he murmured, "but I hate to think someone used a permanent marker to express it."

"You can get it off with alcohol, sir," someone said. "I mean, not you. The janitor will take care of it."

"Sir, can I change my research topic?" another student asked.

"To what? Remember, no serial killers."

"No, sir. But, see, my cousin got his truck stolen at the mall, so I wanted to do it about that."

"About what? Malls? Trucks? Cousins?"

"About vehicle theft, sir."

"Okay, but narrow it down. Vehicle theft on the border, say."

"Yes, sir. They take them down to Mexico. Ford F150s are the ones that get stolen the most. My cousin's was a Ford F150."

"The narcos like those," said a girl. "And Escalades."

"And Navigators and Armadas. Anything big," said another.

Narcos and their tastes was something his students would talk about with pleasure and at length.

"They don't even change the license plates on the stolen ones," someone else said. "They just keep the Texas plates. Even if the cops down there know they're stolen, they don't do anything about it. They're too scared."

"Or paid off."

"So when you see the videos of the shootouts, those aren't Texas people, sir. Those are Mexican narcos in stolen trucks."

"What videos?"

"On YouTube. Or Blog del Narco. Or just go to a narco's Facebook. They like to post them."

As if he knew a narco with a Facebook page. And narcos blogged? He never much liked discussing the narco situation with his students. It seemed to him too unpleasant and sensitive a subject, a minefield of stereotypes about violence and people of color, an invitation to revisit the Evil Mexico tropes. It was obvious, though, that his students kept up with it. He felt nauseated, and the smell of pepperoni pizza crust coming from the wastebasket wasn't helping. A blade of pain pricked the inside of his left brow. He needed to cancel class *right now* and go to the police. But no, wait, he could learn something from them, needed to.

He clenched his jaw, fighting the queasiness as he asked, "Does anybody remember what 'hypothetical' means?"

He wrote the word on the board and waited. As a professor, you had to wait a long time, an uncomfortably long time, before giving up and answering questions yourself. But now the response came almost immediately, from Marisol, who evidently had been absent on the day he had instructed them to please always put away phones and laptops. Absent, or so engrossed with her iPhone that she hadn't heard him then. She was consulting it now.

"'Conjec...' No, here: 'imagined as an example.'"

"Okay, but let's not use devices, okay? Yes, it's like, 'What if'? So here's a what if. What if two Americans went down to Mexico and one of them got snatched. What would the other one do?"

"Snatched, sir?"

The word came strangled from Quigley's throat: "Kidnapped."

"Why did they snatch just one?"

"Well, if they got separated somehow."

"Were they drug dealers, sir?"

"No, no, just visitors. Tourists."

"Because if they're involved in drugs or maybe they're cops or something, like DEA, then it's probably the cartels that got him and he's probably toast. That's called a *levantón*."

"If it's an express, you just have to wait," a female student said. "They'll keep the one they grabbed for twenty-four hours and then let him go."

"Wait, what?" said Quigley. He held his breath. "Express?"

"That's when they get the person to withdraw the max from their account—"

"At an ATM, sir."

"Yeah, and then they drive him around and stuff for another day until he can withdraw the max for the next day. Then they let him go."

"They also call it the *paseo millonario*. That's, like, millionaire's ride."

"But this is an American," Quigley said. "In the hypothetical. Her bank card would work down there?"

"Of course, sir. Credit card too."

"Is it a lady?" asked a boy in the back.

He had a round face, bristly black hair, clear brown eyes, nearly always wore jeans and a Bravo Broncos T-shirt, and rarely spoke. He was one of those students who showed up to class sporadically as if to only to keep tabs on the situation, but who somehow managed to turn in remarkably intelligent papers and end up with a solid B in the course, despite his poor attendance. This dispiriting ability made Quigley question his usefulness as a teacher, while simultaneously prompting him to remember the kid's name—Omar.

"You said 'her,'" Omar clarified.

"Or a man," Quigley said, with a wave of his hand. "Whatever. It's hypothetical."

Omar kept his head cocked as he studied Quigley, but Quigley noticed the sharpness of his curiosity only obliquely, so great was his relief at the information he was getting from everyone.

"What are the chances it's an express?" Quigley asked. "As opposed to something else?"

"Like a ransom thing?" someone said. "Those are the regular *secuestros*. But they don't kidnap Americans for ransom too much."

"Really? Why not?"

"That gets international. Too complicated, sir. It's probably an express."

"Those are pretty simple, right? And nobody gets hurt?"

"Maybe if they resist. You should never resist, sir. It's just money."

"Don't worry about it, sir. She'll be okay."

"The hypothetical she," Quigley reminded him.

"Yes, sir."

An express! That was the likeliest reason she, or the hypothetical kidnappers, hadn't called. And it meant that by tomorrow afternoon, she'd be free. Suddenly he wasn't so keen on going to the police.

He was able to get to the break, at which point he told the students to use the rest of the period for library time. Everyone scrambled out. Everyone but Omar, that is. He lingered, then approached Quigley when the two of them were alone in the classroom. He hung back while Quigley packed his things in his leather satchel and checked his phone.

"Interesting class, sir."

"Yes, it was, wasn't it?"

"This hypothetical kidnapping. Did it happen in La Reina?"

"I suppose so. Right? Hypothetically."

He looked up at Omar's face. The boy's eyes were alive with curiosity, and something in them made Quigley hope the phone might just hold off ringing before he heard him out.

"Did it happen where tourists would go?" Omar inquired. "Like around the main plaza, you know, the square?"

"Well, why not? Why not there?"

"Because that belongs to the Gamboa Organization, and the Gamboas don't go in for kidnapping. They're strict about that."

"Gamboa? Is that a drug cartel?"

"Yeah, but old school. They're only dedicated to smuggling."

"Maybe they've changed. Maybe they kidnap now."

"No, I don't think so."

"Maybe it was someone else, then."

"Maybe. But who? Who were the Americans with? Who did they talk to?"

"Nobody! Each other. The waiters in the restaurant they went to."

"What restaurant? Hypothetically."

"The main one downtown there? Las Brasas?"

Omar stared into the black night outside the window. Or maybe he was examining Quigley's reflection, getting another angle on him.

"They didn't talk to anyone else?" he asked. "They didn't catch a cab?"

"No. They parked on the US side of the bridge and walked across. Oh, maybe they asked a couple of kids on the street for directions."

"Kids? Which kids?"

"Which kids? Just a couple of kids sitting on a wall."

"Which wall?"

Which *wall?* Now Quigley realized that, speaking of walls, there was no more wall between him and this student, this Omar. The fictional barrier had been fully breached, and now they both knew that the other knew they were talking about something actual, not hypothetical. But to confess to a *student?*

Quigley buckled his satchel. "If it's one of those express deals you guys were talking about, anybody could do it, right? It wouldn't take professionals. And in a few hours, the victim is free."

"That's the thing, sir. The Gamboas don't allow just anybody to operate in La Reina. And the kidnappers would have to stash her or drive her around for twenty-four hours and visit ATMs twice, and the cartel would notice that. They have eyes and ears everywhere."

Quigley knew his expression had to be that of a drowning man.

"Sir, half my family lives in La Reina. I know the situation down there. I can help."

"How?"

"Here, draw me a map of where these two kids were sitting," said Omar, handing him a green dry erase for the whiteboard. "And do you remember what kind of sneakers they were wearing? What brand?"

"What brand of sneakers? I don't even know if they were wearing sneakers."

"They were. But that's okay if you don't remember. What about their shirts?"

Quigley shrugged. "T-shirts."

"Any logo?"

"Some car, I think. A rampant lion? Peugeot or something."

"Peugeot, that's funny, sir. Are you sure it wasn't Ferrari? A prancing black horse on a yellow background?"

"Yeah, that's it. Both of them."

Quigley drew the street scene as best he recalled it, like a defendant drawing an exhibit for judge and jury, and he told Omar the rest of the story, including the appearance of the solid-looking bald man and the sinister cop, and the bureaucratic indifference of the CBP agent.

"Oh, hell, I know you're trying to help, Omar, and maybe you can, but I have to go to the campus police right now."

"The campus cops? All they'll do is call your supervisor and rat you out."

"Professors don't have supervisors, Omar. Okay, they do. And the longer I wait, the worse it's going to be. I need to come clean now."

"If you do, the shit will hit the fan, guaranteed, and not just for you."

"What do you mean?"

"The story will get out, and it'll become an international incident and whoever has her will panic. That'll be bad for her. Sir, you need to wait to hear from them and see what they want. If it is an express, which I doubt, they'll just let her go tomorrow and end of story, like you said."

"Why would they call me? For ransom? They'd call her family, wouldn't they?"

"We don't even know who they are. Or what she's told them. If they've got her phone and heard your messages, they'll probably call you. Since you're the one who's worried."

Quigley's cell sagged heavy in his guayabera pocket.

"Sir, sometimes they don't ask for too much ransom," said Omar as he erased the drawing. "Ten thousand, five thousand, sometimes just, like, two. This one uncle of mine, they just told him to drive his Ford F150 over to La Reina and leave the keys in it and walk back to the bridge, so he did. And there's my kidnapped niece, waiting for him at the bridge, you know, crying. Anyway, sir, if you get a call back, make sure you talk to her, to make sure it's not just a virtual."

"Virtual?"

"Virtual kidnapping. That's when they just steal somebody's phone and call the relatives and pretend they're holding the owner. Sometimes the relatives fall for it and pay the ransom. Then the supposedly kidnapped person comes home and says she's lost her phone and wonders why everybody's crying and hugging her."

Quigley was having difficulty processing all this.

"Sir, just sit tight," said Omar. "I know people down there. I can ask around, find out what happened."

"How about this bald guy who got the cab for me? He could know something."

"If he does, he won't be saying. Not to us, anyway. He's security for the restaurant. If something bad happens there, his job is to make people believe it didn't."

"I shouldn't have left just because that guy said I should. I should've made that fucking cop look for her."

Omar shrugged. "Maybe so, maybe not. It's hard to say. That cop could've been involved with what happened to her. Anyway, you did leave. But, sir... there's another reason why you shouldn't go to the cops now, here or there."

"Why's that?"

"They'll suspect you."

"Me?"

"Like if she never shows up? Or if she shows up, you know..."

"What."

"Like not alive? Sorry, sir. You were the last one to be seen with her. The Mexican cops will make all kinds of stuff up to pin it on you."

Now Quigley's whole body sagged.

"If she was just some poor lady going to work the night shift at the maquilas, they'd just write it off as another un-solvable femicide." Omar paused. "Or is it fem*in*icide?"

"I don't know, Omar. Go on."

"Those bodies belong to nobodies. But a white chick, middle of the day, downtown? They'll look into that; you bet-ter believe it."

"She's not white, she's Hispanic."

"Hispanic? What does she look like?"

"I don't know. Slender. Medium height. Dressed in a black suit, you know, a woman's suit. Doesn't look like she's on her way to work in a fucking factory, no way."

"See there. Your first hunch is probably right, sir. Totally. She might have just wanted to disappear. I've heard of that. Or it could be an auto-kidnapping, you know, a self-kidnap-ping. Those happen too. Did you hear about the kid who sent his parents a ransom note from his made-up kidnappers and they replied, 'You know what? We're sick of that kid, all his lies, so we'll pay you half if you'll just disappear him.' So, the poor kid picks up the money at the drop-off and spends it all on drugs till he ODs. The parents later said they knew it was a selfie and were waiting for him to come home and say he was sorry. And he told his friends that he knew they knew and was waiting for them to find him and say *they* were sorry. I guess that's what they call a Mexican standoff, huh?"

"I really can't process that now, Omar."

"I'm sorry, sir. Sir, take this," Omar said, fishing a prescription bottle from his backpack and tapping out a long yellow tablet. "Just half. It'll calm you and help you focus."

Without even asking what it was, Quigley washed the half pill down with a slug from the water bottle he kept strapped to his satchel.

Omar handed him the orange container. "I've got more."

"These aren't going to knock me out, are they? I have to be awake for her call."

"No, sir. They'll focus you. Take another half if you need to."

Omar then reached into the pocket of Quigley's guayabera and plucked his phone out.

"My number," he said, thumbs working the keys. "You're gonna need it."

Chapter Eleven

Minerva waited deep into the night for the men's voices in the street, which had been raucous and alcohol-fueled, to slur down and disappear. Even then she waited, nodding off at times, until her fellow captives had ceased their little groanings and fretting. When only a deep snoring came from two or three of them, she dragged the thin dirty mattress to the door. She folded it accordion-like and stood on it. Fresh night air wafted onto her face from the transom. She placed her right foot on the door handle, grasped the frame and tried to hoist herself up. She slipped, fell back onto the mattress and the door flew open.

She jumped to her feet, lifting the mattress as a shield against the persons who had opened the door from the other side, the ni-nis no doubt, reprising, as some kind of sick joke, the flinging open of the restaurant back door that had propelled her into their clutches to begin with.

No one was there—just an empty, dark hallway. The door, astoundingly, hadn't been locked, and her stepping on the handle had opened it.

Cool, honeysuckle-scented air pulled her into a tiny, gated garden. The spear-point gate opened smoothly and without complaint, and she found herself on a dark street. She ducked behind a stout ebony tree—its whitewashed trunk glowed feebly—and listened briefly to the silence. She scurried from shadow to shadow, vaguely aware of obeying an ancient, rodent instinct. She made her way to a broader street, where a black-and-white sign read, *Puente Internacional 15 km*, its arrow pointing into a solid wall of darkness.

Should she go back for the others? She remembered their apathy, their resignation. They would resist her entreaties to escape with her, and by the time she convinced them to join her in flight, assuming she even could, their captors would be back.

But should she, a woman alone, head into that blackness? Shouldn't she go toward the cluster of orange and greenish lights in the opposite direction? Those lights, by their density and variety, had to indicate some sort of town center. Restaurants, hotels, telephones. Daybreak could not be far off, and then there would be somebody to whom she could tell her outrageous story, who would know which authorities to alert, if not the corrupt local police. Somebody who could drive her to the border, or at least lend her the fare for a bus or a taxi—no, not a taxi, never again a taxi, not in Mexico.

High headlights came bouncing wildly at her, and she dropped into the roadside huizaches. A Humvee or something like that, its grille a sinister grin, no license plate, roared past. Maybe it would be better to avoid the town altogether and hide in this thorn patch with its screaming insects until dawn, when buses to the border would surely start trundling by. But she didn't have a centavo on her, and besides, those border crossings were so busy, especially in the morning hours, and full of their own problems. Who there would even listen to her story, or care? If her alert was to have an effect, it had to be made locally.

She continued toward the town, sidling behind a tree or crouching close to the ground every time the rare vehicle came her way. Storefronts began to appear, their metal curtains drawn down and padlocked to a steel bar set into the sidewalk. Only one, a *carnicería*, had no curtain, as if daring thieves to steal the lone chicken hanging by its neck in the dirty window.

By the time she got to the plaza, dawn had begun to brighten the eastern sky. Backyard roosters crowed. She sought a bench next to a palm and touched the bumps on her arms from the punctures of the huizache thorns. The rising sun shone metallically on the blades of the palms, and the purple bougainvillea climbing up the bandstand lit up as if someone had plugged it in. A metal storefront curtain rose with a rattle, and a gnarled woman emerged and began sweeping the sidewalk. "The timeless rhythms of the Mexican village," as she recalled from some corny old *Mexico on $5 a Day* guide they'd studied in a class on the culture of travel.

A lump on the ground near Minerva grew limbs and yawned: a young shoe-shine boy. When he saw her, he jumped to his feet and pointed at her scuffed shoes. *"¿Boleada?"* His eyes gleamed with a polish of their own.

She wanted to reach out, hug him, tell him everything and at the same time push him away and tell him nothing.

"Me secuestraron," she blurted.

"¿Quiénes?" he asked.

"No sé." She began to describe the house to him, *"Una casa grande, blanca,"* but stopped, suddenly afraid. Those ni-nis sitting on their wall had seemed innocent enough too. The boy edged away, as if he, too, had become afraid.

The lettering on the building across the square read *Palacio Municipal H. La Sal*. It was a beautiful, two-story mustard-yellow colonial building with a clock tower and an elaborate bronze eagle-and-serpent shield centered beneath the lettering. A man on the roof raised the Mexican flag on a shining pole. The sun creeping down the façade revealed the fine grain of the gray stone lintels.

An hour or more passed before she heard further activity from the building, but she waited patiently for it to open, because she knew that was where she had to go. The boy, wrapped in his blanket, watched her from the base of his tree.

The pretty receptionist at the front desk listened with a growing expression of alarm to Minerva's story.

"Permítame un momento," the receptionist said.

She clicked on high heels down the parquet floor to a back office, closing the door behind her. In a few minutes she emerged with a young man in a brown sharkskin suit, his face a burnished brown as well, his eyes large and worried. The man introduced himself as the mayor's secretary and asked her to step into his office, which was bare of any décor except for pictures of his family on his desk. She repeated her story, to which he listened with grave attention.

"I would go to the police, but—"

"No, no, not the police."

In saying so, it was clear he was on the same page as she. Yes, this indeed had been the right place to come. Not to the undoubtedly corrupt police, but to the mayor's office, to people at a higher level and truly concerned about their town and its image.

He contemplated her for a mournful moment, excused himself and went into a back room. She heard his voice, low, talking to someone on a phone. *"Correcto,"* she heard him say.

"You say you can identify the building where you were held?" he asked on his return.

"Yes, yes," she said.

She'd had a good look at it. The safe house, the kidnappery, was one block off the road to the international bridge and around the corner from the sign saying the bridge was fifteen kilometers farther along. "I need to get to the bridge," she added.

"No se preocupe," he murmured, looking down at his hands.

Of course he was ashamed, and the intensity of that shame was no doubt what kept him from apologizing, just yet, for what had happened. She could forgive him for that. A US citizen gets kidnapped in his country a few steps from the border and is taken to his town to be held captive. The apology would come as he escorted her onto the bridge, perhaps followed by a request, she hoped not too groveling, that she not divulge what had happened to her, the implication being that she should show some solidarity with her *raza* and not further darken the already dim view the gringos had of the country of her ancestors.

"Would you like some coffee?" he asked.

"That would be wonderful. And your bathroom?"

"Certainly." They went out to the hall, where he told the receptionist to bring them coffee and, with a bow, showed Minerva the lady's room.

She examined her bloodshot eyes and wounded arms. The punctures from the thorns had swollen, and rope burns still reddened her wrists. Not exactly the best look for a job interview. She didn't need a doctor, but the man could have at least asked if she did. After she went to the toilet, washed her face, hands and arms and had her first sip of the delicious coffee brought to her by the receptionist, she calmed down. Her headache dissolved, and the stress began to recede and give way to a kind of elation as she imagined her fellow captives being liberated by the military or whoever else the mayor's office thought it best to notify. She imagined herself telling her crazy story to the Providencia press and basking in Quigley's, the search committee's and all of Bravo's relief.

The mayor's secretary glanced at her with his mournful eyes and looked down again at his hands. He was a man of few words and smiles. She was fine with being spared chit-chat and niceties. He was obviously simply anxious for her to identify the evil place to him and send her on her way, and so was she. They took a cool staircase down into the parking garage, where he summoned a car, an immense Ford Escalade with heavily tinted windows. A big man in mirrored sunglasses sat in the back with her while the secretary rode up front. The vehicle eased out of the garage and into the brightness.

The Escalade sped along the road she'd walked down earlier, swerving around pickups driven by hard-eyed young men. She got a glance at the carnicería with the single chicken dangling in the window. Before getting to the bridge sign—

was that it up there?—the driver hung a sharp left. She was about to say something, but they probably knew what they were doing. They needed to sneak around to the house by the back way, maybe. But would she be able to identify it from that approach? And if they knew about the secuestradero already—the driver seemed to know exactly where he was going—why did they need her? Just to confirm?

The Escalade lurched down a heavily potholed alley and gave two blasts of its horn. An iron gate halfway down the alley rolled open, revealing the rear of a two-story house in the white stucco of the secuestradero. The Escalade bounced into the bare parking area and two young men rolled the gate shut behind them with a great clang. Minerva whipped around and got a look at them. The two ni-nis.

Chapter Twelve

A space expanded in Quigley's head as Omar walked him to his car. The wind in the palms sounded remote, oceanic.

"I'm already feeling it."

"The pill? You'll be okay, sir. Go straight home, though."

"Yeah, great, get pulled over for DUI and they find her bag in the trunk. Wouldn't that make my day."

"Whose bag?"

"The candidate's. The missing woman's."

"You shouldn't have that in your possession, sir. You need to get rid of it."

"What do you mean, get rid of it?"

"All her stuff. You can give the bag to me, sir. I'll take care of it."

"And when she comes back and all her shit's gone? What am I supposed to tell her then?"

"That your car got broken into? Like when it was parked under the bridge? Just a bad day all around, right? Anyway, sir? This is supposing she's coming back."

"It sure is," Quigley said, outrage clawing its way up from his growing detachment. "Unless she's run off on her own, I sure as hell am supposing that."

"Yes, sir. Me too. Definitely. But until she does, maybe it's not so good to be driving around with her things."

"Okay, so I'll put them in my apartment!"

"Yes, sir," Omar said doubtfully.

Home was only six blocks from campus, and when Quigley got there, having attended carefully to his turn signaling and speed, he plopped her bag defiantly in the middle of the living room floor. No need to hide it, much less get rid of it. It wasn't as though he'd done anything to her!

He then spent the long, wretched night on the couch in a yellow aura of wakeful distance, several times jumping to his phone before realizing that the vibration was only in his mind. The only sound outside his head was the insane night-long singing of the mockingbird in the crape myrtle outside his bedroom window. The energy it must take to produce that song after long, sweltering days hunting bugs and dive-bombing cats and building nests! This was the third night of it, filling the block with patternless piles of warbles and trills. Surely this night song was only a seasonal thing, a spring thing. A birder would know. The area abounded in birders, lying as it did beneath major migratory flyways. How great to be a mere birder down here, blissfully unconcerned with local human affairs. The birders flitted about the towns, interacting with non-birders only to procure food or shelter, and that only when they didn't come down in their own fully supplied campers. Their gaze flew up to tree branches and down to field journals, pausing on another human face only when it was telling them something about avian sightings of interest. Their ears listened almost exclusively for chirps, warbles, trills and quacks, becoming attentive to human vocalizations only when they involved questions and answers about birds.

He could ask a birder, "How many nights in a row can one of these mockingbirds sing without collapsing from exhaustion? I've spent just one night of lost sleep over a disappeared colleague, who I hope like hell hasn't been kidnapped, and I'm about to lose my mind." And the birder would answer, "Aren't they amazing little buggers? I've known them to go on like that night after night. It's the males, you know, marking their territory, looking for mates...." And on and on, and Quigley would wait in vain for the double-take and the say-*what?*

At first gray light of dawn, the mockingbird abruptly stopped its song and swooped down from the myrtle to snap up some winged insect, and Quigley got up to make his coffee and begin his own brutal day.

He'd called Minerva's cell twice in the night, and now he called her again, leaving the same message: "Minerva, William Quigley again, please call this number, we're very worried, this number, please." He repeated the number, slowly. His voice sounded weak, as if he'd been singing all night like that damned bird.

Although he didn't teach any classes on Thursdays, it behooved him to get to campus as soon as possible. He couldn't, without raising suspicions, spend all day loitering around the department offices waiting to intercept any call she might make there. But he should be close by, in his office, ready to provide whatever damage control might be necessary.

Before leaving, he placed her bag in the coat closet by the front door, which was otherwise empty, because no one needed a coat in a subtropical climate like this. It was as if the developers followed the same designs they used back in Duluth. What next, fireplaces? It was sad how closely the architecture and landscaping down here hewed to the suburban American aesthetic. Boxlike brick homes with double garages, surrounded by manicured lawns impaled, in many cases, with staffs bearing American flags, as if to doubly assure everybody that this was still the USA and not Mexico.

He'd once fantasized that as soon as he got tenure and a decent teaching schedule, he'd keep a room in the handsome, Moorish-style Hotel, El Dorado, off the La Reina plaza. He would get his coffee every morning at the Café París downstairs, dine at the Las Brasas or along the "calle del taco," live a quasi-Bohemian life perfectly possible on the Mexican side on his augmented salary. When the narco wars heated up in earnest, he'd abandoned that idea, settling for having to impress his peers at other schools (and ignorant relatives who liked to belittle his profession by saying how remote it was from the "real world") with tales, culled mostly from the local papers, of the danger and violence so close by. Now those stories didn't seem quite so glamorous a backdrop.

As soon as he heard Esmeralda's keys jangling in the department office door, he rushed over from his own office with a stack of midterm exam questions to photocopy.

"Good morning, Professor Quigley!"

She was always sunny in the morning, but her disposition often darkened over the course of the day, so that by afternoon she became the tough, chin-jutting mean girl she must've been in high school. At her most unctuous, she was so exaggeratedly fake that he had the urge to usher her into his rhet/comp class so the students could behold and understand irony personified.

She peeked into the photocopy room, nodded at his papers. "Oh, the work studies will do that for you. You look like you need some rest!"

"That's all right, I've got it. Thank you, Esmeralda."

When she returned to her office, he put the photocopy machine on pause and listened for her to pick up the telephone to check her messages. She spoke briefly to someone, then yelled, "Quigley!"

He rushed to her.

"The candidate didn't check into the Super 8. Dr. Garza thinks someone should call her school and find out if they know what happened."

Quigley wondered if she meant Garza the chair or Garza the dean or if it was actually Esmeralda's idea, not that it mattered. Esmeralda was of one mind with the Garzas, so that if the latter two could be known as the chean, it was really three in one—the *cheanalda*, then.

"But candidates usually don't want their institutions to know they're on the market, Esme. To call her school could be a violation of confidentiality."

"That's for when they're already professors. She's a student! Of course they're going to be wanting her to be looking for a position. Especially her dissertation advisor. We paid for her flight and hotel, so I guess we have a right to know what happened. She better not be lying on the beach at Padre Island!"

"Of course. You're right. I'll call this morning."

"It should be Diosdado to call. He's the committee chair. The phone's not going to bite him. Tell him phones don't bite."

Esmeralda was big on not biting. She herself didn't bite, she made sure everyone knew. "Come on in, I don't bite!" she could be heard calling, with some frequency, from her office to some hesitant student or adjunct. Oddly, if anyone were to bite, it would most certainly be she.

"That's okay, I'll call. It's my fault anyway."

"How is it your fault?" She fixed him with her black eyes.

"Not fault, uh, responsibility. I was supposed to pick her up and…" He held out empty hands.

From his office he emailed Duarte and the other committee members to tell them he would contact Ms. Mondragón's dissertation advisor—one Professor Burris, as he remembered from her CV—to find out what had happened.

He had no intention of doing that, of course. If she had planned to disappear into Mexico, which he persisted in believing was a possibility as if his sanity depended on it, she wouldn't have told anyone she was headed this way. So why worry the folks in New Mexico about her? He could tell the committee that he'd called and left a message, and that the man hadn't returned his call. Or he could say he'd reconsidered the confidentiality thing and thought he'd better consult the EEOC rep first. Or…

The photocopies of the midterm stared up at him from his desk. Question 3: "How does the narrator react to Bartleby when Bartleby says, 'I would prefer not to'?" Which is obviously what he, Assistant Professor Quigley, should have told the chean when the chean asked him to sit on the search committee. "Since I'm on tenure track and need to concentrate on my research, I would prefer not to." But being no Bartleby, he'd readily agreed to serve on the search committee and had even volunteered to pick her up at the airport. Clearly what he should have done then was bring her directly to campus, introduce her to the front office people in the department, leave her with a campus map and let her familiarize herself with the place. But okay, okay, why keep beating himself up about it?

His phone buzzed in his upper shirt pocket. He grabbed at it like he would a heart attack. Omar.

"Sir, I checked out those sources for my paper and I'm doing the research. Could we meet this afternoon? Like maybe at one?"

"Paper?"

"Yes, sir. The paper we talked about last night."

It took Quigley a moment to get the indirection.

"Oh, yes, certainly. Come by my office."

Then he remembered how thin the walls were, how you could hear the next-door lecturer's every word as she explained to students that commodity fetishism meant addiction to shopping and that a double bacon cheeseburger was sublime in the Burkeian scheme of things but a Krispy Kreme with sprinkles was merely beautiful.

"Actually, Omar, let's meet off campus. Is Doña Tota's all right? I'll get lunch."

Chapter Thirteen

By the time Omar arrived, forty-six minutes late, Quigley had drunk two sugary horchatas. He didn't have an appetite, so he skipped his usual gordita. He swallowed yet another yellow pill, which renewed the sense of distance but did nothing to quell the maddening twitching of his eyelids.

"Sorry I'm late, sir, but I've been following up on a weird story," Omar said, after looking around to see that no one could overhear him. "My sources tell me there's this lady in this town just east of La Reina called La Sal who matches the description of your lady. They say she's been kidnapped. The thing is, the Gamboas control La Reina and the towns east of La Reina in Frontera Chica, and like I told you last night, the Gamboas don't go in for kidnapping, like not at all. So I don't get it."

"The Gamboas?"

"The Gamboa Organization. They totally control all those plazas."

"Jesus Christ. Now you're saying drug cartels *are* involved."

"It's always cartels involved on the border, sir."

"But you say they're not holding her?"

"I'm saying they *shouldn't* be holding her. No kidnapping or extortion in Gamboa plazas. That goes back to the days when they wanted to stay good with the community. These new groups like the…" he lowered his voice to a whisper before he pronounced their name, "the Zetas, they don't give a shit about any of that. But I don't think the junior would be changing Gamboa policy."

"The junior?"

"Eduardo Gamboa, *El Junior*. He's the head of the cartel. For now. Ever since his father... Robustiano Gamboa, you've heard of him? No? Well, ever since Robustiano got snatched by the judicial police and the DEA a few months ago and got packed off to the US, the junior's had this thing about kidnapping. Because he insists his dad was kidnapped, not properly extradited."

"So where is this woman? And you're sure it's the candidate?"

Omar gave a slow shrug.

"You don't know where she is, or you're not sure it's she?"

"Oh, I think it's the lady you were talking about. I just don't understand how she could have been snatched in Gamboa territory. Unless El Junior's losing control of the plaza and some of his people are taking advantage of it and are going off on their own, kidnapping people and stuff against his orders. It happens."

"So what you're telling me is that not only did I manage to get the job candidate snatched, I landed her in the middle of some kind of narco turf war."

"It's a developing story, sir."

Quigley took another sip of horchata, but as the cold drink went down, another kind of cold expanded in him, the same cold as when his grad school girlfriend had made it clear, despite much cajoling and tears, that she wasn't going to marry him, even if it meant Bravo University would consider her for a spousal hire. She either couldn't stomach the thought of being his wife, or living in South Texas and working at Bravo, or all three. That realization made the coldness bloom in his own stomach then, just as the realization that Minerva had most likely been kidnapped did now. The walls of Doña Tota's were hung with images from the board game lotería, and Quigley found his gaze lingering on the depiction of a veiny, arrow-pierced *corazón*.

"How do you know all this?" he asked Omar.

"The sources."

"How did you get to the sources?"

Omar thought for a moment before answering. "My family's been here a long time."

"That doesn't answer the question."

"They've been in business on the border since Prohibition. The same business. That's almost a hundred years."

Ah, so a smuggling family, no doubt vastly extended. First liquor, then pot and now, he supposed, the powders and the crystals. That would account for his knowledge about what was going on with the cartels, who were presumably his family's suppliers on the "other side." What else did they smuggle? Immigrants? Sex slaves? Just wonderful.

"I appreciate your help, Omar, I really do. But it's obviously time for me to come clean and go to the police."

"Sir, I don't think that's a good idea. Not right now."

"Well, we know where she is, don't we? La what is it?"

"La Sal."

"And we know what happened, more or less, right? So let me tell them what we know and get it over with."

"No, sir. Things are too… volatile right now. We're not really sure what's happening. We don't want to force anybody's hand."

"So, who has her? The cartel, or this, this hypothetical rogue group?"

"Not sure. It's a fluid situation. I don't think anybody's going to try to ransom her, though. Like I say, the cartel doesn't hold people for ransom, and this other group, what did you call it?"

"Rogue."

"Yeah, rogue group. I don't think they know how to deal with an American hostage. If they still have her, even. Because it seems like she escaped at one point, or they let her go, or something."

Quigley touched the spastic spot under his eye, and it trembled beneath his finger.

"Escaped? How do you know that?"

"A shoeshine boy on the plaza saw her and told the Gamboa people."

"A shoeshine boy?"

"They make good falcons, sir. Spies."

"I've heard the term applied to cab drivers."

"Them too. According to this kid, she went into the palacio municipal, the city hall, and never came out. Sir, this is what I think is going to happen: junior Gamboa is gonna shut down the rogue kidnapping operation immediately, and they're gonna take her to the bridge. Then, hopefully, she calls you and you go get her."

"You're sure about that."

"That's the way I see it going down, sir."

Quigley wanted to believe him. And why shouldn't he believe him? He was obviously well-informed. He could be making all this up, but why on earth would he do that?

"And if they start looking for her before that happens?"

"Who?"

"Friends of hers. Relatives. Colleagues."

"Cross that bridge when we get to it. Sorry, boss. Bad pun."

"Well, speaking of bridges, if nobody wants this gringa, I don't see why they don't just drop her off at one of them and be done with her."

"Oh, no, sir. It's full of roadblocks down there now."

"Okay, so much the better! She can tell the soldiers or police or whoever's manning them who she is and get a military escort the rest of the way."

"Whoever's manning them is the thing. Could be military, straight up. Or could be off-duty or ex-military guys with their own agenda. Could be narcos dressed in military uniforms. Could be *autodefensas*, maybe corrupt ones. Or could be local *delincuentes*, barrio punks. You never know."

Quigley rubbed his eyes. "Oh, God. Okay."

He stirred the ice in his horchata slowly. "You know, I had this hope—I know this sounds bad—that she'd planned to disappear, which means she wouldn't have notified anyone who'd come looking for her."

"I've heard of cases like that on TV," Omar said. "But it's always older guys that've embezzled a bunch of money or something. Except that guy in the story you assigned at the beginning of the semester, the one who came back to his wife after twenty years, no explanation. That was weird."

"'Wakefield,' yeah. Hawthorne. See, it happens. She even mentioned disappearing herself when we were down there, like she was giving me a clue. She's something of a poet, you know, and poets are not known for their sanity."

Omar shook his head in pity.

"Anyway, I've already told the committee I'd call her faculty advisor to ask about her, so I guess I'd better."

"Don't do it, sir."

"Why not? I can ask how her dissertation is coming along, if she'll have it in hand by the time the position starts here, you know, make it seem like her visit and interviews are proceeding normally. Put their minds at ease."

Omar got up and came back with a squeeze bottle of green sauce for his gordita.

"But like you said, Professor. You don't even know for sure if her people back home know she planned to interview here at Bravo. So why alert them to it? Just keep your current story tight. Like in-house? Tell your committee that you called the advisor and that he said she didn't make it because she, I don't know... because she had a mental breakdown, being a poet and all, but that not to worry, she's getting the care she needs. End of story. Your committee will drop it because nobody wants to hire a crazy person, right?"

"Well, that won't work because the committee knows no faculty advisor is going to violate his student's confidentiality by referring to her medical condition, but I get your drift. I'll think of something."

They walked back to campus, a humid wind plastering his shirt to his sweating back. On a bench near the entrance to the humanities building sat Duarte, furtively smoking.

"Thanks for calling Burris," he said, cigarette dangling from the hand at his side. He looked askance at Omar, and Omar took the hint, told Quigley he'd keep revising his paper and moved along.

"Does he know anything?" Duarte asked.

"That student?" Quigley said, voice rising in alarm. "About what?"

"Student, heck. Burris. Does Professor Burris, the candidate's advisor, know anything about why she didn't show?"

Quigley hated conversing in this spot, possibly the hottest spot on campus, a wide swath of brick pavement baking between the south-facing building and the parking lot. But colleagues, especially the smoking kind, always caught you here, where heat wafted off the asphalt as the cigarette smoke wafted into your face and the Pepsi machine—Bravo was a "Pepsi campus"—chugged along, spewing its own machine heat into the mix. Its stupid placement, Quigley had often thought, made it possibly the most hard-working refrigeration unit on the planet. Now he sweated extra with the stress of having to fabricate a nonexistent conversation with Burris.

"Oh. Yeah. Funniest thing. What he says is, 'That's our Minerva!'"

"Meaning?"

"Meaning, I guess, that she's a total flake."

"So does he have any idea where she is?"

At that moment the sliding doors to the building parted and Esmeralda blew out in a volley of polar air.

"The advisor called and, whoops!" she said, covering her mouth. Every once in a while, she became aware of the con-

flict between the occasional need for discretion and her pro-
clivity for announcing things from great distances.

"Professor Burris called," she said, lowering her voice and
drawing close to Quigley and Duarte. "I'd gone ahead and
shot him an email about her no-show, and he called right back
and sounded very surprised and concerned. He said he would
like to talk to you, Dr. Quigley."

Damn Esmeralda for jumping the gun, but so typical of her.
Now Duarte was looking at him quizzically, because hadn't
Quigley just said he'd already spoken to the man?

Quigley had never been good at thinking on his feet, especially since his legs often became rubbery when required
to do so—like now. This was why he'd never considered such
professions as trial lawyer or journalist or floor trader or policeman, and why he was somewhat ashamedly relieved that
his Bravo students rarely challenged what he said, or otherwise put him on the spot, the way he'd heard students at other
schools did, especially those at higher ranked schools.

But the heat and fatigue and the sugary *horchata* somehow
pushed him into overdrive, and he was able to rally his wits.
"Ah, so now that he's had a little time to think about it, he's taking it a little more seriously. Because, as I was telling Dr.
Duarte here, when we spoke this morning, he was all, 'That's
our crazy poet!' I hope he does call me... call me back."

Esmeralda and Duarte nodded, and Quigley felt he was on
a roll. He could deal with this Burris. If he told Burris that
Minerva simply hadn't shown, the man would insist that they
launch an investigation. So, he'd have to tell Burris another
story, something to keep him at bay until the narcos released
Minerva.

As he entered the building, Omar, who had been lingering
by the Pepsi machine as if pondering his choices, turned to him
with a look as expressionless as a fish, giving away nothing.

Chapter Fourteen

The big man sitting next to Minerva in the back seat of the Escalade pressed something to her side, and she had an instant to be amazed at the tiny bolt of lightning and the shower of blue sparks before she collapsed into herself, every muscle losing its meaning, and then started to stretch upward and stiffen. She watched a green-veined hand drag her body out onto the driveway, where they gave her another shock. She went limp again, and two men grabbed under the arms and hauled her into the secuestradero.

They snatched off her shoes and shoved her into a wooden crate, solid except for a few breathing holes drilled into the sides. A padlock clicked in the hasp. As muscle control came back to her, she began to knock on the sides of the box, feebly at first but then vigorously, pounding. She kept pounding and screaming, making the padlock jump, until they snaked a wire into a breathing hole and touched her thigh, giving her a jolt even worse than the one in the car, more acute, burning down her right leg to the tips of her toes. She lay quiet then, like a body in a coffin.

Now she understood what her fellow captive, that middle-aged woman, meant by *"Es todo un secuestradero."* The whole town was one big kidnappery. Even the highest authorities, all those people in the palacio municipal, from the mayor's obsequious secretary to the receptionist, were in on it. And any captive who tried to escape would be shocked and put in a box, or worse.

She should've listened to the woman. She had to learn to listen. Had she finally learned her lesson? One of the rote questions they asked you in job interviews was, "What would you say your greatest weakness is?" In preparing for the Bravo interview, she had considered this and decided admitting that sometimes she didn't listen well was too damning an admission, so she'd decided she would give her interviewers a rather more anodyne, though not unrelated, response: in class discussions, she probably didn't give the students enough time to answer the questions she posed before answering them herself. The interviewers would nod, acknowledging that they were often guilty of the same sin, because it was the hardest thing in the world for a teacher to do, to endure the silence.

All she could do now was listen, lie in her pseudo-coffin and listen. The men who had stuffed her into it had gone. For a while there was just silence, only interrupted by a slow-buzzing fly bouncing dementedly off the box. No, wait, there was one man left, grunting now at a woman, ordering her to make a call. A moment later, the woman was asking someone on the phone how much ransom money they'd gathered, and she told the man, "*Diez mil.*" The man told her to tell them to take it to a certain street corner immediately, and when she had done so, the man commanded, "*Vámonos.*"

Diez mil—ten thousand. That was it? Surely, they meant dollars and not pesos, but even so, it was nothing for a kidnapping ransom. It gave her hope. She just needed to bide her time, and when they let her out of the box, she would tell them she could get ten thousand dollars. Because they had to let her out, didn't they? How long did they think they could leave her there? A wave of nausea burned up her throat, but she forced it back down, swallowing hard. She couldn't let panic take hold of her. Of course they would let her out. They were angry with her, justifiably so, but that would pass. This was their business, and they were reasonable businessmen, and just wanted money. As soon as she heard the man return, as soon as she heard any of the men, she would call out to him, in the calmest voice she could muster, that she would like to make him an offer.

A pair of cockroach antennae waved in the hole they'd sneaked the wire into. She closed her eyes. She'd wet herself a little when they'd shocked her, and she concentrated on the clammy discomfort to distract her from the hideous image of them carrying her out in the box like pallbearers and burying her alive in the ready-made coffin.

Some time later, she had no idea how long, a door slammed, the suddenness of the noise sending a shower of blue sparks like those of the stun gun inside her eyelids. Running feet slapped across the floor below. Popping sounds outside, getting louder and closer. A vehicle roared down the street, followed by another. Angry voices shouted orders. And then the angriest voice of all from down below: "*¿Dónde está?*"

Somehow, she knew the voice meant her. The infuriated man was asking where she was. And it didn't sound like he was coming to negotiate a deal.

"*¿Dónde?*" the man demanded again, growing closer.

"*¿Dónde estás?*" She remembered her idiot high school boyfriend yelling that in his jealous rage, before finding her cowering in her closet and breaking her jaw. His assault had propelled her to the dojo, where Sensei had taught her *Kyokushin* with every possible variation of *ichigeki hissatsu*—one blow, certain death. For two years, Minerva had practiced, practiced, practiced, though she'd slacked off since entering the final stretch of her dissertation. Now she had to see if she remembered, if her body remembered.

"*¿Dónde?*" the man demanded again, growing closer. She'd practiced many a kata with those syllables pounding in her ears. She'd never cower before them again.

She attacked from her supine position as the man lifted the box lid. Attacked the sack, as Sensei enjoyed putting it, in the way Sensei had taught her, aimed not at the testicles but through them and beyond, her fist driving into his body at an upward angle. As he went down, she sprang up in a single fluid, choreographed motion. The man's companion reared back in amazement at this hellcat released genie-like from the box, his throat wide open for her spear hand, his head snapping down an instant too late to protect his trachea. *Fast, committed, devastating* — she hadn't forgotten the mantra. Now her heel came down with all the force of her torqued hips on the first man's temple as he lay in a fetal position, hands folded prayer-like at his groin.

A spray of bullets from the street pierced the foil on the window and thudded into the ceiling. Minerva dropped to the floor, hugging it with her ear pressed hard to the tile, panicked footfalls thudding below, gypsum dust floating gently down on her.

Chapter Fifteen

Professor Burris cradled the receiver of his office telephone gingerly after speaking with Assistant Professor William Quigley and watched students flick a Frisbee across Smith Plaza. What a strange and disturbing conversation. The things this Quigley said about Minerva Mondragón did not sound like her at all. This business about her needing to go off and "get her head together" or "find her center" or whatever it was. He couldn't imagine such hippie-speak from her. True, she had that martial arts thing going on and he supposed those dojo folks spoke of "centering," but the overall story Quigley spun just did not compute with what Burris knew of Minerva. For her to have gotten off the plane and immediately start talking to Quigley, a virtual stranger, about her need to "find herself" before she committed to the tenure track, to confide in him her doubts about an academic career in general—when she had never expressed such doubts to Burris, her very mentor and advisor!—and finally to ask him to drop her off at the Providencia bus station with no plan as to destination.... None of that rang true.

Quigley sounded young and unsure, with a voice that started out firm but lapsed into a quavering and a cracking that betrayed his lying, and she might have been able to persuade such a man to tell the Bravo search committee that she simply hadn't shown. And catching a bus into Mexico— Quigley had hinted it might be Mexico—on a lark would not be unlike Minerva. But the Minerva he knew would go on such a jaunt only after her interviews and upon making arrangements with the department secretary to change her return flight to Albuquerque. She was adventurous, yes, but not irresponsible.

"Or maybe she's spring breaking on Padre Island, who knows!" Quigley had said, by then with a near-hysterical note in his voice.

Burris could see her taking an anthropological interest in spring break, appraising it in an amused, detached way. But to be partying on the beach with the kids in celebration of having abandoned her academic career? Nope, he couldn't see that. Certainly wouldn't want to.

Another odd thing was the man referring to her as a "poet," implying that her erratic behavior was par for the course for poets, and that everybody on the committee understood and was even prepared to forgive her for it. Minerva a poet? Burris remembered how he'd explained to her that a CV, unlike a résumé, was a kitchen sink kind of thing, and when she mentioned she'd published a couple of poems and a short story, he'd recommended she list them as well, perhaps under a new heading, "Creative Works." No, it wouldn't be "padding," he assured her. Kitchen sink, remember?

Minerva was the first Ph.D. candidate in the program he'd helped establish, and she had what it took to succeed. She was not the kind of student Burris worried about. He had called Bravo only because the department secretary had emailed him to ask if he knew why she hadn't shown for the campus visit. The secretary, Esmeralda, told him that the man who was supposed to have picked her up from the airport, this Quigley, would be calling him. Burris tried calling Minerva, to no avail, and then Quigley had called him with this crazy story that she'd gotten cold feet about the job and taken off on a bus to Mexico, asking that Quigley cover for her by telling the committee that she hadn't shown at all.

The Bravo job, Assistant Professor of Border Studies, sounded perfect for her, and he'd alerted her to it. The ad for the position had popped up in the MLA Job Information List just when Sandra Crowley, Principal Investigator and Director of the Center for Intelligence Education, had begun meeting with him and the Center's other dedicated faculty about laying the groundwork for getting the ODNI grant extended for another five years. To keep the grant, they needed to show the senior advisory board metrics, outcomes and results, *deliverables*. Burris knew that the ODNI, the Office of the Director of National Intelligence, was keen on expanding its Intelligence Education Centers to other campuses, particularly to the Historically Black, the Tribal, the Asian-American-Serving and the Hispanic-Serving Institutions. Bravo already had a smaller-scale Intelligence Center for Academic Practice and was seeking full IEC certification. The Bravo ad stated that the successful candidate would be expected to help develop and launch a cross-disciplinary Border Studies Program. Such a program could play a pivotal role in establishing a full-scale Center, Burris had told Sandra, with Minerva as one of its dedicated faculty, perhaps eventually its administrator. Would that not be a "deliverable" for which New Mexico could take some credit?

Sandra had allowed that it would, but she was skeptical about Minerva. "Advisors often have expectations of their students that the students don't share," she had told him in that textbooky way of hers. "Have you talked to her about participation in the Center at Bravo?"

Burris admitted that he hadn't, yet. But there would be time to pitch it to her once she had the job.

"How sure are you that she'll be hired?" Sandra had asked.

"Bravo clearly wants the position filled. This is a second-round ad. None of the respondents to the fall ad worked out, apparently. There probably hadn't been many applicants.

Border Studies is, after all, a new field, if you could even call it a field yet."

His enthusiasm was such that he'd hinted to Sandra that she might want to alert the Dean of Humanities at Bravo, or even the provost, that they had a job applicant with the potential for securing some serious federal monies for their school, but she'd demurred, saying something about jumping the chain of command.

ICAP at the University of New Mexico had an office in Mesa Vista Hall. Burris headed there now. He found Sandra dressed in leggings and running shoes and jabbing at her keyboard while peering closely at her oversized computer screen. As soon as he mentioned Minerva was missing, she jumped up and grabbed a track jacket.

"Let's take a walk, shall we?"

It wasn't the first time she'd asked him to walk with her while they talked, which he took as commentary on his gut and his sedentary ways.

Once outside, she said, "Sensitive conversations are best conducted in sparsely populated outdoor settings. Hold your thoughts till we get to Johnson Field."

What made her think what he was about to tell her was sensitive? More likely, she just wanted to get out of the office and was disguising it as a "teachable moment." As if he were a student and not a full professor a good fifteen years her senior. But a mere professor of cultural linguistics, of course, whereas her field was something called Social and Decision Sciences. She'd been president of the Society for Risk Management, and she had received the Defense Intelligence Agency's Civilian Expeditionary Medal for intelligence gathering in Afghanistan.

Boots on the ground there, sneakers on the ground here. She walked fast, arms pumping at her sides. He had to break into a trot to keep up with her. It was an unpleasant, wispy-clouded day, the raw high-desert wind whipping across the playing field.

As she did her stretches, palms against the trunk of an elm as if trying to push it over, he gave her the scoop.

"You're sure this Quigley's hiding something?" she said. "You don't think it happened just like he said… she got cold feet?"

"Minerva doesn't get cold feet. She's tough, she's persistent. You know her story. Grew up in a single-parent home in the South Valley, went straight through undergrad and graduate school without a hitch. When I told her a doctorate from the venerable UNM Spanish and Portuguese Department would honestly be more marketable than one from our brand-new cultural studies program, she took it as a challenge and stayed with us. She doesn't dither around 'finding her head.'"

"Well, if she doesn't show, I can have one of our people down there look around, see if his story holds up."

"She *hasn't* shown. Well, she has, but he's the only one who's seen her, or so he says. And I suppose our people are expecting her as well."

"Why would they be? You didn't give anyone at Bravo the head's up about her, her potential value in getting an IEC going there?"

"Nope. Well, I might've shot the department chair and the dean something along those lines."

"That's breaking the chain of command, Douglas."

"Well, I couldn't exactly say it in my letter of rec. Who knows what anti-Americanism lurks among that search committee faculty. Spy school! CIA on campus! But the admins, they understand and respect the external funding that comes with it, as you know."

"You're jumping the gun with this girl, aren't you, Douglas?"

"No, I don't think so. Didn't I tell you she helped me do some language work for IARPA?" IARPA was an obscure federal agency with an appropriately convoluted name, Intelligence Advanced Research Products Activity.

"Unwittingly, I hope."

"Sure, but so what? It was all unclassified stuff. And Snowden leaked the rest anyway."

"Yes, I'm aware."

Burris was also sure he'd told Sandra what a good conference organizer Minerva was. This year and last, she'd been instrumental in making the annual Southwest Popular/American Culture Association conference in downtown Albuquerque a success, helping with logistics from panel scheduling to off-site happy hours. It went without saying that she could be useful in pulling together conferences down on the border that could attract scholars from Latin America who could in turn be recruited by US intelligence services. These conferences would be funded by what Sandra called "cutouts," intermediaries through which intelligence agency funds could be laundered, as it were, so that they weren't traceable back to the agencies.

"Douglas, I know she's one of your stars and you have high hopes for her, but the Center has her down as a potential-potential at this point. The Center's involvement and obligations are currently quite minimal regarding Minerva Mondragón. But you've come to us for help, and we will provide it. So, first off, who's going to start worrying about her? I don't imagine her mother will."

Sandra made it her business to know about persons of interest to the Center, even those as marginal as Minerva. She no doubt had read the statement of purpose in Minnie's application to grad school. In that letter, written in the novelistic style supposedly required for such documents to stand out from the pack—to his old-school mind, it was way too personal, but young people spilled their guts publicly and without a second thought on social media these days—she'd addressed her very conception, which allegedly took place on a moonless night on the summit of a Oaxacan pyramid to which her "Toltec" father and Chicana hippie mother from Santa Fe had ascended following some sort of mushroom-laced ceremony. The "Toltec" father vanished (the scare-quotes were Minnie's because Toltecs may have never existed except in Aztec mythology, she noted, careful to distance herself from the woo-woo) to be replaced by a series of dysfunctional stepdads. Her mother gave Minnie her maiden name, Mondragón, and they ended up in Albuquerque's rough South Valley. By then, Santa Fe had become too gentrified and expensive to move back to. Minnie's academic career was sparked by a conference she stumbled across as a college freshman: the annual meeting of the Southwest Popular/American Culture Association. She had gone to the conference hotel in Old Town with a boyfriend to deliver a bag of weed to a grad student who would be giving a paper on *Buffy the Vampire Slayer*. (She had wisely omitted the drug dealing detail from the essay, and he'd been flattered that she'd confided it to him when retelling the story to him later.) She'd been amazed that popular culture could be the subject of serious study at universities, and she'd snuck back into the conference the next day, sans boyfriend. That day of panels and readings had changed her life, setting her on an academic track that she hadn't wavered from since. As a grad student, she became an important organizer of the PCA/ACA conference for several years running.

"You are correct, her mother's not the worrying kind," said Burris. "But if she tries calling Minnie and can't get through, she'll probably call me to find out why."

"Anyone else to be concerned about her? Boyfriend? Girlfriend?"

"Not that I know of."

"Okay. If the mom calls, tell her what this Quigley told you. Hopefully she'll buy it and not go file some missing person report before we've had time to look into it. Meanwhile, we'll root around in Minerva's emails to see if we can find any clues there."

"You're going to *hack* her email?"

"Her .edu account isn't hers, Doug. It belongs to the State of New Mexico. Nobody's email here is actually private. I trust you know that?"

"Can't you track her cell phone? By GPS or whatever?"

"We'll put a stingray on it."

"What's wrong with a missing persons report? Maybe we ought to let local law enforcement down there handle it."

"And who do you think they'll interview first? Quigley. He'll just tell them what he told you, that she took off on her own, and that'll be it. Case closed."

Sandra checked the Fitbit on her wrist, waved goodbye absently to Burris and took off in a jog down the running track. He trudged back to his office, hunched against the wind, disappointed that Sandra hadn't seen Minerva's potential in quite the way he did— "potential-potential," what the hell? That's why she hadn't given the Bravo administrators the heads up about Minerva's application. Burris indeed wanted her to get the job on her own academic merits, but in this tough job market it never hurt to have her candidacy eased up the chain of command by administrators keen on getting an Intelligence Education Center at Bravo. Now all he'd done was give Sandra a reason to spy on Minerva's emails and find out all kinds of private things about her—including things she said about him, probably.

Until today, Burris' involvement with the Center had been so uncomplicated. All he had to do was suggest a few language and linguistics courses for the Security Studies Program, send students to Center-sponsored colloquia, help organize a study abroad to wherever. The grant monies that came with this involvement had been low-hanging fruit, nice plump figures to add to his own CV and the External Funding line on his Annual Merit Review form.

Burris dialed Minerva's cell from his office phone, but once again no answer, and he couldn't leave a message because her voice mail was full. Another reason for her mother to call him, and when she did, he would dutifully do what Sandra had instructed him to do and relay Quigley's lies to her, in the interest of buying the Center some time.

Chapter Sixteen

Minerva remembers it this way: ninja-like men in black ski-masks, balaclavas or whatever they were called, bursting into the secuestradero, dragging out the men she had attacked, yelling orders. Now those among her fellow captives who had cell phones were shouting into them, repeating the address that one of the soldiers had given them. The women without phones clutched at those that did, begging them to let them borrow them. Cars screeched up to the building, and the freed captives piled in and rushed from the scene.

One of the masked men spoke into his phone, voice muffled, lips moving wormlike beneath the fabric, clear brown eyes fixed on her. "*Sí, patrón, es ella.*"

Later she would realize that a real soldier wouldn't call his superior "*patrón*." At the moment, she assumed they were Marinas, which she remembered Quigley as having said were the only law-enforcement group that could be halfway trusted. She allowed them to lower a Kevlar vest over her head and hustle her into an armored vehicle that looked like a cross between a Jeep and a Brinks truck. They roared off with her, gunfire popping behind them, the air inside rank with exhaust and sweaty bodies. She was glad for the masks covering their noses, because maybe they wouldn't smell the odor of stale urine rising from her crotch.

"*¿Está bien, señorita?*" the man beside her asked.

"*Sí*." The numbness in the fingers of her spear hand had spread up her arm, and the heel she'd kicked the enraged man with throbbed.

He opened a bottle of Topo Chico for her, and it bubbled up and spilled on her knee.

"*Perdón*."

"*Quiero ir al puente*," she said between gulps. The bridge, the bridge, just get me to the bridge.

"*Sí, señorita*."

Only the amber glints of animal eyes gave the black night depth. The driver killed the headlights and swung onto a dirt road, and the soldier riding shotgun shone a flashlight through the windshield, barely bright enough to illuminate the contours of the potholes. The road was so narrow that tree branches brushed the vehicle on both sides, thorns screeching on the paint. When they got to another, wider dirt road, the headlights came on again, and the speed resumed. But it did not look like they were headed to any kind of town.

"*¡Al puente!*" she repeated.

The man who had given her the water explained that it was dangerous to go there directly. He brought his trigger finger from the stock of his rifle and curled it in front of his eye. "*¡Pum pum!*"

Yes, she had heard the *pum pum*. And no, she didn't want to go toward the *pum pum*. She rubbed life into her own fingers, squeezed them.

She couldn't make sense of the radio chatter. One of the men sitting in the back with her kept a receiver to his head, grunting monosyllables into it, cutting his grave eyes to her. The one riding shotgun kept glancing at her too, as if trying to make sense of her.

They pitched down a deeply rutted, dusty road parallel to a high stone wall. The driver radioed ahead and a solid steel door in the wall slid open, and they drove onto the grounds of a Mediterranean-style villa surrounded by gigantic nopales, waxy yellow cactus flowers and whitewashed walls glowing in the headlights. What was this, some high-ranking officers' quarters, a rich politician's home? A place requisitioned from the narcos? Another iteration of the secuestradero?

Rather than shock her to limpness and haul her out as the men had done at the first secuestradero, the masked man beside her offered her a courtly arm to help her down from the armored vehicle. He gently lifted the Kevlar over her head and, guiding her off the sharp gravel and onto the brick walkway, escorted her to the front door of the villa.

"*Buenas noches,*" he said, two fingers saluting from his helmet. He turned and clambered back into the vehicle, and he and his men disappeared into the darkness.

A young woman in a French maid's uniform cracked open the heavy door. "*Pásele, pásele.*"

Minerva entered, warily. What else was she going to do, take off barefoot into the night?

"*¿Cómo se siente, señorita?*" the maid asked. "*¿Quiere que llame al doctor?*"

"*No, gracias. No hace falta.*"

Her arm and foot still throbbed, but she was not seriously injured. She didn't want anyone touching her at the moment, not even a doctor. Leave her body in peace. But where had that body landed now?

"*¿Dónde estoy?*"

"*No se preocupe, señorita. Ahorita llega El Júnior,*" the maid replied, then quickly corrected herself: "*Digo, el señor.*"

Evidently this junior *señor* would explain everything to her as soon as he arrived.

"*Pásele, pásele,*" the maid said. "*¿Desea un caldito?*"

Caldo. Broth. Synonymous with sustenance, in either language. Minerva nodded.

"*¿Y un tecito? ¿Té de manzanilla?*"

Yes… chamomile tea… exactly what her mother would have given her. This was all so strange.

The maid led her across the marble floor to a dining room and a glass-topped table surrounded by massive, high-backed chairs, the same heavy colonial furniture as in the restaurant Quigley had taken her to, where this weird nightmare had begun. The maid brought her the broth, which she served out of an ornate silver tureen. No, it was much more than broth: chicken soup with *fideos* and carrots and that indefinable flavor she'd only found in Mexico and had never been able to replicate in her own cooking.

Her own stink of rancid urine and sweat barged in on the unnamable fragrance. The maid stood at a distance.

As soon as Minerva sipped the last of her tea, the maid said, with a little nod, "*Venga, señorita,*" and led her up a broad flight of stairs and into a large bedroom with a canopied bed, crystal chandelier and a grouping of brocade chairs and loveseat.

A man stood motionless in a darkened corner, and her left leg eased instinctively forward into front stance, *kamaete!* Wait, no, not a man, but an empty suit of armor. *Yame.* Relax.

A few hours ago, Minerva had been forced to use the filthiest, most vile bathroom she'd ever seen. This one, with its green onyx toilet, granite double sink and gold-plated fixtures, was the fanciest. A delicate jasmine scent wafted in from the open window. If this mansion was another secuestradero, it was a five-star one.

The maid turned on the golden faucet and water steamed into the marble tub.

"*¿Cómo te llamas?*" Minerva asked her.

"*Juanita,*" the maid replied, looking down. "*A sus órdenes.*"

Juanita, being a servant, was of course obliged to address her formally. Minerva had never gotten used to the formal verb forms. Growing up in New Mexico, she'd used Spanish exclusively with friends and family, using the "*tú*" informal all the time. Once when waiting tables in Santa Fe, she'd asked "*¿Y para ti?*" when taking an order from a Mexican woman not much older than herself, and the woman's sputtered objection—"*¡igualada!*"—had made her burst out laughing.

Damned straight I'm your equal, but you're right, I'm the one taking orders—so what'll it be, milady?

"*Yo soy Minerva,*" she said to Juanita.

It was probably wrong to introduce oneself by name to a servant, forcing her to be "*igualada*" by suggesting she call her anything but "*señorita.*" But it would be nice to close the distance, somehow get some amicable indication or assurance that this was not just another trap like the one at the palacio municipal.

Juanita was having none of it. "*Sí, señorita,*" she said, still not meeting her eyes. "*Bueno, aquí está su baño.*" She gave a little curtsy and left.

Minerva stood immobile in the bathroom, listening to the gushing water and breathing in the fragrant steam. Yes, those shits at the palacio municipal had also been formally hospitable, giving her coffee and letting her use the toilet before delivering her to the men who had stuck her in the box. But the tension there had been palpable, whereas Juanita seemed guileless and genuinely kind. And she represented this junior as someone benign who, as soon as he arrived, would set things straight.

Wary as she was of disrobing in this strange place, she yearned to get the stink of the kidnappery off, scrub it away, even though she had no change of clothes and would have to put on her sour, urine-stained Jackie Brown, as she called her black suit with its pointy-collared white blouse. On the granite vanity stood an array of travel-sized notions, lotions and potions. Yes, she'd bathe but make it quick. She locked the door and gingerly peeled off her sticky clothes. The scratches from the thorny bushes she'd hid in the night before had scabbed to black, but the three sets of twin dots from the cattle prod, or whatever it was they'd shocked her with, still shone red on her ribs.

She sank into the tub.

Chapter Seventeen

As soon as Minerva got out of the water, she heard a tapping at the door. "*Señorita, señorita.*"

She unhooked a thick white bathrobe, monogrammed "R.G." in gold, wrapped herself in its plushness and unlocked the door.

Juanita handed her a stack of clean clothing: soft periwinkle drawstring pants and a baby-blue T-shirt, topped by a pair of pom-pommed pantuflas for her feet. Minerva almost stopped her from gathering the Jackie Browns, but putting that fouled clothing back on her clean body was out of the question. She let Juanita take away her power suit, which was probably ruined anyway. She tied the bathrobe over the pastel softness. It gave the feeling of a karate gi and restored to her a sense of strength.

She sat in one of the brocade chairs, listening to the remote pop-popping of what was no doubt gunfire. The broth and the bath and the tea had revived but not relaxed her. She was still running on adrenaline, and she sat forward in the chair, prepared to spring from it. The knight's sword looked real enough, and she half-rose to examine it when a knock on the door came, a tapping even more timorous than Juanita's.

"*¡Adelante!*" she called, as if this were her room.

A man entered cautiously, deferentially. He couldn't have been over thirty. In his oversized horn-rimmed glasses, he looked like a nerdy but serious young professor or grad student. *This* was the guy in charge? The patrón? The señor? She might have expected a mustached rancher type in pointy snakeskin boots and a shiny silk shirt, but this man wore penny loafers and a white twill dress shirt neatly tucked into his jeans. She could see why Juanita had called him "junior." His only concession to the narco look was his silver-threaded black pita belt, but even that lacked the typical oversized buckle.

"S'okay, s'okay," he said, as if to soothe a wild animal. He was watching her hands. "Very sorry about the violence," he added. He pronounced the o's long, as in "woe."

Strange way to open a conversation, but it was good to hear English, her mother tongue, and to know she could speak it to him. It empowered her. She let him continue."The attack had to be…" He searched for the word. "Definitive. But everyone was rescued." His worried eyes stopped wandering and rested for a startled moment on the monogram on Minerva's bathrobe.

"The kidnapping victims?"

"Yes," he said, hands smoothing the air. "All free."

"So where am I? What is this place?"

"It's okay here. It's secure."

"And who are *you?*"

He hesitated. Finally: "Call me Eduardo."

"I need to get back home, Eduardo."

"Yes, I know. But not immediately. The plaza is too hot."

"Too *hot?* It's nighttime."

"Hairy," he clarified.

"Hairy?"

"Yes, hairy," he said, doubling down on the word as if to insist that he'd found the right colloquialism. "It's not safe."

"Soldiers brought me here. Marinas. In an armored truck. They can't take me to the bridge? It can't be far."

"What did they look like?"

"The soldiers? Like soldiers look down here. With masks on their faces."

"Yes, of course."

"You don't know who they are? But someone here opened the gate to them."

"Yes, yes. But they weren't soldiers. They were clones."

"Clones?"

"Guys dressed in Marina uniforms."

"And you're the patrón they spoke to on the radio?"

Eduardo gave an impatient cluck of his tongue, as if to say he'd already said too much. "We'll get you to your bridge. You think on top of everything else we like having a missing American woman on our hands?"

"Who is 'we'?"

He didn't answer that, either, but whoever this Eduardo was, his exasperated tone made her believe he wanted to get her back as much as she wanted it.

Minerva was an unexpected problem for him, it seemed, one he would want to resolve as soon as possible. A buzzing exhaustion began to fill the space left by her receding fear.

He plucked a walkie-talkie-looking thing from his belt and told someone to bring her "bolso." A moment later, a teenage boy slipped into the room, handed him her shoulder bag, slipped back out.

She rummaged through it. Everything was there except for her cash and cell phone.

"And my phone?"

"It's been destroyed."

"You destroyed it?"

"It could be traced."

"Well, if I'm no longer being held against my will, then can you get me some kind of phone so I can tell my people that I'm okay?"

Eduardo radioed for a "prepago," and the same boy reappeared, this time holding a cheap-looking orange cell phone.

"Tell them whatever you want," Eduardo said to Minerva, "but you shouldn't worry them."

"Thank you for the advice." She couldn't help but add, "Yes, it might be a little much to explain that I'm hanging out in the mansion of some junior whoever you are whose clones have rescued me from some really bad guys but not to worry, he's bringing me back as soon as things calm down a little."

"Yes, that's too much," Eduardo agreed, oblivious to her sarcasm. "That would complicate matters. That could create an international incident."

Minerva had no intention of telling her mother or the Bravo people all the details. For now, all they needed to know was that she was safe. She didn't have Quigley's or the Department of Languages and Literature's number but supposed this Eduardo might be able to find them for her.

"At least give me an idea when they can expect me back," Minerva said as he passed the phone to her.

"One day," he said. "Or two."

"So, no ransom? You sure?" she said as she poked out her mother's number.

"Don't offend me."

Her mother answered with her customary airiness. "Speak, Unknown."

"Mamá, it's me."

"So why are you Unknown, m'ija?"

"I had to borrow someone else's phone. But I'm fine."

"I know. I called your Dr. Burris to see why you weren't picking up. He said your phone didn't get coverage way down there, so I figured this might be you." Her mother's voice held a note of indulgence. "He seems to think it was irresponsible of you not to interview at all, but I think you did exactly the right thing. If you know right off you don't want the job, why waste everybody's time pretending?"

Pretending? What was her mother talking about? Was she even hearing her right, or was the exhaustion playing tricks on her?

"I think it's perfectly reasonable," her mother continued. "Other people might not think so, but—"

"What exactly did he tell you?"

"He told me what the professor who picked you up at the airport told him. That you'd had second thoughts about committing so soon to a permanent position. Traveling can get you to thinking, don't I know it. Ahora, if it were me, I might have gone to the campus and let them know from the horse's mouth. No, I take it back, if it were me, I would've done exactly what you did. Deliver me to the bus station, kind sir! Or I guess these days people rent cars. You didn't want to rent a car? Where are you now, m'ija?"

"Just traveling."

"Well, you have the Gulf not too far. Uy, I miss the ocean. Don't go into Mexico, though, not alone. Those days are over. Remember when we took the Cinco Estrellas to Guadalajara…"

When her mother was done giving travel advice, Minerva stood for a moment with the phone hanging from her hand, stunned, before returning it to Eduardo.

"No one else for calling?" he asked.

"No." Her mind was racing again now, the adrenaline back.

"The professor, perhaps?"

"That son of a bitch."

"Why?"

Her anger kept her talking. "He's been telling people I'm okay."

"You are okay."

Eduardo bent the burner phone in his hands, absently destroying it as if this were something he did often.

"He's making it seem like I'm some kind of flake who blew off the whole campus visit."

"He would say this, instead of looking for you?"

"Maybe that's what he thinks I did. Ghosted. We were joking about that sort of thing just before it happened…. Wait a minute. What if he was in on it? Quigley, I mean. It's like they all were. The creepy old waiter, the taxi driver... What if, when Quigley asked the ni-nis where the restaurant was, that was the signal? Then the creepy old waiter tricks me into going out to the loading dock where the ni-nis and the taxi were waiting for me—"

"The ni-nis?"

"The kids who snatched me. That's what Quigley called them. *Ni trabajan, ni estudian.*"

"Ni-nis," Eduardo repeated. He seemed to savor the expression, or these gringos' knowledge of it. Because, Chicana though she was, she was still primarily a gringa in his eyes. A pocha, to put it rudely. After all, she spoke to her mother in English, didn't she?

"He knows they don't have me anymore, so he can't demand ransom. He's just trying to buy some time until he figures out what's going on."

Eduardo shook his head. "A gringo professor conspiring with these ni-nis to sequester a student looking for a job? There is craziness down here, but that is ridiculous. No, he has nothing to do with the kidnapping. He is probably just scared for himself, worried he'll get in trouble for taking you here."

Okay, okay. Eduardo was probably right. She was getting carried away. A dizzying wave of fatigue rose in her.

"Your mother didn't seem worried, no?"

"She's not a worrier."

"And she's right because there's nothing to be—"

"Worried about. Yes, you said."

"There are three rings of security around this house."

Not until the next day would she have the wherewithal to reflect that needing three rings of security around them, whatever that exactly meant, might itself be cause for worry.

"You must rest. You have been through a trauma. We'll talk in the morning."

"Could you turn that thing around before you leave? I don't like him looking at me."

"This guy? No problem."

He turned the suit of armor to face the wall. As soon as he left, she dragged one of the heavy chairs over and braced it against the door.

Chapter Eighteen

Minerva's mother called Professor Burris the next morning to report that all was well. Minnie, she told him, had called from a borrowed phone because, like he said, her own phone didn't get reception way down there.

"Of course, in our day, what phone, right? Much less email, credit cards, any of that. Traveler's cheques, if you remembered to get them. Otherwise, it was cash in your sock and a fake wallet for the thieves. Professor, are you still there?"

After Minerva's mother was through with her report, Burris called Sandra to arrange a meeting.

"What's up?" Sandra said. She was eating something crunchy.

"Over the phone?"

"Is it sensitive?" Crunch, crunch.

"Maybe. It's about that grad student."

"Oh, yeah. Go ahead."

It seemed to him insensitive that things regarding Minerva might no longer be regarded as sensitive, but he proceeded.

"She called her mother last night."

"Keep going. What'd she tell her?"

"That she was okay and traveling."

"Like the professor there told you.... What's the name again?"

"Quigley. By the way, when you hacked her email, what kind of activity did you notice there?" he asked.

"Not hacked, Douglas. Took a look. Nothing sent or opened by her since the night before she left."

"See, that's just not like her. She doesn't do social media much, but she's big on email."

"Well, it's in keeping with Quigley's description of her state of mind, isn't it? Wanting to get away from it all, take a break? You know, Doug, she wouldn't be the first twenty-something to put things on hold to take stock of what she really wants to do with her life."

As if he hadn't dealt with his share of twenty-somethings over a thirty-year teaching career. He knew what Sandra was thinking: that his pride was so wounded by his star student's not telling him about her career crisis that he insisted on believing something more sinister was going on.

"She didn't use her own phone," he said.

"Which accounts for her not receiving your messages. What number?"

"If she'd left a number, don't you think I would've called it? It read UNKNOWN, her mother said."

Sandra's chewing abated, as if she were pausing to assess the degree of his annoyance.

"Burner phone, probably. Forget trying to geolocate. Here's the elephant question: did anybody get on and demand ransom?"

"Obviously not. Didn't I say her mother said she was okay? And what's an elephant question?"

"Well, that's the elephant in the room, isn't it? Kidnapping? She's not covered by our kayinar, by the way, I looked into it. I mean, why would she be? She's not part of the Center or any of its programs."

"Kayinar?"

"K and R. Kidnap and ransom insurance. Any of your frequent travelers to the Mexican side of the border are gonna want it, your maquiladora execs and so forth." Her swallow slid into his ear. "When she said she wanted to travel in 'the area,' do you think that included the Mexican side, La Reina or Monterrey or places like that?"

"How would I know? Probably! Quigley mentioned Padre Island."

"That makes sense. Spring break, blow her ya-yas out."

"She's not eighteen or the kind of woman that needs to blow… Look, are you going to help look for her or not? Did you use that stingray or whatever you called it to find her cell?"

"Let's give it a couple of days, Doug. Because she's not exactly missing, is she? And, you know, there's a reason for having a waiting period before you can file a missing persons report, in any jurisdiction. I'm sure you can understand why."

It was all he could do to keep from hanging up on her. He, a full professor, wasn't going to be talked down to by the non-academic head of the campus spook program. If she wasn't going to look for Minerva, he would. He'd drive down through all that south Texas "no country for old men" and wring the truth out of this Quigley.

Chapter Nineteen

After another wretched night, Quigley, head still thick
from the yellow pill, tripped into the Stripes convenience
store, poured himself a 16-ounce coffee and got in line for
his fajita taco. Tonight, Friday night, folks would fire up their
barbecues and the whole town would smell of grilled meat.
He was rarely invited to a backyard barbecue, as those tended
to be family affairs, and he had no relatives for a thousand
miles. The fragrance would recall his Minnesota childhood,
redolent of summer cookouts, and once again he'd feel the
depth of his isolation.

He and the other faculty were always nagging at the students to become less provincial and strike out to find their
fortunes in more economically promising areas, but he understood the students' resistance to this pressure. For what?
To end up like him, a thousand miles from everyone you grew
up with, with no one around to confide in, tell your troubles
to? Except, in his case, a sketchy student.

According to the hallowed HOP, the university's *Hand-
book of Operating Procedures*, he shouldn't be "fraternizing"
with students anyway, whatever that meant. *Oh, you'll make
new friends wherever you go*, he told his students, but this was
easier said than done, as he well knew. He'd made one truly
good faculty friend at Bravo, just to have her take a tenured
position in Seattle, at the opposite end of the country. Friend
or not, would he really have confided in her his present

predicament, she being a fellow faculty member and all? For the present purposes, maybe it was a good thing he didn't have any colleague he could confide in. The fewer people that knew, the better. Omar was in on it, for better or for worse, and Omar was quite enough.

He hitched up his pants and proceeded to the cashier with his foil-wrapped taco. At the checkout counter, the *El Mañana* newspaper from La Reina blared, "NUTRIDA BALACERA EN LA SAL." He bought a copy, although the only part of the headline he understood was La Sal, the town Omar said Minerva, or the Minerva look-alike, had been taken to.

He sat at a decrepit picnic table by the ice machine outside, in the shade of a palm, and entered the headline into Google Translate, which returned "nourished shootout in the salt." He tried to decipher the article. Something about marines and armed groups and sequestered people liberated. He scalded his tongue with a gulp of coffee and called Omar.

"I hear salt's unhealthy," he said, without identifying himself.

"Yes, sir," Omar replied. "But not for everybody. Where are you?"

"The Stripes with the empty antacid boxes in the gutter, not condom wrappers."

Omar's silence suggested this was a little too cryptic.

"The one by the courthouse, not the campus," he clarified.

"Got it."

Omar had set him up with an app called Signal, which supposedly encrypted their conversations. Even so, Quigley thought, it was good to get in the habit of speaking in coded ways, just as it was good to converse in places like this, next to a grumbling ice machine that could confound eavesdroppers.

Quigley pulled long fingers of fajita from the tortilla and chewed them worriedly. Something weird was happening in La Sal, and he needed Omar to hurry up and explain it to him. Black ashes almost as long as the meat floated in the air. Were they still burning sugar cane fields? Could be anything; something was always being incinerated over in Mexico, the toxic smoke and ashes drifting over the river. A cicada sputtered to a start, then sputtered out, the morning air not quite hot enough to allow it to reach the sustained pitch that the writer Paul Bowles called the "sound of heat itself." The Bowleses, Paul and Jane, a couple more authors to add to his expat lit syllabus, if they ever let him teach that course again. And if, after his current ordeal, he could still stomach reading about the trouble the gringo characters in those books tended to get into.

Omar wheezed up in a grey car so nondescript that even "grey" seemed too specific. A blurry car. As always, he was dressed in baggyish jeans neither old nor new, and today's T-shirt was off-white without image or logo. Quigley was beginning to get the picture: if the narcos in Mexico were ostentatious in their dress and choice of cars, everything look-y'all sharp and gold-accented, those involved in the smuggling trade on this side went under-the-radar drab. Different presentations for different business models, he supposed.

"So," Quigley said, tapping the headline. "La Sal."

"Yes, sir, I've already heard. Just as I thought would happen, the Gamboa people shut down that kidnapping operation."

"With a healthy shootout."

"Yes, but all the hostages were rescued. Including our lady."

His heart jumped. "Where is she?"

"She's safe. I don't know where they've taken her, exactly, but she's okay. Like I said before, as soon as things calm down a little and the plaza cools off, they'll drop her off at the bridge."

"How do you know? I mean, I have to believe you when you say you've got informants or whatever you want to call them down there, but how can they be sure what this, this organization, plans to do?"

"What else could it do, sir? The junior, Eduardo, doesn't want to antagonize the gringos. They've got his father. He needs to do a make-nice gesture and let her go."

"A goodwill gesture, you mean."

"Aha. So we just have to wait for it to happen."

"And how long will that be?"

"Hard to say. The Marinas are all over the Frontera Chica now, and when they withdraw, the Zetas or the Gulf Cartel or whoever could pounce. So, yeah, it's hot. It's a waiting game, sir, till things cool down a little."

"Surely they can find a way to get her here. They're smugglers, aren't they?"

"That's true, profe," he said noncommittally as he scanned the article. "How did your talk with her professor go?"

"Burris? Fine. Suspicions allayed." He recalled with a wince how he'd lost his steeliness and let his voice crack during that conversation.

"What did you tell him?"

"That she'd gone off to find her head." Yeah, great phrase considering the current vogue in Mexico for decapitations. "Find herself, find her center, think about what she really wants to do with her life. And that she'd asked me to tell the committee that she simply hadn't shown, which seemed better to her than telling them she'd shown up and then got cold feet."

"Maybe better to have told him that the secretary was mistaken," said Omar. "That of course the candidate was here, everything was going great, only that her phone didn't get reception way down here. But she says hello and will tell him all about it when she gets back."

"I thought about that, but then if she wasn't back in New Mexico in a couple of days, we'd be back to square one, wouldn't we? By the way, do you know if she's gotten any of *my* phone messages?"

"No idea, sir. But if she didn't activate her international roaming, she can't call you. Even if the junior let her."

"Shit. Because I'd really, really like it if she'd call back so we can get on the same page with all this." He was conscious of a whining having crept into his voice. "Talk to me, agree to tell the committee that she came in on an earlier flight and bopped down to Mexico to do some shopping and got snatched. Or whatever! But leave me out of it."

"She doesn't owe you, sir."

"It's called collegiality. Oh, what do you know about this business, Omar!"

"I understand, sir. You beginning professors need to stick together, until you get the tenure."

"That's right! Why would she let this ruin my career?"

Omar let the selfish complaint air out its stink for a moment before gently pointing out that Quigley now had two different stories, one for the committee and one for Burris.

"That's true, but it's not Burris I'm worried about."

"Maybe you'd better, a little. We gotta hope he buys it and doesn't file a missing persons. That will get hairy quick with an airport involved."

"What do you mean?"

"*Ay, ay, ay,* with the security. They got TSA there, and that means Homeland Security. The two flights a week from Monterrey make it an international airport, so you have your Border Patrol, your CBP. Air marshals. And they all got nothing to do, I mean like nothing, they just sit—"

"Okay, understood. But I told Burris I picked her up, so if he at least buys that, he'll file the report with the Providencia police, who we can hope are busier and less competent than the feds."

"Where'd you say you dropped her off?"

"Downtown by the bus station."

The Providencia bus station was a big one, housing Greyhound and the regional carrier and a bunch of big Mexican lines. Omar seemed to find this satisfactory.

"Sir, have you heard about the Matamoros bus station? The baggage claim kept getting full of unclaimed baggage. Like 400 suitcases. Finally, they looked into it and found out these were the bags belonging to the people the narcos took off the buses. They roll boulders into the road or shoot at them to get them to stop and then they get on and say, 'You,

you, you, come with us.' The drivers and the rest of the passengers are too scared to say anything when they finally get to Matamoros, and the bus companies don't want to pay out insurance on all those disappeared people, so the suitcases keep piling up. Sucks, huh?"

"Yes, it sucks, and I wish you hadn't told me that, Omar."

Omar searched the heavens as if needing a blank slate of sky on which to work out strategy.

"You're right, sir. You and her need to talk before she talks to anyone else. Work it out, like colleagues. Because if there's an airport video of you two, then you can't say you never met her, and if there's a bridge video, then you can't say you didn't go to Mexico. You could say she decided to pull her disappearing act in La Reina, but then what about the border guard you freaked out to? How is that covering for her? At least she won't have any eyewitnesses to back her kidnapping story up. The waiter isn't going to admit anything bad ever happens at that restaurant. That guy on the plaza? Twenty dollars shuts him up. The ni-nis? Lucky if they're still alive."

"Okay, okay." The memory of that nightmare afternoon, on top of the fajita and too much coffee, churned in his stomach. "The search committee's meeting in half an hour. I have to go."

"Search committee?" Omar looked at him alarmed.

"You know, hiring committee. Yeah, no, not what you're thinking, my God."

"Scared me, sir."

Though it was Friday, when few professors taught or held office hours or were otherwise on campus, the chean had insisted the Border Studies search committee meet to "wrap things up." What this meant, DeWitt informed the group, was that the chean had suspended the search and that they needed to finalize the paperwork and lock away all the dossiers.

"This couldn't have waited till Tuesday?" Cindy Wheeler said. Tuesdays were when most faculty committees met. What was the hurry?

"They want to sweep up and reallocate the funds allotted to this appointment," said DeWitt. The chean was fond of sweeping up and reallocating. They really enjoyed that shell game.

"They're gonna do that over the weekend?" she grumbled.

Like DeWitt, she was a holdover from the days when the school was a junior college. She was a stocky, gray-haired hippie with a house on stilts by the Rio who seemed mostly interested in her papaya and guava trees.

At one particularly hard-ass moment the previous semester, the chean had ordered the faculty to be on campus every weekday from nine to five and had only backed down after the Faculty Senate erupted. It seemed obvious to Quigley that requiring committees to meet on Fridays was petty payback for that defeat, but he wasn't about to jump in and interject.

"No doubt they're eager to divert the funds to some pet project, such as 'assessment' software to spy on our online activity," Wheeler said.

The EEOC rep, who as Engineering faculty had no dog in these Humanities fights, held up his hand. "If I can be allowed. From what I understand, they want to suspend the search, not cancel the line. You can readvertise in the fall."

"What if this one applies again?" Cindy Wheeler asked, meaning Minerva.

"No, uh-uh," DeWitt said. "She's blown her chances."

Duarte turned to Quigley. "Her advisor implied to you that she just must have gotten cold feet and deserted us, right?"

"Actually, he said something about 'personal issues,'" Quigley said, his voice flattened by the lie.

"Personal issues?"

"Some kind of family emergency, I guess? He didn't go into detail."

"Which is all we need to know," said the EEOC rep, holding up another cautionary hand. "We don't need to get into medical matters."

"All I know is that she's made us eat a plane ticket and waste our time and hasn't bothered to call us personally with an explanation. I think that might speak to her job performance, don't you?" DeWitt fixed his heavy-browed gaze on the rep, forcing the old engineer to look away.

The meeting over, Quigley wandered back to his office and sat contemplating the only brows more daunting than DeWitt's, those of the Fridas in the student gallery below. If luck was with him, Esmeralda would close the department office early, as she often did on Fridays, and then the danger of Minerva talking to office staff before talking to him would be over until Monday. The campus, a commuter campus with few dorms, would become quiet in a couple of hours, with just a handful of research-happy professors scuttling about the halls. Like Norbert, the Mexicanist upstairs in History.

Chapter Twenty

Within the History department, Norbert Gottlieb was the go-to geek on all things Mexican, and the great thing was that he supposed everyone else was as fascinated as he was by that country. You could ask him anything about it and he'd fill you in without wondering for an instant why you wanted to know. Heck, you didn't even have to ask him. You just had to be within hailing distance and not take off before he reached you with fresh news about the scandal in the Something Something Party or the elections in Nuevo Whatever or the shakeups in the federal police force, as though anybody on this side of the border gave a damn about any of that.

All Quigley had to do was waylay him in the hall and pretend to read the *El Mañana* article about the La Sal shootout—Norbert read Spanish and assumed everybody else did—and they'd be off and running.

Norbert's habits were as regular as Immanuel Kant's, and at 3:15, just as Quigley predicted, he came sidling down the empty hall towards his office, his head projecting turtlelike from his rounded shoulders and appearing to whisper to the Grande latte he'd brought from the Starbucks kiosk in the Student Union.

The sight of Quigley contemplating the photograph of the bullet chewed La Sal city hall brought him up short.

"Isn't that something?" Norbert said. "What we're witnessing here is the demise of a vertically integrated criminal structure. The inevitable result of the kingpin strategy."

"Kingpin strategy?"

"The kingpin—in this case, Robustiano Gamboa—gets extradited to the US and his organization splinters into warring factions. You cut up a centipede and each piece grows into a new one. My educated guess is that some Gamboa rogue faction, or maybe some completely new group, decided to set up shop in La Sal, and what's left of the main organization went after them. La Sal is the heart of Gamboa turf, you know. It's always been their plaza."

What Norbert said jibed with what Omar had conjectured. Quigley followed him into his office.

"That La Sal situation," Norbert continued, nodding at the paper, "involves a secuestradero, a kidnapping operation. Like extortion, it's never been a Gamboa thing. They're almost strictly dedicated to smuggling. Or as *Forbes* magazine delicately says about the source of the family fortune, 'shipping.'"

Norbert plunged into his enormous office chair and perused the article. Quigley contemplated the stack of exam blue books teetering on his desk, an open one festooned with meticulous corrections in red ink. It was a vaguely depressing sight. Did Norbert really think the students did anything beyond flipping to see the grade on the last page? But like Norbert's prattle, those marks were all about Norbert repeating to himself what he already knew.

"Their spelling's getting worse, don't you think?" Norbert said, catching Quigley staring at the exam books. "I heard one kid teasing his friend, 'Güey, your spelling's worse than a narcomanta!' You know, one of those warning banners the narcos hang on the overpasses next to the dangling bodies? Called 'piñatas,' by the way, those gibbeted corpses. When criminal culture starts making inroads into everyday language, you know the society's in trouble, right?"

"I guess so."

"Though the spelling is invariably atrocious, some of the more detailed messages the bad guys staple onto the piñatas can be wonderfully expressive," Norbert added wistfully.

He handed the newspaper back to Quigley. "What's strange is that the Gamboas would choose to heat up the plaza like that. That's what it's called when you shoot up a town, 'heating up the plaza.' If I were them, I'd want to keep a cool plaza by quietly eliminating the rogue operation, not go in full blast. Makes me think there's a third party involved, someone who wants to stir things up, hoping that when things do cool down, they'll end up on top."

"Who would that be?"

"Oh, goodness. Any number of comandantes within the organization eager to shove the junior aside and take over."

"The junior?" said Quigley, trying to sound only vaguely interested.

"After Senior, Robustiano, was spirited away to US federal prison, Junior stepped in to replace him as head of the Gamboas. El Junior, real name Eduardo, is not exactly the Michael Corleone of the family. That would've been his brother Reyes, who reportedly died in a stupid hunting accident in the Sierra less than a year ago. Pardon the redundancy: all hunting accidents are stupid. It might have been no accident, of course. You never know with these people. Not to be unkind, but Eduardo's more like the Fredo Corleone. Well, maybe that is a little unkind."

Yes, let's not be unkind when speaking of narcos, Quigley thought sourly.

"The truth is, he wasn't brought up to be the head of the cartel," said Norbert. "I mean, even his given name, Eduardo, doesn't exactly scream capo, does it? Narcojuniors like him are sent to study at universities abroad and then start overseeing the family investments: equities, hotels, what have you. They create foundations, contribute to philanthropies, set up shell companies. Those are used to launder money, as you can imagine. From what I know, this kid has always kept a low profile. His brother was the sports-car-driving, night-club-hopping playboy of the family."

Quigley pictured both brothers as what his students called "fresas." A fresa was an upper-class Mexican of the polo-shirt-and-loafers variety. *Fresa* meant strawberry, and a few of them indeed had strawberries-and-cream complexions, light skin with pink cheeks. Some of their Mexican-American classmates considered them stuck up, said they talked like they had potatoes in their mouths. Toward Quigley, the fresas were invariably polite, and some of them were among his best students, despite their serious problems with punctuation and punctuality.

Norbert rattled on: "Like many kids born into organized crime, they often feel trapped but don't know how to get out of these families. It can be pretty tragic. The Eduardos will become the legitimate face of the family, investing family money in legal businesses and so forth. And there's plenty of money to invest. I take it you've been following the Zambada case?"

"Not really. No."

"Vicente Zambada, son of El Chapo's No. 2 man, pled guilty in New York to a number of charges, and you know how much in assets he agreed to forfeit? $1.38 billion. That's billion with *b grande*. Of course, the government actually getting their mitts on those assets is another thing. Treasury's Office of Foreign Assets Control can only do so much. Good luck seizing hotels in Cuba, casinos in Venezuela, all the off-shore accounts on islands you've never heard of."

"So what do you think this Eduardo's going to do now?" Quigley asked, still trying to sound casual.

"Oh, I imagine he'll want things to cool down as quickly as possible. Which makes me wonder why he let them get as hot as he did and why he took down that secuestradero, that safe house, with such a show of force. Maybe an oblique warning to the DEA and the Mexican authorities that he's not to be trifled with and that he won't be taken as easily as his father? But it doesn't sound like he has those kinds of huevos, frankly. Like I said, I think we're seeing a power struggle between a couple of Gamboa comandantes, the one who set up the kidnapping operation and the one who took it down, with the junior watching helplessly from the sidelines. He's got the Gamboa name, and they'll respect that for now, but the longer big daddy Gamboa's in a US prison, in solitary confinement no less, the more precarious the kid's situation gets."

Norbert was known not only as a Mexicanist but also as a "narcologist," a designation Quigley didn't know how seriously to take, although it apparently encompassed a field of knowledge as full of arcana as any other. Now in full lecture mode, Norbert commenced to detail cartel structure and hierarchy. The comandantes or jefes de plaza were in charge of cells of four or five lieutenants who ran the intelligence networks, paid the falcons and, in the case of the La Sal operation, maintained safe houses. Beneath the lieutenants were the sicarios who did the actual hits and kidnappings. Quigley supposed that the suspect ni-nis were sicarios.

"That's the traditional structure, anyway," Norbert went on. "It may be changing as some of the cartels move to more of a franchising model. Which I understand Robustiano was trying to do after the demise of the competent son and heir apparent. Basically, he'd lease the Gamboa name to independent operators—not just the name, but warehouses and other infrastructure, political goodwill down in Mexico, contacts on this side of the border, all that sort of thing. Even their logo, a rampant horse, is leased out. Find a dope brick stamped with that and you know it's the good stuff. It's not unlike our own Bravo mascot, come to think of it."

Norbert lifted a three-ring binder from his desk and contemplated the Bravo bucking bronco embossed in gold on its cover. These were the binders the chean required for submission of materials for annual merit review, and Norbert, to Quigley's consternation, had two of them, his meritorious accomplishments unable to fit into just one, apparently.

The lecture was not over. "The Gamboa cartel has been around a long time, going back to Robustiano's father, who started the business during Prohibition as a *bulega*—a bootlegger. Robustiano went on to import marijuana, then the harder stuff. Over the years, the Gamboa organization became practically a parastatal or quasi-governmental entity. Gamboas funded public works projects, built churches, heck, probably built that La Sal city hall."

He paused and glanced at Quigley's lap as if expecting to find him taking notes.

"For all those years, there was minimum fighting between cartels, compared to now, anyway. Each cartel had its turf, everything organized as vertically as the government itself. Now things are less centralized in Narcolandia. Bosses are being taken down and plazas are coming up for grabs. My understanding is that Robustiano, like I said, had been trying to preempt this by turning the organization into what you might call a franchise, but he didn't get a chance to before he was arrested and extradited to the US. Just a few years ago, his extradition would have been unthinkable. The Mexican government wouldn't have allowed it. Now you're seeing the Mexican federal authorities coordinating with the DEA and other US law enforcement agencies to locate and capture guys like him."

Norbert took a sip of his latte. "Even so, it's a tricky business, this franchising, if that's what you want to call it. You want your franchisees to be independent to a point. But if you're old school, like the Gamboas, you want them to stick to the Gamboa brand, which is drug smuggling. Some people smuggling. But no extortion, no kidnapping. No black-market organ trafficking, and no stealing of oil from pipelines.

"Take Starbucks here," he said, caressing the mermaid's green bosom with his thumb. "It can't have one of its franchisees start selling cigars, right? Dim the lights and encourage people to light up in a back room? That's not the brand. As you saw in the article, a bunch of kidnapped people were found in a secuestradero in La Sal. Kidnapping, nope, not the Gamboa brand. Robustiano fancied himself something of a Pablo Escobar, a man of the people. Their protector, not their abductor. The fact that these abductions took place in the middle of Gamboa turf shows a weakness within the organization, obviously. And I would chalk that weakness up to the junior being in charge now."

"What if he's holding some wild card?" Quigley blurted. "Some bargaining chip."

"Who?"

"The son. The junior. Eduardo."

"Like what?"

Shouldn't have used the word "holding," dammit, but the alarming picture Norbert painted of the situation had punched it out of him. For a hideous moment he imagined throwing himself at Norbert, confessing all to him: the wild card the junior was holding was an American hostage, a young woman that he, Quigley, had foolishly taken across the border, where she'd been snatched. No, don't be stupid. Norbert would likely have valuable insight into how Minerva's situation might unfold, but Quigley couldn't risk telling a fellow faculty member about her.

"Well, there could always be something," Norbert said, stroking his long, smooth chin, evidently trying hard to think of what this bargaining chip might be, as if he himself had brought it up and now found himself in the awkward position of not being able to answer his own question.

Quigley got up. "Okay, well, you've been a lot of help!"

He realized that this, too, was an odd thing to say, even as he enhanced its oddness by holding out his hand. Norbert shook it firmly, as if they'd sealed some kind of deal. The quizzical look in Norbert's eye suggested that Quigley had managed the rarest of feats, which was to get Norbert, who was surely on the spectrum and not much interested in other people personally, to wonder what made this colleague of his tick.

Chapter Twenty-One

Minerva awoke in the canopied bed from a sleep so profound that for a moment she didn't know who or where she was. The chandelier crystals shattered the morning sunlight, jiggling rainbows around the room like those thrown by a mobile she'd had in her childhood bedroom. She stared at them uncomprehendingly until she heard again what had woken her: a nudging of the door against the brocade chair blocking it and a timid voice, *"Señorita... señorita..."*

Minerva unblocked the door, and Juanita stepped in, glancing puzzled at the displaced chair before addressing her with her customary solicitousness. Did the señorita want *¿juguito, tecito, cafecito? Huevito?* Words diminutive, motherly.

"Quiero hacer caquita," a baby voice in her head said before she snapped fully awake.

"Té, por favor. Gracias, Juanita."

The hot tea was there when she came out of the bathroom, as were her Jackie Browns, laundered and neatly folded. Had Juanita somehow been able to get them dry-cleaned in such a short time? They smelled fresh and felt great and, even more remarkably, the thorn tears had been sewn invisibly closed with minute stitching. At the foot of the bed were half a dozen pairs of shoes for her to choose from, good shoes, Ferragamo or at least Ferragamo knock-offs, pumps and mules and ballerinas, one pair of which fit her nicely, black ballerinas like the ones she had lost, but far more expensive if the real thing. She dressed quickly, and when Juanita came back, she thanked her for the clean clothes.

What she needed to do now was check her email. She would fire off a message to Quigley: What the hell was he doing telling people she was okay and just "traveling around?" Had he gone to the police? Was this part of their strategy? Or was he just trying to cover his ass? Until he answered her questions, she wasn't about to tell him what had happened to her and where she had landed.

"Ahorita llega el señor Eduardo."

"Ahorita" was a diminutive you had to be wary of, the "little" in the "while" an unintentionally ironic warning that the wait could in fact be a long one. But wait she must; the maid left no doubt that Eduardo was the only person empowered to give her access to a computer.

Minerva ate breakfast by herself in the dining room below, only picking at the feast of papaya and chilaquiles and pan dulce, her attempts to get information of even the most basic kind from the servants meeting with the invariable *"ahorita llega el señor."*

Minerva returned to her room and waited. Quigley, she surmised, must surely have gone straight to the police, and the police, for procedural reasons of their own, had concocted that story of her decision to travel around rather than interview for the job. Devious, but then the police could be that way if it helped in the investigation, couldn't they? Well, good. If the police were on it, all the more reason for Eduardo to get her to the bridge pronto and release her. Where the fuck was he? Another diminutive came to trouble her mind: *muertito*, a word she'd heard used to refer to the victims of the narco wars.

The desert sun seared its way up the cloudless sky, and the room grew hot. She turned on the ceiling fan, and the flow of air tinkled the chandelier crystals. Finally, Eduardo arrived, unshaven and disheveled, as if he'd slept in his clothes. His nervous, reddened eyes stalled for a moment on the knight turned to face the wall, naughty knight on time out.

Minerva sprang up from her chair, buoyed by relief, ready for action. "I have to check my email."

"We don't have internet here. For security reasons."

"They can trace it, like my phone?"

"Correct."

"Well, you'd better get me to the border bridge immediately. It seems obvious to me now that the police are working on my case. To buy themselves some time, they must have had Professor Quigley call my mother and my advisor and tell them I'm okay."

"That's not how the police work."

"What do you mean?"

"Unless this professor told them that he saw you get snatched, which we know he didn't, they're not going to know it was a kidnapping. The first thing they will do is ask the people closest to you if they know of any reason why you would choose to disappear. They won't hide anything from them."

"What if a witness has told the police they saw me get into that taxi? Until there's a demand for ransom, wouldn't it make sense to work quietly on the case without worrying friends and relatives?"

"First of all, they're not going to get such a witness. Not in La Reina. Not in all of Mexico. Anyway, I don't think this Professor Quigley has contacted the authorities."

"How do you know?"

He hesitated. "Let's just say I have a guy up there keeping an eye on things. Keeping us informed."

"A guy?"

"A student. The professor confides in him."

"A Bravo student?"

Guardedly: "Right."

"And this student has told him I'm here, presumably."

"In good hands."

"In good hands, you say."

"Yes," Eduardo said haughtily. "In good hands."

Quigley *was* just trying to cover his ass, if Eduardo was to be believed. Quigley, satisfied she wasn't in danger, wasn't about to tell anyone now what really happened or where she was. After all, she was in good hands!

"How come you're a junior, anyway? Who's senior?"

"He's in prison in your country."

"So who is he? Explain it to me. I need to know what's going on or I'm walking out, and your 'good hands' aren't holding me back."

Eduardo gave his cluck of impatience again, looked at her hard. For a moment she thought he was going to call her bluff, invite her to walk out beyond those high walls and take her chances at getting back to her country safely.

"He's my father. They have him in solitary confinement. A cell not much bigger than the box those guys put you in."

"And who were those guys?"

"People who are very sorry now, believe me."

She thought of the ni-nis. Were they among those he was making feel very sorry? Most likely. She, in turn, almost felt sorry for them. They were just poor little shits, following other guys' orders.

"The people at the palacio municipal in La Sal were in on it too," she said.

"Yes, I know," he said unhappily. "Believe me, all this would never have happened if my father was here and not in isolation in your country."

"How did you find out about me being in the box? About the secuestradero in La Sal?"

"The shoe-shine boy you talked to. He informed us."

"Bravo students, shoe-shine boys. You have spies everywhere."

"Information is everything."

"But until I came along and told your shoe-shine boy, you weren't aware?"

"Information is not always complete."

"Also, you're saying that if your father were here, the kidnapping would have never happened."

"Correct. That's not the business we are in."

"Your business is, let me guess, drug smuggling."

"You never smoked the weed or did a line, Minerva? It's a victimless crime. For me, people can decide for themselves what they want to put into their bodies. Oh, who fucking cares what you gabachos do to yourselves, anyway! Imperialist pigs."

She hadn't expected such an outburst. She laughed, and he turned red. She had a knack for making guys blush. Quigley had blushed too, more than once—at what she couldn't remember now, it seemed like so long ago.

"If you need anything, ask Juanita," he said brusquely, before turning to leave.

"Because every imperialist pig needs a maid, right?"

He paused, back stiffening, continued on.

Chapter Twenty-Two

The route Burris took to Bravo University in the deep south Texas town of Providencia was Google Maps' second suggestion, taking him south of I-10 and plunging him into the heart of No Country for Old Men territory where he whiled away the sunblasted hours searching vainly for radio stations that were neither Christian, country nor rightwing talk and making up Cormac McCarthy parodies in his head. *The sun deployed in unmoved moving above the barren ungodded unsaged despoblado drawing forth tottering crenellations of towered heat and yielding no right passage to any amphibious hominid emerging from the moated division of that ruined desert....* According to Minerva, every Southwest Popular/American Culture Association conference had to have at least one panel on McCarthy's novel *Blood Meridian,* and thanks to her he had finally gotten around to reading it. He couldn't decide whether its genre was horror, satire, straight-up western, or some hybrid thereof.

By the time he got to that moat, the Rio Grande, and followed Highway 277, catching whiffs of the river's heavy, snaky smell, his thoughts turned to Quigley and to what kind of a man he might be, and how to approach him. For starters, what would have motivated him to take a teaching job way down here? Couldn't get hired anywhere else? It made sense for Minerva, what with her command of Spanish and her scholarly interest in Mexican and border culture, but there was little in Quigley's CV, which Burris had read on Bravo's website, to make the man an obvious fit for a Hispanic Serving Institution like Bravo. Nothing in his personal background or scholarship revealed either an academic interest in the region nor the kind of missionary zeal that compelled a certain kind of teacher to benighted areas like this. Quigley was from Minnesota, an Americanist with a special interest in the literature of the Beats. It was hard to imagine that movement of disaffected, self-congratulatory white young urban men of the 1950s having a lot of relevance to the people down here. Unless, of course, one wanted to understand the origins of modern American drug culture, which arguably had its roots in the Beat generation, and which unarguably had a profound impact on the border economy and culture.

He braced himself for the crosswind impact from a string of semis roaring towards him in the narrow opposite lane: six trucks with Mexican plates and heaped with purple onions in white mesh bags. Now, how hard would it be for smugglers to bury a bag or three of powder deep in those loads? Unless they got a tip, would customs agents ever search such shipments? Would a drug-sniffing dog really be able to detect the dope?

Doubtful. The only way the war on drugs could possibly succeed, if interdiction was the solution, was through intelligence. Only tips, surveillance, infiltration—all the stuff of espionage—would turn the tide. But drug war aside—and, personally, he would like to see more resources devoted to addiction treatment—intelligence was necessary for any country's survival and well-being. How did they get Bin Laden, if not through intelligence?

A convoy of three armored vehicles painted in desert camo, followed by two green-and-white Border Patrol vans, zoomed by. Despite there never having been an actual connection between Mexican drug cartels and international terrorism, politicians of the build-the-border-wall variety were using this fantasy as one excuse to throw billions into militarizing the border—easy spillover money for any Bravo University program even remotely related to security. It was assuming a lot, he knew, to believe Minerva would be eager, or even willing, to participate in the ICAP or any other intelligence education program at Bravo or any other school. Sandra was right to think he was jumping the gun a little there. On the other hand, Minerva had never mentioned to him her opposition to such programs or participated in any of the "spy school" protests on the UNM campus. Sandra would have known about that and promptly removed her from any consideration. Even if Minerva were to have misgivings about such programs—the CIA's sinister initials were always the first thing to leap into the minds of the uninitiated—he would try to assuage her, as he had others, by telling her that she would be positioning (he had been advised to avoid the word "recruiting") students for work in benign-sounding places like the Open Source Center and World News Connection. And if the CIA affiliation still stuck in her craw, he'd remind her that the arch-feminist Gloria Steinem had worked for a CIA front organization, the Independent Research Service, which she called "liberal, nonviolent and honorable," and had recently said she had no regrets about it.

But okay, okay... before he could bring Minerva into the intelligence community, he had to *find* her. So, back to Quigley and how to squeeze the truth out of the man. To try to get an idea of who he would be dealing with, he'd searched for him on social media, but found no presence for him there, which suggested he was either too cool, too shy or too afraid.

Burris had then taken a look at Quigley's Rate My Professors evaluations. If students had an expectation of privacy, professors could expect no such courtesy on sites like this. One student said of Quigley, "He acts like he needs to get laid," while another, in reply, gave Quigley a red chili pepper for hotness and said he actually shouldn't have any trouble in that department, despite his unfortunate penchant for "goofy beret hats." One rated him "Awesome" and said the course was an "Easy A," while another gave him an "Awful" for the same composition course and wrote, "Easy F!!!" Another detractor wrote, "Your beter of taking someone else your warned."

A "Good," this one for Quigley's Intro to Literature course, allowed that he was "passionate about his subject." That was a common judgment. Burris got quite a few of those on his own evaluations, as had Minerva for the Spanish 101 courses she'd taught as a teaching assistant. The students citing "passion" rarely went so far as to claim that the instructor inspired any in them; it seemed sufficient only that the instructors evince passion, as if they were being paid to act that way for the students' entertainment.

Maybe he was getting cynical. But not so cynical as to believe that Minerva, for one, was incapable of inspiring true passion in her students. She had what it took: charisma, presence. Sandra was the cynical one, with her snide comments about Minerva being his "star pupil." Well, how did she think she got to be his star, if not through her shining?

Anyway: William Quigley. Young assistant professor of English, with a specialty in Beat literature. From the Courses Taught listing on his CV, which by state law he had to post publicly, he hadn't yet to teach a single course dedicated to this subject. He'd been able to sneak some Burroughs and Kerouac into his sophomore lit survey, as evidenced in his syllabus, which was also required by Texas law to be posted online so that the public could scrutinize the subject matter being fed to Texas youth by liberal professors. Burris wondered if Quigley, as an expression of his "passion," played the role of the cool hepcat, slouching behind his desk in his jaunty beret before jumping to his feet and bopping about to make a point. The point being something like, "Man, you have to reject conformity and question authority, question the Man, man, you dig?" In which case he'd have to explain the irony of his being hired by the Man as the authority on anti-authoritarianism.

If Quigley's story about Minerva's disappearance was true, wouldn't he have to have something going for him to have inspired her to confide in him her doubts about her career, and to trust him not to tell his committee that these doubts were the reason for her no-show? And why would he so readily lie for her and tell the committee Burris had told him over the phone that she'd had to cancel the interview because of a family emergency? If Minerva was having some kind of career crisis, why hadn't she come to him, her longtime advisor and mentor, with her doubts? If the choice was either not to believe the guy or be jealous of him, Burris was inclined, out of pride, to not believe him.

In defiance of the GPS, which patiently redirected him until falling silent in defeat, Burris took what looked on the map to be a shortcut to Highway 83. A few miles in, he stopped in the middle of the road to pee—no shoulder, but no traffic, either. And no more insect noise, just an oceanic silence broken only by his splashing on the tarmac, the odor of urine mingling now with the oily smell of the hot pavement and of the leathery vegetation *emanating from a flatness of earth unrounded and utter in its heretofore unmictorated silence now profaned by the xanthous spatterings from that lone pilgrim....* The popping of an unhealthy engine intruded, and he wrapped things up and got back in his Acura just as a terrifically beat-up red station wagon like the one in Peckinpah's *Bring Me the Head of Alfredo García,* a pulpy cult movie Minerva had lent him on DVD, zoomed past with at least seven burly guys jammed inside. He wondered if he shouldn't have told Sandra where he was going in case she wanted to take a little K & R insurance out on him.

Chapter Twenty-Three

Midday silence descended within the villa. It was a spacious place, full of dark Spanish mission-style furniture and faded oriental rugs, but hardly one of those narco mansions you heard about, immense palaces with cupolas and caryatids and grand double staircases—"narchitecture," she'd heard it called. The Gamboa family crest hung above a swept fireplace, three elm-like leaves on a yellow shield—should be marijuana leaves, Minerva thought. A pool in the back, but a modest one without fountains or waterfalls or silly neoclassical pool house on the side. No topiary in the shape of dollar signs. Beyond the pool and the high stone wall spread the thorn forest, baking in the heat. Noisy with insect stridulation out there, but quiet inside the house. No sign of an exotic animal zoo or hippodrome or crocodile pond or any of those things so supposedly dear to narcos. Presumably, Gamboa cartel men lurked out there somewhere in the "three rings of security" Eduardo had alluded to.

And Eduardo himself? Why was he lounging all day on the leather sofa in the living room, staring at the ceiling fan, looking totally lost? Didn't he have business to attend to? The two-way radio at his side crackled occasionally with indecipherable messages, which he answered mostly with grunts when he answered at all. But where was the bustle one would expect around him? Where were the henchmen and the toadies? Even the servants had made themselves scarce. And why wasn't he working harder on getting her out of there?

Maybe he was just giving his people time to mop things up, as the revolting military idiom went, in La Sal. Meanwhile, he too was trapped, a prisoner in his own home, waiting for the situation triggered by her escape to shake itself out.

"Es todo un secuestradero," she blurted from the doorway.

"What's that?" he said, sitting up.

She was again glad he spoke to her in English. It gave her an extra edge.

"That's what the kidnapped women in La Sal said. It was all one big kidnappery. *Todo, todo.*"

He considered this and began to nod. *"Todo un secuestradero."* He gave half a laugh. *"¡Todo un puto secuestradero!"*

So she was right? The two of them were also now sequestered, trapped?

"Do you remember that show 'The Prisoner'?" he said, reclining with the memory. "That big beach ball thing would always bring the guy back to the island whenever he tried to escape."

"The Village."

"The Village! I loved that show." Reflections from the ceiling fan's whirling blades glanced off his glasses.

"So that's what this is? The Village? A beach ball is going to bring us back if we try to leave?"

"Beach ball," he said to the fan and giggled.

She waited.

"So, what do you think of a people who like to kidnap others as much as we Mexicans do?"

"I don't understand."

"Maybe it's just an acting out of our internalized kidnapping. By our mothers. By our fathers. By the gringos."

Was he on something? A narco could get any drug he wanted, she supposed.

He sat up again and asked her, lucidly, eyes gimlet behind the big lenses, if she'd tried to get any of the other women to escape with her.

"Yes, but they weren't interested," she replied.

"Passive people."

"Well, if they knew the whole town had them captive, why even try?"

"Of course. Why even try."

"Even so," she said, "if we'd tried it en masse, our guards might not have been able to control it."

"Collective action. Good idea. Doesn't work in *nuestro México*, however."

"What do you mean?"

"We're all individualists here. Everyone prays to their own saint."

She thought back to the kidnappery, the women on their phones, negotiating their releases, hardly talking to each other. Had she not gotten the better of the men who'd broken into her box, and had Eduardo's people not burst into the room at that moment, would the women have intervened? Or just let them rape her, kill her, right there in front of them?

"Sometimes looking after number one is the best way," he said. "What do you think would have happened to you if you had just minded your own business and had not gone back to try to rescue those others?"

She pictured herself continuing out of town along that road, perhaps picked up by a Good Samaritan and taken to the border. Whisked over the bridge as soon as the authorities realized who she was. Taken to FBI headquarters or the State Department or who knows where for a debriefing, bombarded with attention from the media. Bravo administrators coming to her on bended knee, offering her the job at full professor salary, as well as Quigley's head, in the hope of diverting her from a lawsuit.

"Would you have liked that?" she said. "My not going back? Then you wouldn't have learned about the whole kidnapping operation, and none of this would have happened. Ignorance is bliss."

"Yes, it's all your fault." He said it in such a deadpan way that she couldn't tell if he was joking or serious. He added, "But you don't really believe that. You're glad you went back. Not just because the kidnapping operation got disarticulated and everyone was saved, but because now I know what was going on behind my back."

"Why would I care what you know or don't know?"

"*Por eso*. I put a stop to the kidnapping, didn't I?"

Well, somebody did. From his present attitude—talk about passive—it was not altogether clear to her now that he was the one deciding things. Once again it occurred to her that maybe she'd been dumped on him without his having asked for it.

"I don't think you even know for sure who brought me here."

"Ignorance is bliss," he said, dreamy again. "You said it. But knowledge is power. Isn't that what you teach your students?"

Actually, no. She was more likely to alert them to the Dunning-Kruger effect, in which incompetent people exaggerated their knowledge and competence because they didn't know what true knowledge and competence involved; and unfortunately for the rest of us, this self-confidence often got them promoted to positions of power.

Is that what was up with Eduardo? The Dunning-Kruger effect? That didn't jibe with his apathy, though, or did it? She needed him to keep talking; each of his revelations added to her knowledge of him, her power over the situation—and over him.

"How about you?" she asked. "Are you just praying to your own saint?"

"Me? I have people."

"I don't see them."

"They're out there."

"Ah, the three rings of security. I've been thinking.... Maybe their job is to keep us in as much as it is to keep others out?"

"Where do you get that?" he said, straightening up. "Those men work for me, they work for the Gamboa family!"

"I believe you," she said, and she did, to a point. But the nerve she'd hit suggested he was not in control of the situation, and that he knew it. His father in a US prison, men out there fighting over Gamboa territory and keeping him on the sidelines as they slugged it out...

"Where's the rest of your family? Besides your father."

"My mother and sisters live in Spain. My brother should be right here, but he died a year ago, a little more. I'm the Gamboa in charge now, and these plazas are my responsibility. Even the government respects that."

"Your brother should be here instead of you?"

"Of course. He was my older brother. He knew these operations far better than I. The day-to-day."

"So do you live here, alone, in this place?"

"Me? I live in Mexico City. Panama. All over. I look after other businesses."

"Like what?"

He lay back down. He was through answering her questions.

She trudged upstairs and lay down as well. The ornate grandfather clock in the corner opposite the knight read four-fifteen, the sun outside dropping but still fierce. What would she be doing now if she'd just prayed to her own saint and not gone to the palacio municipal to alert people about the kidnappings, if she had instead made it safely and inconspicuously back to the Bravo campus? A second wind having powered her through her teaching demo and her interview with the dean, she'd likely be back in her motel room, resting before going to the final dinner, masturbating the stress away. The next morning, they'd take her to the airport, and by noon she'd be back on the quiet spring-break UNM campus, plunged anew into her dissertation and anxiously awaiting Bravo's decision, just as she now anxiously awaited word from Eduardo that it was safe to take her to the border.

But it would seem Eduardo was himself awaiting news about what was going on outside the walls of this villa in which they were both sequestered. She wondered again why his people had unloaded her on him instead of just dumping her by the side of the road. Had they done so to place an extra burden on him and distract him from their struggles for supremacy? Or being still loyal, had they done it to protect him, placing her here as a kind of human shield against the enemy, who wouldn't dare attack for fear of harming her and perhaps bringing the gringos down on them? The same went for those vaunted rings of security. Were they there to protect him, keep him prisoner, or both?

Whatever the case, here they were, she and Eduardo, in it together. She thought of him down there on his couch, lost and alone.

Was she just going to stay up here, praying to her own saint (as if she had one)? Should she give him his space or go back down and offer solidarity?

She went back down.

Chapter Twenty-Four

"Kidnap's a funny word, isn't it, profe?" said Omar. "Like it's not just kids who are napped. And why 'nap'?"

"Shhh!"

Normally he'd be delighted to talk things etymological with Omar or any other student, but what if the office was bugged? Then again, why would it be bugged? Anyway, he needed Omar to concentrate on the task at hand, which was erasing the searches about kidnapping in Mexico from Quigley's computer. Yes, yes, short of dousing the hard drive in acid, those searches were probably always going to be lurking there, not to mention in the Cloud, but surely Omar could do a better job of deletion than he had.

Omar was cleverly leaving Quigley's searches for "disappearing in Mexico" and his perusal on Amazon of the book *How to Disappear Completely and Never Be Found,* because that would bolster his story, should the authorities inspect his computer, that he knew nothing about her kidnapping, only her disappearance.

The idea was for Quigley to repeat to the authorities, should it ever come to that, exactly what he'd told Burris: that she'd asked him to drop her off at the bus station and to tell people she hadn't shown. Why had he gone along with her request? they'd ask. He didn't know, he'd say, hanging his head. Out of a sense of collegiality, maybe. And she was persuasive. She had that kind of charisma about her.

He had a hunch, Quigley would tell them, that she intended to disappear into Mexico, hence those searches on his computer, dated the day of her disappearance.

Forgetting about the potential bugs, Quigley said to Omar, "What if when she shows up... we're still assuming that, right? Sooner rather than later? What if when she shows up, she's not as collegial as we're hoping, and she's mad at me, doesn't give a damn about my career and insists on telling it exactly as it came down? That I took her to La Reina, put her in harm's way and then lied about it?"

Omar shrugged. "Your word against hers. If we have to, I can get a guy to say he saw her at the bus station."

"You sure no witnesses from the restaurant will come forward to back up her version?"

"Nah. No one down there is going to risk talking with US authorities."

"And bridge videos of us crossing that morning?"

"On foot? I wouldn't worry about it. Good thing they didn't run your passport when you came back over, though."

"What about that customs agent I talked to about her?"

"Uy, profe, you're pouring a lot of cream on the tacos. Everybody's just going to be happy she's back, don't you think? It's all good."

"All good. Right. You don't know the academic world, Omar. It's a snake pit. These so-called colleagues of mine will never let it go."

Omar swiveled in the office chair to face Quigley. "Okay, maybe, but what's for sure, professor? You didn't get any help from me with this shit. That's an understanding between us." He fixed Quigley with raptor eyes that showed how well he'd survived in a business that had plenty of snakes of its own.

At least the office door was closed. No one in the hall could hear them. You were supposed to keep your office door cracked open whenever you had a student inside, but under the circumstances, screw that. Speaking of the office door, he now remembered a dream from this morning, one of many disturbing ones. In real life, the water in his bathroom pipes was making a knocking sound again, and in the dream he heard it as someone rapping on his office door; when he opened it, a student kneed him in the balls. Not a good start to the morning.

Despite the bad dreams and Omar's chilly warning not to rat him out, he felt better as he talked things through with Omar and rehearsed his story to keep it straight. Recall and review, as he admonished his students to do. Minerva could tell people anything she liked, but he had his story, and he was sticking to it. Obviously, he wished her the best and hoped for her release asap. He continued to hope that upon her release she'd contact him before anyone else so they could get on the same page, which meant that she'd agree to leave him out of it, just as he agreed to leave Omar out. Be collegial! In any event, there was no way he was going to take responsibility for putting her in harm's way. Gallant though that might be, it would follow him throughout his academic career and kill his own chances of being hired elsewhere. If Quigley had learned anything from being on Minerva's search committee, it was that in a marketplace as competitive as the academic one, any application with even the shadow of a stain went on the reject pile.

"What you have to watch out for," said Omar, taping a square of masking tape over the computer's camera lens, "is cyberespionage. Don't open any emails from people you don't know. And don't open any from her."

"I thought you said they weren't allowing her to use email."

"Exactly. So those emails wouldn't be from her."

"Then who the hell *would* they be from, Omar? Tell me what the hell's going on!"

"It's just a precaution, sir. The Mexican government has this state-of-the-art spyware from the Israelis called Pegasus that's activated when certain emails are opened."

"The Mexican *government*? What would the Mexican government have to do with anything?"

"They know about her. They know who has her and how she got there, and they're gonna be following things. But *you* don't know all that, right? You've got your story, and you're sticking with it."

"I just don't understand why they, why this junior, hasn't let her go already. If the plazas are so hot, there must be Marinas and other military people running around all over. How hard can it be for him to hand her off to them?"

"It's a good question, sir."

A knock came on the door. Omar clicked out of his cleanup task, and Quigley opened, not to the student from his dream but to a bearish man he'd never seen before but whose presence, as soon as he intuited who it was, came as another kind of kick in the balls.

Chapter Twenty-Five

Professor Burris had waited until Professor Quigley's office hours to pay him a visit, because if he was a normal professor, you wouldn't be able to find him in otherwise, especially in a building this uncomfortably cold. Now Burris understood what they meant by the "Texas winter," the season when Texans showed off the extent to which they could splurge their abundant fossil fuel energy on air conditioning. It was a cavernously empty building, as Burris half expected after ascertaining from the Bravo class schedule that many, if not most, professors in the department taught their courses either fully online or with "reduced seat time." He doubted Minerva would teach her eventual classes remotely—or at least he hoped not. She was just too good one-on-one with students to squander valuable face time with them; besides, these deserted halls needed livening up with her laughter.

And lo, there Quigley was, keeping his hours like a good boy, and with a student no less, though it was odd how fast the student ducked out of the office as soon as Burris identified himself.

His office was only moderately messy, as professors' offices went, with a stack of student papers on the desk, a coffee cup with the Bravo bucking bronco logo, and a shelf devoted to the Beat writers. The black beret that students had referred to in their Rate My Professor evaluations hung from a hook, next to it a broad-rimmed Panama hat. His window looked down upon a gallery of some sort—a gallery of student work, to judge from the garishness of the paintings.

Quigley's alarmed expression, his lips turning pale, was proof that the man had something to hide. He offered Burris a seat in an overstuffed blue armchair, and turned to face him, crossing his jeaned legs and his thin, hairy arms. Quigley would no doubt have preferred his desk defensively between them, but his furniture wasn't arranged that way, probably so as to seem friendlier to students. Thumbtacked above the young professor's head was a quote from Kerouac: "Everything belongs to me because I'm poor."

"That sentiment must be a tough sell down here where people are actually poor," Burris said.

Quigley swung his head around and stared at the phrase as if he'd never seen it before, then turned back to Burris and blinked almost spastically. No, he was no cool cat, no devil-may-care beatnik, maybe just the opposite. Burris had been in academia long enough to know that scholars' areas of interest did not necessarily reflect their temperaments; at his own school there was a Romanticist who hated the outdoors and an accounting professor who purported to be an anarcho-syndicalist and played in a punk band.

"So... Ms. Mondragón is on the road, is she?" said Burris. Maybe not a good idea to start out with so mocking a tone, but he couldn't help it. Young Quigley annoyed him, and he was feeling cranky after the long, hot drive.

"I suppose so."

"Traveling around to... how did you put it? Get her head together? Find her center?"

"I think that's how she put it."

"Doesn't sound like her."

This was Quigley's chance to either level with him and calmly tell him what really happened, or unlock those arms and throw them up in exasperation and cry, "What can I say? What more do you want?" Instead, he stopped blinking and kept his gaze fixed on Burris, waiting.

"How was she acting?" Burris persisted. "What was her state of mind?"

"State of mind? I'm not sure I know—"

"She told you she didn't want the job? That she was reconsidering the academic life?"

"More or less, yes."

"Everything would belong to her then, because she'd be without a job and poor, right?"

"I'm not following. Look, Dr. Burris, even though the search has been suspended for this year, I'm sure the position will be relisted next year, and the committee will be glad to consider her application again at that time."

It wasn't the fact of the suspension per se that outraged Burris. He himself had been on search committees whose searches had been summarily suspended or even canceled by administrators even as they were about to offer a candidate the position. What galled him was that his enthusiastic recommendation of Minerva hadn't brought her more time. He had sent it directly to both the dean and the provost, with juicy hints of Homeland Security external funding should she be included in Bravo's intelligence program. And it had meant nothing! But then again, damned Sandra hadn't followed up with her own plug, as he'd hoped she would, so that the Bravo people could really get it into their heads that to hire Minerva was to tap into a pipeline for some serious federal monies.

"Or maybe they'll re-open it if she comes back," Quigley said.

"Reschedule her interviews, teaching demo, return flight?"

"If she comes back soon, of course. These things happen, right? She's a good candidate."

Really, Burris thought, after suspending the search altogether, they'd open it anew when she decided to waltz back in? What self-respecting search committee, or chair, or dean, or provost would ever accept such behavior, even from a trophy candidate?

"You haven't been in this business long, have you, Assistant Professor Quigley?"

"Not long, no." Quigley looked down, now playing the newbie counseled by a senior.

"Because that seems like an unlikely scenario," Burris said.

"Hasn't she called anyone to say she's okay?" Quigley said suddenly. "Her mother, maybe?"

"Her mother? Why her mother?"

"Everybody has a mother!"

"Everybody?" Burris said in the patronizing tone movie cops used to gaslight suspects. "I don't have a mother."

Burris had no idea if he was going down the right path with his goading, almost sing-song tone. It sounded bad cop, but to have a bad cop you had to have a good cop, and where was his good cop? Could you have both in one? As a suspect, Quigley seemed to be playing a dual role himself, alternately defiant and chastened.

Did he know about Minerva's phone call to her mother? It sounded to Burris as though he did. And still, Quigley remained hermetic. His refusal to level with him enraged Burris to the point of triggering what he had explicitly, on his drive down, thought of as the nuclear option.

"Dr. Quigley, have you ever heard of IGNU?"

"Agnew? Nixon's crooked vice president?"

"Integrated Global Knowledge and Understanding Collaboration. Operates under the auspices of the Office of the Director of National Intelligence."

"I don't think I've had the pleasure."

"You have several programs right here at Bravo connected to it, including Global Security Studies. And you'll soon be getting an Intelligence Center for Academic Practice. They're both IEC's—Intelligence Education Centers."

"I'm impressed."

"Well, you should be. And let me also impress upon you that Ms. Mondragón and I both are assets thereof. And see, she hasn't lost her center, the Center has lost her, and it wants her back."

Sandra would've laughed out loud, less at this witticism than at his misappropriation of spy craft jargon. "Ah, you and your student, two cloak-and-dagger assets, field agents for the National Clandestine Service perhaps, practicing your dark-world magic?" she would say, sardonically. Well, fuck you, useless Sandra. He, if not Minerva, was indeed an intelligence asset, in the most general sense of the term. Anyway, one used whatever language worked for the mission at hand, right? And from Quigley's return to pallor, it was indeed working.

"I'm surprised your dean didn't advise you of her partici-pation in these centers," Burris continued. "Which, as you can imagine, enjoy much federal largesse. Deans like those grants, especially in underfunded colleges like yours, right? You've heard of the Patriot Act, I assume. Look up Title IV of that leg-islation, 'Protecting the Border,' and Title IX, 'Improved Intel-ligence,' to see some earmarks relevant to this region."

A moment of silence followed this barrage. Only the faint tapping of someone assembling a frame in the gallery below could be heard. Quigley had stopped jiggling his leg and, his gaze wandering above Burris' head, seemed to be searching for a way to weasel out of his mess.

"To be blunt, I'd hate to have to get Homeland Security in-volved in Minerva's disappearance. Unless you tell me…" Then he lost it, was on his feet, "… what the hell really happened!"

Burris hated losing his temper, but his having to exagger-ate Minerva's involvement in intelligence, to lie about it, just to get this man to level with him made him see red, because despite the phone call to her mother that seemed to corrobo-rate Quigley's story, he could not accept that story, could not accept that Minerva had confided her doubts not to him, but rather to this dweeb, this stranger. Now he'd done it again, lost it, his voice reaching its loudest thunder on the penulti-mate syllable.

Quigley scooted back in his chair, as if from the force of Burris' breath alone. Burris knew immediately that far from cracking Quigley open, the outburst was more likely to have sealed him shut, at least for the moment. And, depending on how thick the walls were here and who was on the other side, someone might come to the door to see what was going on, and then the conversation would be over for sure. He hesitated, tried to formulate an apology, but couldn't bring himself to it. There was nothing more he could do right now but, as in all the cop shows, drop his card on the man's desk and ask him to call him if he "thought of anything."

As soon as Burris left, Quigley got on the computer to try to verify what Burris had told him, but he was so shaken that he couldn't remember the acronyms the man had spouted or what they stood for. Academic Intelligence Centers? Intelligence Studies Centers? Norbert upstairs would know, but Quigley was too rattled to go up there and ask without giving away the game.

He googled Homeland Security Investigations, and it took him to an ICE page and a picture of an HSI Gang Unit cuffing a Hispanic-looking suspect. Omar's signature one-two knock came on the door.

"I heard that guy yelling," Omar said, eyeing the computer screen.

"Yes. But if he is what he says he is, he wouldn't yell like that. They train them better."

"What does he say he is?"

"Some kind of intelligence agent. Or asset, I think he said, whatever that means."

Omar fixed his raptor gaze on him again. "Like a spy? Like CIA?"

"He didn't say that, exactly. Just that he and the candidate work in some kind of intelligence program."

"The candidate, meaning Minerva Mondragón."

The metallic flatness with which he said it gave Quigley pause. "Yes. But it has to be bullshit. Spies don't say they're spies, right?"

"But he works for Homeland Security," Omar said, nodding at the computer just as the stars of the screen saver burst on.

"Works for? Those programs he's talking about get funding from them, is what he said."

"Spy programs."

"I guess so. I mean, I don't know! That's what I'm looking up."

He didn't want Omar there any longer, didn't want his collaboration right now. He'd already said too much. And Omar, whose gaze had now landed on Burris' business card, seemed just as eager not to be there. In a phrase Quigley would ding as cliché on a student paper but couldn't get out of his mind the next day as he marveled over how stupid he'd been to tell Omar about Burris: "And Omar bolted without another word...."

Chapter Twenty-Six

There was a hideous story to explain Stockholm syndrome: the mouse so frightened it went to the cat for love. Minerva was not, would never be, such a mouse. As she watched Eduardo's peaceful face and listened to his slow breathing, she thought of how shyly he'd responded to her at first. She was sure that he was not that cat.

Where had her lust—his lust, their mutual lust—come from? Maybe it was just the need for stress relief and nothing more. Being trapped in this deadly, quiet place, waiting for news about whatever was going down outside its walls, unable to make a move until things settled down, they needed release, and they had found it. Simple as that. No need to start theorizing about the perverse relationship between eros and thanatos. She could imagine the obscene scenario in which the victim prostrates herself before her captor, her gratitude for his sparing her life translating into sexual excitement and even a kind of profound spiritual love. Yeah, no. This was not that kind of scenario.

If there was more to it than lust, then it perhaps followed Sensei's admonishment to "grab the enemy by the belt." Conscious of this strategy or not, she had quite literally grabbed his silver-threaded belt to draw him to her for their first kiss. Behind this may have been a desire to buck him up, snap him out of his lethargy and empower herself by doing so. They'd tripped up the stairs to her bedroom, where he'd touched her gingerly and tensed a little when she'd reached for his cock with the hand that—perhaps he'd heard—had driven like a piston into the groin of the man that had released her from the box.

Now Eduardo lay on the jumble of satin sheets, snoring gently. As the sun had died, drawing long, golden light across the polished furniture, he had called for Juanita to bring them something to eat. Within minutes, bolillos and serrano ham and queso manchego and thin slices of melon materialized on the marble top table by the door. If Juanita had even glanced at the two of them, she'd done so with enough tact that Minerva hadn't noticed. Now the tray held only crumbs, and the room had gone dark as a half-moon rose.

On Mexican telenovelas, servants were either extremely discreet or extremely gossipy, depending on the plot. If Juanita was the gossipy sort, the word would have spread that the patrón was sleeping with the rescued Chicana. How would that affect his people's, and his rivals', view of her?

What mattered more was how Eduardo himself now perceived her. Before they became lovers, if that wasn't too heavy a word for what they were now, it was clear that the only desired outcome for all involved was her immediate release. Had her impulsiveness, her going downstairs and grabbing him by the belt without a word, complicated this picture? It took a certain post-orgasm clarity of mind to wonder all this, and to appreciate the irony of it. It was funny what rash things one did to get the relief one needed to reflect soberly on their rashness.

She watched his breathing—so deep. She suspected this was the first time he'd gotten real sleep in a while. She felt a pang of renewed desire; it turned her on to have brought him this rest. Thinking clearly now, maybe her desire to see him comforted arose from her own desire to survive. Maybe it wasn't so far, after all, from the case of the mouse so frightened it went to the cat for love.

Minerva contemplated his clavicles and the little valleys they formed at his neck, one of the most vulnerable parts of a man, and the most endearing. She watched the pulse beating just above. He looked so smooth-browed and innocent, it was impossible to believe he was predatory in any way. Maybe it was naïve of her, but she struggled to believe he'd ever been on the violent side of things, and easy to believe what he'd told her in their conversation in the room below: that he'd always been kept away from the "day-to-day," that he'd been thrown into this situation by force of circumstance and wanted out for himself as much as he wanted it for her.

He hadn't spoken to her of any specific plans to extricate himself from the situation, but it had been obvious all along that her presence was an impediment to that exit. Was it still? Now she imagined him dreaming of her in another common *telenovela* role, the drug queenpin. In his version it would be the story of a lowly graduate student teaming up with a hapless cartel junior to become La Reina del Norte, or Este, or whatever it would be here... La Reina de La Reina... *Ay*, Minerva, what have you done?

She nudged him awake.

"¿Qué, qué?" He groped for his glasses, his unguarded eyes panicked.

"No, no, nothing, just... what's going to happen to me?" She needed to hear from him that nothing had changed, that everything was on track and her release imminent.

He sank down again, mumbled into her breasts. "I already told you."

She eased him away. "Tell me again."

He propped himself up on his elbow. "You don't believe me? Some guys will come. My guys. They will tell me they have secured the plaza. Then we can move freely."

"What if the guys that come aren't your guys?"

"Not mine?" A hint of fear gave the lie to his incredulity.

"Your father's in prison in the US, you said. In isolation."

"Yes. *¿Qué tiene?* What are you getting at?"

She didn't need to spell it out. He himself had as much as admitted that he didn't command the kind of control over the cartel that his father had. And his father, being in isolation, couldn't exercise any control at all now, obviously. So leadership of the organization was up for grabs.

"Don't worry," he said, a little bitterly. "Everybody will want the credit for freeing you."

"What about the La Sal people? The people that put me in the box?"

"Those people are crushed. It's not them who would be coming. Anyway, they don't want you either. They just didn't know what to do with you after you didn't make good on your escape and turned back to rat them out. Believe me, nobody wants you down here."

"What about you?"

He blinked, and she could see he had misunderstood her question.

"I mean, what will you do if somebody other than your guys come?"

"Oh." He gave a self-conscious little laugh. "Oh, I have plans. I've got a tunnel under here, and at the other end I've got some guys of the very most *confianza*."

"And you always have plenty of warning? Shoe-shine boys everywhere?"

"Yes. And this always by my side." He patted the two-way radio on the bedside table.

"Escape from the authorities is always especially easy," he added. "They always take the toll road, and every single Humvee and patrol car is required to stop and pay the toll. A falcon will notify me, and I'll have plenty of time. *Ay, México.*"

This got him started about his country's deficiencies: the glacial bureaucracy, the corruption, the lack of a sense of civic duty and of working together for the common good. She'd heard this litany of complaints before from Mexicans she'd met on her travels as well as from a Mexican student or two at her university. It was an odd set of grievances to come from a narco, or even the most reluctant son of a narco, but she held her tongue. The best response was to nod and say nothing. If you were American and agreed too readily, they'd turn on you for representing Mexico's other big problem: US imperialism.

"So naturally you couldn't organize an escape from that secuestradero," he said. "We Mexicans can't even put together a decent fútbol team."

She nodded just enough to say she understood, not enough to say she agreed. She waited for what she'd come to refer to as "the crab thing," and, sure enough there it was:

"We Mexicans are like a bucket full of crabs, one gets to the top—"

"And the others pull it down, yes."

But it wasn't really true in his case, was it? His rivals would be perfectly happy for him to escape the bucket and leave the plazas to them.

"That's the *envidia*," he said. "But you know what our main problem is? No trust. The main thing I learned in business school is that for things to run well, there has to be trust. You were right to trust the municipal authorities and the police but look where it got you. Right back to where you started."

"Who do you trust?" She immediately regretted the question, fearing he might say, "I trust you." It made her cringe inside to think he might have begun to imagine her as his reina.

"The guys at the end of the tunnel, like I said. They've been with my father all their lives, and they will die for me, a Gamboa."

"How nice." Relief had a bad habit of making her sardonic.

"Death is nothing to them because the dead don't know they're dead. That's what they tell me. It's not that '*la vida no vale nada*' like in the song, but that la vida has nothing to do with la muerte."

"They're Epicureans! 'As long as we exist, death is not with us, but when death comes, we do not exist.'"

"Nah. It's just machismo."

"Machismo doesn't need philosophy," she said. "It's pre-theoretical."

His turn now to be wry: "Machismo is pre-theoretical. Yes, professor."

Even spoken in irony, it sounded good to her to be called professor.

"Like any proper Mexican man," he said, getting back to his Mexico-bashing, "they're captivated by machismo. That's their secuestradero. Machismo is their safe house."

"'Machismo is their safe house.' I love it. Unpack that, class."

"Speaking of death," he said, finger circling the tattoo on her thigh, "why do you have a tattoo of Coatlicue?"

He was the only guy she'd been with who knew it was Coatlicue, the mother of gods and mortals.

"We got good instruction on Aztec deities in grade school," he explained. "Except all I remember is that her daughter rallied her four hundred brothers and sisters to decapitate her, but then the daughter herself got decapitated and her head became the moon. Or something like that. We Mexicans like the decapitations, ¿que no?"

Minerva laughed weakly and tried to gather her thoughts to explain to him the dialectical ins and outs of the "Coatlicue state," as elucidated by Gloria Anzaldúa, her favorite Chicana scholar whose alma mater was, happily enough, Bravo University. How the goddess represented life and death together, both part of the same process.

"My teacher told us she's the precursor of La Santa Muerte, the saint of the narcos," Eduardo said. "She's the comforting deity who teaches them to be unafraid of death."

Minerva demurred. "But were the Aztecs even afraid of death in the way those guys might be? Did they pray to her for their own private, individualistic salvation? We don't know what kind of inner life the Aztecs had."

She was rekindling her professorial self and liking it. Then his radio crackled with something indecipherable to her, and he sat up. He gave her a funny look as he pulled on his clothes and went out to deal with it.

Chapter Twenty-Seven

Losing one's temper almost always led to a setback, if not a total torpedoing, of one's objectives, as Burris well knew. It had been a mistake to have gone directly to Quigley's office; after the long, hot, over-sugared and over-caffeinated drive, he should've checked into a motel and cooled down with a drink and a nap before seeking the man out. But what was done was done, and if he hadn't learned to control his temper, he'd at least learned to wait out the delays it incurred. With luck, the young professor would take his anger—he revisited the stunned man propelled back in his chair from the force of his outburst—as a sign of the seriousness of the situation. Sooner rather than later, Quigley would pick up his card and call him, ready to spill the beans.

What he had to do now was find that motel, and a bar, and give it a little time. He jumped back on the freeway and cruised a while, the forward motion calming him as he kept an eye on the roadside signage. One billboard—and they were all gigantic things aloft massive steel posts—offered women the vaginal rejuvenation that would "keep him happy." Another announced, against the silhouette of an enormous assault rifle, an upcoming gun show and swap. A third read, in bold white letters on a black background, "DON'T MAKE ME COME DOWN THERE! — GOD." Below these signs stretched the strip malls with their dollar stores and pawn shops and payday loan joints and fast-food drive-thrus.

Beyond that, cookie-cutter suburban homes built of peniten-tiary-gray brick sprawled across the flat, featureless topog-raphy. Even the gray-bottomed clouds were flat, like irons pressing hotly on the land.

Well, hell, maybe there were no beans for Quigley to spill. Maybe Minerva had done just as he said she had, looked around and made an executive decision to ditch the job in this ugly place and hightail it to... where? South Padre Island? San Antonio? Mexico? It wasn't that she *wouldn't* do some-thing so impulsive, knowing Minerva; it was just that she wouldn't do something impulsive until *after* she did the re-sponsible thing, i.e., the job interview. If that made any sense?

She wouldn't have come to Texas looking for natural beauty, anyway. If that's what she was after, she'd never leave New Mexico. She wanted to be on the border, immerse her-self in border culture, study this remote place. They called it Deep South Texas for a reason. If you went directly west, where those flat-bottom clouds were now tinged pink with sunset, you'd be far into Mexico. If you kept going east across the Gulf, you'd hit Miami. The big Mexican city of Monterrey was closer than any large US city. No doubt white Texan money still dominated down here, but the population itself was overwhelmingly Hispanic. This was where the rich-est country in the world butted up against the developing world, with all the cultural hybridity you'd expect. He re-called the students chattering in Spanish as much as English as they streamed along Bravo's mandevilla-festooned breeze-ways. No, she *couldn't* have just walked away from this.

Finally, a billboard he could relate to, Buchanan's whisky, amber waterfall splashing over boulder-sized ice. In the shadow of the sign sat a midcentury modern motel, the Capri, with a lounge attached: Capo's Cantina. Plenty of semis and muddied pickups in the parking lot, but what did he expect? Minivans of families on vacation? He hoped the rooms didn't stink too much of smoke.

The lobby had a noirish feel to it, with multiple trophy heads, including a warthog's, staring glassily from the walls. A gaunt, bespectacled man checked him in, taking his credit card with long, careful fingers and returning it with a voucher for a free cocktail at Capo's.

He hadn't given much thought to the name, but as soon as he entered the bar, the gangster theme whacked him: framed movie posters of Marlon Brando as the Godfather and of tough-guy James Cagney. Behind the bartender was a row of tequila in bottles shaped like submachine guns.

"Welcome to Capo's!" the barman called cheerily. "What'll it be?"

He was a sandy-haired young guy, very gringo-looking, unusual in these parts. He appeared to be just opening, setting up. There was no one else in the joint.

Burris ordered Buchanan's on the rocks.

"You've got the *onda*, as they say around here," said the bartender, taking the voucher.

"What do you mean?"

"Buchanan's. Narco liquor of choice. Hey, I'm Alex. Where you from?"

"New Mexico."

Alex deemed this awesome. When he came back with the drink, he said, "So whatdya think?"

"About what?"

"The decor!"

"Well," said Burris, "it looks like you have a theme."

"That's for sure! You know who that is in the corner?" He tilted his head at a skeletal figure in white ensconced in a grotto behind the bar. "La Santa Muerte. The White Lady. And over there's St. Jude Thaddaeus, patron of lost causes and desperate situations. They're both narco saints. A month ago this was a truckers' bar. Goodbuddy's, one word. Booori-iing! Now we've got the *movimiento alterado* crowd."

"Not familiar with the term."

"That's people who like to play narco. You'll see them when they come in, the snakeskin boots and silk shirts. Actually, now it's Big Pony polo shirts. Narco polos. The chicks in these, like, tiger-stripe outfits and butt-lift jeans. In real life they're farmworkers and shit like that."

"That's…" Burris searched for the word, "… sad."

"Nah, it's all good. It's only make-believe. Cosplay. If they were the real thing, they'd leave offerings and shit to the lady and the saint. I've found, like, three bucks for them in the whole time I been here."

"Which you kept."

"Hey, well, that's another thing. The tips aren't that great here. If these guys were the real thing, I'd get a Benjamin every now and then."

Minerva would really get a kick out of this place. There was a paper and a presentation right here. A book chapter.

"Tonight's doggy corrido night," Alex informed him. "*Corridos perrones*, the ballads with the really violent lyrics. They've outlawed them on the Mexican side, you know."

"I think they kinda like having a white guy like me serving them," he said. "Role reversal. I'm only half-white, actually. What they call a coyote. Refresh?"

Burris nodded, and the kid poured a gigantic slug over the old ice.

"Despite the lack of tips and offerings," said Burris, "how can you be sure some of them aren't actual narcos?"

"I don't think a real narco would want to call attention to himself by going to a place called Capo's, do you?"

"Maybe they would enjoy the irony," Burris said. "A hidden in plain sight kind of thing."

"You're thinking it too much," said Alex. "You a professor?"

"Yes, actually."

"Yeah. I went to our university over here for a semester. Bravo. Not for me. I'm gonna graduate from the University of Life!"

"Or the University of Death, as it were."

"Naaaw…"

He left Burris alone and moved down the bar. If Burris were a proper sleuth, he'd have brought a picture of Minerva to show him. Knowing her, and her nose for weird manifestations of popular culture, she'd already been here. Maybe he'd see what images he could scare up of her on the web to show around, see if anybody recognized her. But that was for tomorrow. The drive and the encounter with Quigley and the scotch had hit him, and he could only think of bed. As he was leaving, Alex let blast a narco ballad just as the first young "capo" and his date arrived, the guy wearing a fawn-colored Abercrombie tracksuit and blue-mirrored sunglasses, she in a leopard-spotted miniskirt and six-inch stilettos.

Chapter Twenty-Eight

Hot morning sunshine slashed through the crack in Burris' motel room curtains. As he made himself in-room coffee, a persistent scrabbling and pecking sound outside his window got him to peek out: a cardinal attacking its own image in his car's wing mirror, a green gecko eyeing it cock-headed from the pavement. Reptile and human continued watching the stupid bird for a while. Burris guessed it was programmed by instinct to attack anything red and moving in its territory, especially here in the springtime. Following its script, like animals did.

Well, maybe Quigley was right and Minerva had walked away, in the unpredictable way of humans. Maybe she wasn't automatically following the program, the script: undergrad to grad school to teaching; tenure track, tenure, full professor, emeritus, death. Grant applications, merit reports, one- and three- and five-year plans, the playing footsie with administrators and the likes of Sandra and the rest of the bureaucracy. Good for her for being fluid and human, for thinking twice about that life and career. And hadn't her mother reported her as sounding fine, if rather exhausted, as one might naturally be after taking such a step back and reevaluating one's course in life?

Minerva's mother, for her part, had sounded almost triumphant on that call, as if to say this proved the fruit didn't fall far from the tree, daughter as adventurous and nonconformist as mother.

He'd had high hopes for Minerva's academic career, whether or not she worked with him to expand the intelligence centers. But she was young and had every right to rethink her life's path.

His phone buzzed on the bed, the number lighting up with the local area code. A surprisingly aggressive Quigley unleashed right off, voice quaking with an indignation that didn't quite jibe with his noir-novel diction.

"Tell me one thing, Burris. Why should I be the fall guy for some hot-to-trot spy-cum-job candidate who got me to take her to Mexico, and now finds herself in over her head? Or maybe not so over her head—I understand she beat the shit out of her kidnappers, and I'd say now she's exactly where she wanted to be, and where you'd want her to be, in some narco's lair. Gathering intelligence, presumably. Sorry if your communication's broken down, but it seems like she was able to call her mother, yes, so you might want to call the mom and get all caught up, but I can tell you, your girl spook's fine. Setting a honey trap—isn't that what you call it?— for the big narco's son. So, I'll tell you what I'm going to do. I'm going to go to my chair and dean and tell them exactly how I've been played, and you're welcome to come along."

"I don't... I have no idea what you're talking about, Dr. Quigley. No. Don't. We need to meet before you go to anyone."

Fifteen minutes later, Burris found himself across from a wild-looking Quigley at a table in the middle of Pato's Tacos, on the main drag across from the Bravo campus. The *taquería* was busy, the air steamy and eggy and loud enough so that the other customers couldn't hear them, although Burris sensed that Quigley was ready for the world to hear his story.

Burris tried to speak calmly. "Look, William... can I call you William? I'm sorry. I exaggerated. Okay, I lied. She has nothing to do with intelligence. I do, to a very limited extent. But not Minerva. If she's a spy, why would she call her mother and not her handlers? Now, what's this about a kidnapping?" That last word came out in a kind of choked whisper.

Quigley looked at him the way a reared-back horse looks at a snake. His hand was trembling enough to slosh his coffee out of its mug. He was beginning to infuriate Burris all over again.

"Either you tell me now or *I'll* be the one to go to the police with what you've told me," Burris said. "She's been kidnapped? How, where?"

"She *was* kidnapped. Now she's whatever she told her mother."

"So you knew about her call to her mother?"

"And you didn't?" Quigley said.

"Yes, we did. I did."

"So you must know what I know! Why are you stringing me along like this?"

"That's all I know," Burris said. "She called her mother, said she was fine. Didn't say where she was. So you're saying she's being held against her will?" He wanted to reach out and throttle the guy, but he let him vent.

"You don't know anything that's going on, beyond what she told her mother? What was all that about you guys working for intelligence?"

"That's what I'm trying to tell you now. I get a small grant from Homeland Security for a language research project, and I thought Minerva might participate in that here at Bravo. That's it. She's not actively involved in any kind of intelligence gathering. She doesn't even know I was thinking of her for that grant. I exaggerated our involvement to get you to talk."

"Goddamn you."

Goddamn *me?* But Burris let Quigley keep talking, his dread growing as the story came out. She'd been snatched during lunch in the adjoining Mexican city of La Reina. Then she was rescued, if you can call it that, by a drug cartel hostile to the kidnappers. And the cartel planned to release her as soon as they could find safe passage for her to the border.

"Why the *hell* didn't you tell your committee right away that she'd been snatched?"

"I didn't *know* she had, at first!"

"So what did you tell them? Same as you told me, that she'd bailed on them?"

"I told them she hadn't shown. And that I'd contacted you, and you said it was due to a family emergency."

"Great. What did *you* think had happened to her?"

"I don't know! Gone native or something."

"Gone native? What's that supposed to mean?"

"Wandered off! Like a poet."

"Like a...?" Could be the kid was certifiably nuts. "How did you learn she'd been kidnapped, and how do you know this narco family has her now?"

"Well, okay. Okay. That student you saw in my office? He's my go-between."

"Go-between? Between you and the narcos?"

"He keeps me informed, and them too. But yeah, now you've fucked it all up."

"How have I fucked it up?"

"He overheard you. Now it's going to get back to them that she's some sort of agent or spy or something!"

"He overheard me, or you told him?"

"What does it matter? Now he's spooked, and I haven't been able to contact him since he left my office."

"Well, you sure as hell better keep trying, Quigley. They've got to know it's not true!"

Quigley had his phone out already, his finger pecking on it as sharply as that cardinal had been pecking at Burris' rearview mirror half an hour ago, a distant time in the past when, having stoically accepted Quigley's story of Minerva's disappearance, Burris had been a quick shower away from getting in that car and heading back through the no country for old men and home.

Chapter Twenty-Nine

After Eduardo's radio squawked and he'd left to deal with it, Minerva lay in bed a while, thinking about some of the things they'd talked about. She'd told him about being raised in New Mexico by her single mother, who for all her New Age woo-wooism and partying and deficiencies as a mother, had been aware of Minerva's intellectual bent and encouraged her to pursue an academic career. He told about how he'd been raised as the "respectable" son, also encouraged to go to college and then pressed into managing family businesses: hotels, real estate, offshore accounts, shell companies. His first school? Bravo University, no less, though when he got confident enough in his English, he transferred to U.T. Austin. The business school, of course; he wasn't going to get away with studying something as useless as cultural studies. No offense, he'd added quickly—those would be his father's words, not his.

"Business school didn't teach you all you need to know, though," Minerva said.

"What do you mean?"

"Money laundering. Isn't that what your businesses are for?"

He paused before answering. "You'd be surprised what you can learn getting an MBA," he said. "By the way, do you know what is our government's latest plan to stop money laundering? Get rid of the $1,000-peso bill and leave the $100 as

the highest denomination. The one thousand bills are easier
to smuggle, is the thinking. They take up less room."

"Ten times less, I would guess."

"But there's one little miscalculation they're making."

"What's that?"

"It's the dollars that need laundering, not pesos!"

She laughed, but he didn't. He was too worried about his
father for merriment. A month earlier, his father had been
spirited away in the middle of the night by the Marinas and
the DEA. No extradition request. Just like that—disappeared.
Kidnapped. Now he spent twenty-three hours a day in a cell
the size of a parking space.

"The US does not respect the UN Mandela rules, which
limits solitary confinement to fifteen days at a time," he said.
"Talk about an outlaw country. A rogue state, as they say."

It was then that he'd caressed her tattoo of Coatlicue, the
Aztec goddess with a skirt of writhing snakes and a necklace
of hands, hearts and skulls. Eduardo made the questionable
comparison of that goddess with La Santa Muerte. He wasn't
interested in her disquisition on Coatlicue as a deity of life
and death in dialectical relationship; he wanted the tattoo to
signify Minerva's toughness, her lethality, because once again,
now stroking the calloused edges of her feet, he marveled at
the way she'd burst from her box to take down those two
"putos." Her attack was becoming legendary, he'd said.

Minerva sat up in bed and asked herself again what she
was becoming in his mind, and in the minds of his people. If
Juanita had gone to them with the gossip that El Junior and
the Chicana were fucking, what form might the legend now
be taking? Was he allying himself with some pocha who,
after having brought down his rivals' kidnapping operation
and set the plazas ablaze, was now emerging as some possible reina who would help save the Gamboa cartel?

With that unnerving thought, Minerva got up to shower
and dress. If he wasn't back by the time she'd made the bed,
she'd sit and wait for him as patiently as she could. When he

returned, her body language would acknowledge that yes, they had fucked, that had happened, it was fine, it was good, but it had been nothing more than a lull in the one story that should occupy them now, the story of her release. It had been a pleasant interval, something to temporarily kill the anxiety of waiting for the inevitable outcome. It would not lead to anything but getting her to the damned bridge.

She took her clothes with her into the gigantic bathroom—best to reappear in the bedroom fully clothed—and placed them on the granite vanity. She stepped into the shower's powerful stream. She thought she saw a shadow through the frosted door but did not call his name—best not to invite any may-I-join-you playfulness. But when she emerged from the steam, she saw that the game was on. Her clothes were gone.

"Okay, Eduardo, bring them back," she called. "Seriously. I want to get dressed, now."

Silence. What was he doing, sniffing her panties or something? She dried herself, her hair.

"Eduardo…"

She put on the plush bathrobe, went to the door and on the handle. The door was locked from the other side.

She didn't like games. Not card games, not board games, not sex games. Whatever game this was, it was in extremely poor taste. What was he thinking, locking her in, after her traumatic confinement in the box, after all his talk about his father's isolation in a tiny cell?

She pounded on the door. "Eduardo, open!"

A cold tingling ran through her limbs as she considered that something else was afoot, that having been lured away by the radio call, other people had taken over, and that was not him at all out there.

But then his voice came, almost mournful. *"Me viste la cara."*

She knew the expression. You saw my face. My *pendejo* face. You took me for a fool. It was strange hearing him speak in Spanish to her, and it shifted power in his direction.

"¿Cómo?"

He repeated it, louder, a shout.

"No entiendo," she said.

He went back to English. "You know Douglas Burris?"

"Yes, of course. He's my dissertation advisor."

"I think 'handler' is the word you people use."

She crouched at the door, shivering now, as he spun his outlandish story. Apparently, she was a spy working for Homeland Security. What particular agency was unclear, but the DEA most likely. She'd gone down to Bravo University to interview for the teaching job as a cover for her spying, and she'd managed to let a couple of common criminals snatch her. Which didn't say much about her abilities, did it? Still, she'd lucked out, because here she was, in a narco's lair, springing a honey trap, gathering information.

"Eduardo, you can't be serious. That's just... paranoid. Open the door and explain it to me. What makes you think this craziness?"

"What happened is that your Burris went to Bravo University to look for you and stupidly blew your cover. He doesn't know I have eyes and ears all over."

"That student... Quigley's student. Is that who you mean? He's been talking to my academic advisor, who's told him I'm some sort of spy? This is seriously insane!"

What she thought was him finally unlocking the door was instead the sound of some sort of brace being placed against it.

She rattled the handle. "Eduardo!"

"Cállate... ¡Puta!"

The epithet stung. Classic. She was the "easy," whorish gringa now. Yes, she had been beyond easy with him, considering it was *she* who had jumped *his* bones. But she hadn't sensed any contempt from him until now. She thought him too sophisticated for crude slut-shaming. But of course she would be a kind of prostitute in his eyes if she had fucked him because, as he insanely believed, she was some sort of spy out to get information from him.

Eduardo left. She heard the click of the bedroom door lock behind him.

A flying kick to the bathroom door—and the bathroom was big enough for her to get a running start—might do it in. But then what? Another encounter with a stun gun? If she lowered herself out the window, she would find herself in the garden dressed only in a bathrobe. And what then? She could perhaps force him to come in and get her if she stoppered the marble tub and sinks and let the water flow, flooding the bathroom. But that would just infuriate him more, and besides, she was afraid of electrocution. Who knew how the place was wired.

Better to wait it out until he cleared up the misunderstanding, talk again to this student. Demand to talk to Burris!

She lowered the heavy onyx toilet seat. She sat down and stared at the colognes and perfumes in cut glass vessels on the vanity. How totally ridiculous this was. Well, at least this kidnapper's bathroom was a step above the last one with its turd-choked toilet and bottles of urine. How did the saying go? The first time it's tragedy, the second time farce?

Before long, she heard the bedroom door unlock.

"Eduardo!"

"Shut up."

"What are you doing?" she said through the bathroom door. "Let me out!"

"Because I'm not the pendejo you take me for, I'm looking for devices in your clothes. Like tracking devices. *¿Cómo ves?*"

"Don't tear them! Those are my interview clothes."

"You still think you're going to have an interview? You're not in reality."

"Juanita cleaned that suit and she would have found any such 'devices' then, don't you think? Anyway, if they were tracking me, why would they be looking for me?"

In her mind she heard an *oh, yeah* in his pause.

"Eduardo, listen. You remember my call to my mother? If I am who you say I am, don't you think I'd have pretended to call my mother and instead called my handlers or whatever they're called with a coded message saying I'd stumbled on to something good? Why would they put me in the position I'm in now by crashing around the campus looking for me? Wouldn't they be more discreet? Are you listening to me?"

"Who says crashing around? Burris went logically to Quigley, the last person seen with you. Too bad for you people that I have ears up there!"

"Eduardo. Remember when I thought Quigley might be part of the kidnapping ring? That was crazy, as you yourself said. I wasn't thinking straight. Now it's you who isn't thinking straight."

"No? The difference is, I have evidence for my story, in the form of this Burris."

"Let's talk to him, Eduardo. Let's talk to him and clear this up right now. I know his number."

"I'm sure you do. And we're going to talk to him, you can be sure of that. We're going to negotiate. Let's see what he'll exchange for his puta."

There was that word again. *Puta.* A lot of insult packed into those two little syllables. Now she sought to really wound him back.

"Hey, Eduardo... What would the DEA want from a loser like you? What do they care about the crumbling Gamboa operation? You're a nothing, a nobody, *don Nadie*, and you know it. Why else would you be lying around with this 'puta' instead of taking care of business, or what's left of it? Letting a couple of ni-nis take it over. *¡Puto!*"

She heard his labored breathing. Had she gone too far? What did the insults gain her? The homophobic slur *puto* rang nasty in her ears.

"Eduardo," she said, trying to sound conciliatory. "Do you really trust this informant of yours? Do you believe him

over me? How do you know he's not working for your enemies now, the ones who want to take over the plazas?"

"Of course I trust him. He's my cousin. I don't even know
you!"

He slammed the bedroom door behind him.

Chapter Thirty

No return call from Omar, so Quigley set out to find him and try to stop him from passing Burris' lies on to her captors, or to beg him to rectify what he might have already told them. Surely Burris' exceedingly un-spy-like behavior—his barging into Quigley's office, his yelling—was proof enough that the man was bluffing, that he was no sly secret agent. Minerva, by extension, could not possibly be one either. There was danger, of course, in Omar's not only believing they were spies but in suspecting Quigley's attempt to dissuade him from this belief was proof that Quigley himself had gone over to that dark side. But he couldn't allow that fear to derail his search. He had to find that kid and use his professorial skills of persuasion, meager though they be, to convince him of the truth.

Quigley remembered Omar mentioning in class that he was from El Mesquital, an unincorporated community about five miles north of the Rio Grande. Considering the business Omar and his family were in, a stranger asking around for him, especially a white guy, was going to be awkward. Perhaps identifying himself as Omar's college professor would soften people up a bit.

The respect he got for being a "profe" had enchanted him at first, but today, as he considered matter-of-factly how things were spinning out of control and how his days at Bravo once again appeared numbered, he decided sourly that people down here respected only the title "Professor" and not what lay behind it. Like the fancy scalloped walls and ornate gates around the small, bedraggled ranches he was driving past, it was all about façade. About what you were on the outside. About signaling. Did his students truly want to learn? Some of them, sure. But most just wanted the title of college graduate, which signaled to prospective employers that they were able to show up regularly at a specific place and sit and perform clearly defined tasks. Certified proof that they could be captured and kept. "Just tell us what you want us to say!" one exasperated student had cried last semester, wondering what it was the profe didn't understand about this game.

The best way for a profe to survive and get ahead, everyone agreed, was to cultivate higher-ups. Norbert the Mexicanist had, in avuncular, mentorish fashion, taken Quigley aside at the fall faculty convocation and told him that "*personalismo*" was a thing "in the culture down here" and that Quigley'd do well to hobnob with the chean and other administrators, develop personal relationships with them. In other words, it was not advisable for Quigley to hole up and work on his scholarship, as it would be at a more research-intensive school, but to make connections and "network." Quigley took Norbert's advice to heart, and though he wasn't skilled at hobnobbing, he figured the next best thing would be to demonstrate his camaraderie by doing a lot of visible service, such as serving on search committees. What else was he supposed to do? Go to their churches, find out who the drinkers were and hang out at their bars, get married to someone in their circles and have kids their grandkids could play with? Well, maybe! Just think how different his present situation might be if he were real buds with the chean, the provost, heck, the president. Every one of them had deep roots in the area. Who knew what behind-the-scenes machinery, what influences, extending into Mexico, they could bring to bear on his behalf?

But he hadn't gotten to be their friend, so here he was, on his own, trying to track down the only local person he knew who could help him, his undergrad student Omar.

The midday heat had reached its zenith, but he had an ice-cold Topo Chico in the console, cold and fizzy enough to give him a jolt whenever the sun-slick highway threatened to hypnotize him. The map on his phone instructed him to take Business 83, so he exited and came to a stop at a light so ridiculously long that he had time to study the sign on the *yerbería* across the way. In addition to the usual herbs, votive candles and amulets, the store offered the white magic services of a shaman who, if Quigley was translating the sign correctly, specialized in bringing people "submissively" to one's side. He imagined the shaman needing, as in voodoo, one of the desired person's possessions in order to work his magic. Before Quigley could stop himself, he thought of the silk panties he had touched when rummaging through Minerva's bag in search of her phone.

It was said that people couldn't blush alone any more than they could tickle themselves, but Quigley felt his face get distinctly warm even with the A.C. blasting from the dashboard. Not only was it completely unacceptable to entertain such thoughts about Ms. Mondragón, but it was also perverse picturing her as submissive, which seemed so out of character for her. It was embarrassing to realize that after all his derision of superstition in class—and he was amazed at how superstitious his students were—here he was actually thinking a shaman's "white magic" couldn't hurt. Wow, he really was desperate—no atheist in this foxhole! But of course he didn't believe such things, not even enough to place a Pascalian wager on them. On the other hand, Omar probably did believe in it, and what would it hurt for him to know Quigley had a little magic working in his favor?

The inside of the yerbería was a wild tumult of candles, oils and unguents, brass buddhas, amulets, medicinal herbs and statuettes of every saint imaginable. The person who emerged from behind the counter was not the gnarled witch or pigtailed shaman he expected, but a voluptuous young woman in a tight red dress who did not, alas, speak English.

Half amused, she patiently awaited his floundering attempt to make himself understood.

"*¿Amarre?*" she asked, making a tying motion with her many-ringed hands.

Amore? No, no, it wasn't like that. But, yes, Minerva had been tied up, is that what she meant? Very clairvoyant. And she needed to be released to him, yes, that's right!

"*¿Foto?*"

He showed her his ID. Was she wanting to sell him that would require he identify himself?

"*No, no, ¡foto de ella!*" Now she was openly enjoying herself.

"*¿Ella?*" Oh, right. No, he didn't have a picture of her.

"*¿Ropa? ¿Alguna prenda?*"

Back to the rope. This woman was good; she knew Minerva had been tied up. *Prendre*, capture, that's right! Wait, wasn't *prendre* French? And *ropa*, now he remembered, that was Spanish for clothing. She indeed wanted a bit of Minerva's clothing for casting her spell or whatever. Quigley again flashed on the silk underwear he'd scrabbled around in, looking for her phone.

He left the yerbería clutching the large votive candle the woman managed to fob off on him, his face burning hot enough to light it. Its thick glass holder was stamped with the image of San Judas Tadeo, patron saint of desperate situations, or so said the label.

According to Google Maps, he was now in El Mesquital, which appeared to be just another centerless border community with a Stripes convenience store and an RV park for winter Texans—snowbirds, as they were referred to back in his home state of Minnesota, a term now almost as politically incorrect as was wetbacks for people coming from the opposite direction. A couple of brick McMansions, belonging to relatives of Omar perhaps, stood on barren land. Quigley imagined their tidy business: drug mules trudging up from the river, Omar and his people expertly hiding the goods in the snowbirds' Winnebagos (which the Border Patrol would never search), the snowbirds returning with rolls of cash for all. Probably not that neat and easy, but what did he know?

He spotted a party barn, one of those drive-through beer stores that always seemed to him to make a mockery of drunk driving laws. He intuited that its attendants were as likely to know Omar as anyone.

"Could I have, ah, a quart of Bud Light and, ah, a Topo Chico?"

"Forty do?"

"Uh... yeah." What? Fortitude? Yes, fortitude! What an odd word for a young guy like this to use. Probably knew Quigley was a profe and wanted to show off his vocab. For a while he'd been afraid that his tierra caliente outfit—the bone-colored linen pants, the Hawaiian shirt—made him look like an undercover cop, like Don Johnson in *Miami Vice*, the first grown-up TV show he'd gotten addicted to, back in the 80s. This kid wouldn't even know who Don Johnson was. Anyway, was there any way to not look like a plainclothes cop without looking even more like a plainclothes cop?

The attendant returned with a forty-ounce bottle of Bud Light and the beverage Quigley really craved, a fresh, sparkly Topo.

"Thanks, bro. Hey, bro? You know Omar Garza?"

"I know like three Omar Garzas."

"This would be *the* Omar Garza. Know what I mean?"

"No." The guy turned away with a brusqueness that shouted a silent "I sure do!"

Maybe he'd drink some liquid fortitude, ha ha, and come back by in a little while and ask the guy again. But as soon as he found a blot of shade, his phone pinged with a message from Omar himself: "Meet me at Pins & Cues Bowling in Weslaco. Just you."

Omar was taking every precaution, obviously. Even if he thought the CIA or DEA was following Quigley and planned to send an agent behind him toting one of their ultra-sophisticated eavesdropping devices, the bowling noise would surely disrupt the recording. Just as one of them was about to say something incriminating, boom, strike! Pretty slick. Omar had game, Quigley would be the first to admit.

Quigley's job, obviously, was to disabuse Omar of the notion that what Burris called the "intelligence community" had any interest in Minerva's situation. And to help him convince Omar of Minerva's innocence, Burris had prepped him with all kinds of background information on the genesis and operations of intelligence programs on college campuses, which Quigley had listened to patiently, though it seemed irrelevant and mostly smacked of bad-faith justification for Burris' own involvement in that business. The OSS, the virtuous precursor of the (admittedly sometimes) not-so-virtuous CIA, had started recruiting academics from all kinds of disciplines for its operations during WWII. As the Cold War revved up, the CIA began funding academic programs in American Studies and other disciplines to counter Soviet cultural propaganda. When the CIA got involved in "regime change" and assassinations around the world, student protests succeeded in curtailing its presence on campus, but after 911 and the Patriot Act and the formation of the Department of Homeland Security, programs like Bravo's Intelligence Center for Academic Practice were established at numerous universities. Particularly at minority-serving institutions, because in the rather unfortunate phrasing of a member of the congressional committee allocating the funds, "we need spies that look like their targets."

"But it's not just about recruiting spies," Burris had hastened to add. "It's training in open-source intelligence gathering and that sort of thing. And it's not all CIA. That's only one of the fifteen agencies under Homeland Security—fifteen!"

As if being only one of fifteen made the CIA seem less daunting. Burris' point, apparently, was the rather cynical one that there was low-hanging fruit ripe for the picking from this bloated, disorganized bureaucracy, and that academics, especially in the perennially underfunded humanities, would be foolish not to take it. This kind of Faustian bargain, if you wanted to put it in such melodramatic terms, was the only way to keep their disciplines viable.

Pins & Cues Bowling, announced from miles away by a giant bowling pin atop a mighty metal column, was housed in an enormous prefab metal building off Business 83. Omar sat munching on a mound of nachos in a dimly lit booth next to the exit he would presumably have darted out of had Quigley arrived with Burris or anybody else.

"I get it," said Quigley as he slipped in opposite him. "The bowling noise kills bugs, right?"

"But not the ones on you."

"You don't think I'm wearing a wire, do you?"

"Nah, nah. Put your shirt down, profe."

Omar's nonchalance came as a relief. He must have digested Quigley's messages and come to believe him when he said the whole Minerva-as-agent story was a concoction by Burris to get Quigley to confess the truth about her disappearance.

"Because why would Burris blow her cover if they had her exactly where they wanted her, spying on this junior narco? That wouldn't make sense."

"Yes, sir, I know. You don't have to keep explaining. She's not a spy, and neither is he. I've done some research."

That didn't just mean internet searching. Omar had a snoopy source in the Bravo ICAP, a graduate student and cousin of his on a Global Studies research assistantship. It seemed everybody was everybody else's cousin in this neck of the woods, when they weren't something closer. One of Quigley's students had even written about a "microcousin," though what he meant, of course, was "microcosm."

Omar's cousin in the ICAP had sneaked a few peeks at a file of unsolicited requests from random people, most of them cranks, recommending themselves or others for "service."

There was the student going on summer study abroad to Russia who wanted to know if the program needed him to do any "intelligence work" in that country. There was the disgruntled lecturer in chemistry who wanted to know when someone could meet with her to hear her out on the suspicious laboratory equipment ordered by her "Islamicist" department chair.

"And, get this," Omar said, "there was a letter from a professor in New Mexico wanting to give them the heads up about a job applicant for a new faculty position in Border Studies, a field he thought might fit in nicely with Bravo's ICAP."

"A professor named Douglas Burris."

"There you go."

The ka-bloom of downed bowling pins matched the ka-bloom in Quigley's mind as he realized the implications of Burris recommending Minerva for the job at Bravo. Burris was trying to go around the search committee and get this intelligence program to put in a good word for his gal with higher administrators!

"According to my cousin," Omar said, "the ICAP people weren't too impressed with either him or her. They realized Burris was just a professor who teaches a couple of courses in the intelligence program at his school, and she has zero experience in areas of interest to them. So basically, what Burris told you is true. He's just an overjealous professor trying to get his student a job and some influence for himself."

"Overzealous."

"Exactly. So, they just filed his letter away. They don't know anything about what's going on with her."

"Well, they do now! Your mole cousin does, anyway."

"Mole cousin. I like it. Name of my next rock band. Except that moles are very quiet, so that would be, like, ironical. Everybody in my family is extremely discreet, sir."

Yeah, right. So why was this cousin opening up to Omar about his snooping, and, more important, why was Omar confiding in his professor about this cousin? For some reason, he wanted Quigley to know he was now sure of her innocence.

"You told that junior she was some kind of agent, didn't you?"

"What could I do, boss? That's what Burris said she was. Gamboas needed to know. But I've corrected that. Now they know he was just bullshitting you. Just so *you* know, profe, she was never in any real danger."

"How do you figure?"

"After the Camarena thing? No way. Did you see *Narcos* on Netflix?"

"Nope."

"In the 1980s, the Félix Gallardo organization tortured and killed an undercover DEA agent named Enrique Camarena, down in Jalisco. Yeah, you don't wanna do that. The gringos came down on them like holy hell."

Quigley didn't buy that she was never in any danger. But that was moot now, if indeed Omar had convinced the junior of her innocence. He felt his body relax into the Naugahyde booth, practically melt into it.

"You know what's crazy, sir? For a while the junior was thinking you and the kids who snatched her were part of a conspiracy to get her planted in his place so she could spy on him."

"Me! What gave him that idea?"

"Don't look at me, sir! I just told him what Burris told you. But people get going on their conspiracy theories. Did you know that Minerva also at first thought the reason you didn't report her kidnapping to the cops was because you were in on it?"

"Jesus Christ."

"I know. Still, sometimes things aren't as innocent as they like to seem."

"What do you mean?"

"Well, like this program my cousin's in. The one that Minerva is definitely not in? It *is* about making spies. Like, ultimately."

Quigley rubbed his temples. He needed one of Omar's yellow pills.

"Okay. But Ms. Mondragón's hosts, so to speak, understand that she's never been directly involved in these programs, right?

"Correct."

"And everything's back on track to release her?"

"Yessir," Omar confirmed, bowling balls rumbling behind him. "Just a matter of time."

Chapter Thirty-One

A tapping on the bathroom door drew Minerva out of a fitful sleep and up from the bedding of bath towels she had laid on the floor. There had been nothing to do but wait for him, as calmly as she could, to clear up the absurd misunderstanding and come to his senses about this idiocy of her being some sort of American agent.

By the gentleness of the tapping and the forgiveness in his tone—*Minerva, Minerva*—he had done just that. Unless it was some trick... but what need had he of tricks?

"S'okay, s'okay," he murmured, the same first words he had spoken to her, utterances to soothe a cornered animal. "Come out and I will explain."

She wrapped the plush white bathrobe firmly around herself. Its gold-stitched monogram, she at last realized, stood for Robustiano Gamboa, Eduardo's father. She'd slept in it, if that turmoil could be called sleep, and now she double knotted its sash as she would her gi. Every time she'd woken up during the night, she'd tried to center on her breathing and cultivate *fudoshin*, imperturbable spirit. She had also rummaged through the medicine cabinets for some chemical that might calm her. All she found were prodigious amounts of Tums tablets and pink-crusted bottles of Pepto Bismol. Someone must have had a tremendous case of indigestion, and as she hadn't noticed Eduardo taking any of those remedies, she imagined it to be his father, the middle-aged capo whose robe she wore.

She opened the bathroom door. Eduardo glanced apprehensively at her hands, just as he'd done when they'd first met the night of her rescue, and said "s'okay" again, lifting his own hands in surrender. It was as if the clock had been reset and they were once again strangers. Except that now he knew something about her professional life she had no clue about: her program's involvement with the US government. As he revealed what he knew, a sense of estrangement from the person she had most trusted in that life, Dr. Douglas Burris, grew in her.

Eduardo told her he'd had a long talk with his contact at Bravo—his "ear," as he called him. The ear had retracted the warning he had raised about Minerva being an agent or spy for the US government. That warning had been based on fabrications Dr. Burris had told Quigley about her importance to the government's clandestine services, apparently to frighten Quigley into confessing what he'd done with her. The ear had investigated and discovered that Minerva had no such role. She wasn't even involved in Burris' program, though Burris had high hopes that she would be and had told his contacts at Bravo University as much.

"You don't know about that program?" Eduardo seemed skeptical. "For training spies?"

According to the ear, a number of US universities had centers devoted to teaching espionage and training spies. Burris was involved in the New Mexico center and had advised administrators at Bravo that Minerva had a lot of potential for theirs.

"I mean, really, you had no inkling of his plans for you?"

She thought back. She and Dr. Burris had discussions about many things in his paper-heavy office, in the sunny student union, in the classroom, and, yes, politics had come up, the Iraq war, Afghanistan. He'd been against the Iraq war. He'd deplored either the lack of good intelligence leading up to it or the Bush administration's ignoring of that intelligence, she couldn't remember which. It didn't occur to her until now that he'd been sussing out her own views on those things. Yes, the war was stupid, on that they had agreed. The footage of a bunch of nineteen-year-old American soldiers dressed up like space aliens trying to bludgeon an ancient culture into embracing their own told her how stupid it was. As far as developing better intelligence to prevent the kind of terrorist attacks that triggered such wars? Well, yes, that would be a good thing, she concurred, and she now recalled the look of satisfaction on his jowly face as he contemplated her.

One day, they'd gazed out the window at a group of students gathering on the plaza for an anti-war protest, and he'd asked if she went to any of those. She admitted she didn't, and he'd nodded, not so much in approval but as if to confirm something in his mind. "I just don't know what good protesting does," she remembered saying.

"You didn't remind him of the CIA's depredations in Latin America, all over the world?" Eduardo said now. "Their plots to assassinate world leaders and overthrow democratic governments? That water torture they use, what is it… waterboarding?

She'd heard of waterboarding. Dr. Burris himself had mentioned it as the kind of thing that could be stopped if the "right people" were in charge of intelligence gathering. He'd never alluded to those other things, the Latin American coups and assassination plots, but she imagined he'd dismiss them as things of the past, products of the Cold War, and, again, perhaps preventable had the "right people" been in charge.

Eduardo kept at it. "In all your studies, you never learned of the CIA coup against Arbenz in Guatemala, its role in overthrowing Allende in Chile, the hundreds of assassination attempts against Castro?"

"My field isn't political science," she said, and realizing how lame this sounded, corrected: "But of course I knew."

And she did, more or less. Though she'd never explored them in depth, those events lurked darkly around the edges of her consciousness, not that she could do anything about them.

"You think the shocks those guys in La Sal gave you hurt? You should feel the *picanas* the CIA uses. They have a voltage—"

"I seem to remember something about the CIA helping the Contras smuggle cocaine so that they could finance their war against the Sandinistas," she retorted. "I guess you drug lords would know about that."

That shut him up. Who was he, given the business he was in, to get on her case about politics? She was pissed, but she realized it was no longer at Eduardo, whom she could now forgive for suspecting her, but at Dr. Burris, not only for putting her in danger but also for taking her for granted as a future participant in his spying curricula.

"Maybe he was only trying to help you get the job," Eduardo said quietly.

"He didn't think I could get it on my own merits?"

Now she realized it wasn't even to help her so much as to keep his precious grant money coming in. He took her, but not his grants, for granted, ha ha. These were desperate times for the humanities, she remembered him saying more than once; they were being hurt by budget cuts, and anyone involved in them had to seek external funding to survive. "You'll see, Minerva, if and when you get into this business."

Now she better understood his confidence in her getting the Bravo appointment even without a dissertation in hand, and his assurance that "they" were going to like her, "they" being the administrators. He had a peculiar fixation on administration. The only way to get ahead in academia was through administration, he had told her many times, especially for faculty in marginalized fields such as hers. Administration led to a fatter paycheck, lower teaching load, assistants and, most importantly, a say in the direction of the university. She remembered thinking, why would she want less teaching in exchange for more bureaucratic paperwork? She loved teaching! But now she saw that he didn't have her desires in mind, but his. No doubt "placing" her in one of his spy programs redounded to his own administrative advancement. How many other students and advisees had he tried to pimp out like this?

She eyed the wadded clothes on the bed, the clothes for interviews she was suddenly not so keen on.

"I'll have Juanita iron those," he said. "And I'll call my ear to tell Quigley and this Burris that we've cleared up the misunderstanding."

"Wait," she said, her hand on his arm. "Don't have him tell them that. I have another idea."

He looked at her quizzically.

"Didn't you say you wanted to see how much Burris would pay for his *puta*?"

"I was angry. I thought—"

"I know. Now, listen."

Chapter Thirty-Two

Burris called Sandra with Eduardo Gamboa's demands for Minerva's release: that his father, Robustiano Gamboa must be freed from solitary confinement and that the US must not seek Eduardo's extradition.

Sandra laughed dryly. "The Bureau of Prisons is not terribly open to being told how to run its facilities, Douglas."

"Letting one guy out of solitary? How much of a threat does he pose, anyway, being in—what do they call it?—the general population?"

"It's easier for him to reorganize his business if he's not in solitary. Right now, he's not permitted to have unmonitored phone calls, receive mail or communicate with anyone except his lawyers."

"Reorganize? You said there's not much left of the Gamboa cartel to reorganize. As proven by the fact that the Fredo Corleone of the family's now in charge."

"The Fredo, that's funny. Where'd you get that?"

"That's what Quigley calls him," said Burris.

"Well, he has a point. This was the wrong son to step in, but the Michael Corleone of the clan's dead. It does look like the cartel is splintering. Maybe he's desperate to talk to Papá and get instructions on how to get things back on track."

"Maybe Papá can talk some sense into him. Like tell him to let the girl go?"

"Yeah, no. More likely when the kid tells him he's angling to get him out of solitary, Papá will tell him to apply this or that evil thing to the hostage to make it happen. Latinos hate solitary more than anybody. Not to stereotype, but they're very social and hate being alone. Speaking of desperate, how desperate did Minerva sound to you over the phone? You say she didn't say how they were treating her?"

"It was brief. She's upset, obviously. She didn't go into particulars. She requested we meet his demands. Demanded it, more like."

"Demanded? It's hardly our fault she was snatched, or that they believe she's some kind of agent."

Good, Burris thought. It hadn't occurred to Sandra that the way he had gone about looking for Minerva had alerted her captors to her supposed ties to intelligence.

"And what about the punk's no-extradition demand?" he said. "He sounded like a real asshole, by the way."

"Because guys making ransom demands never sound like assholes, right? Actually, there's never been an extradition request for him, and if this goes the way we're hoping it will, there won't be."

"Why wouldn't the US seek his extradition? After he abducted one of our citizens?"

"Because if we did, it would come out that we made a deal for her release, and the US doesn't negotiate for the release of hostages. Usually. Besides, the Mexicans would never go along with it. If anything, they'll try to protect the kid, if just to defend their sovereignty and all that good stuff. As it is, the way we snatched the father right from under their noses and without warning the politicians at the top got us dangerously close to getting all our DEA people down there PNGed."

"Peeyenjeed?"

"P-N-G-ed. Declared persona non grata. That would've been disastrous."

"Right. Okay, so you'll take it to whomever? Tell them what you have to. Tell them she's a highly valuable asset!"

"I'll talk to DOJ. But it's going to be hard working around PPD-30. That's the directive that says no negotiating for hostages taken abroad. No concessions."

"But it *can* be worked around."

"Read my lips. It's hard."

"Some concession, letting a guy out of solitary. Which is cruel and unusual punishment, by the way. Cruel, anyway. Look, if DOJ's not gonna play ball, why can't we just handle it directly?"

"Like send a batman and a skyhook down to extract the girl? You'd want to take that kind of risk?"

"Or cultivate someone on the inside, one of his people, to snatch her away from him."

"What does the word 'cultivate' make you think of, Douglas? Time, right? Takes time to cultivate. Plant the seed, wait for harvest. And who might you have in mind, anyway? This go-between, what's his name, Omar? How would this rescue work?"

"Omar, yeah. He seems genuinely convinced of Minerva's innocence."

"You sure about that? I thought you said you haven't even met the kid."

"He's skittish. But according to Quigley, yes, he realizes she's not an agent of any sort. And he's told her captors as much."

"So maybe they realize she has no value for us and they're just playing us. Or would Eduardo Gamboa seriously believe US law enforcement is interested in infiltrating his organization, now that we have his dad, the kingpin? I'd be curious to know how he came to this conclusion, if that's what he really believes."

Burris couldn't bring himself to confess his role in Eduardo's coming to believe Minerva was a spy.

"What does it matter?" he said. "He believes it, and we have to deal with it."

"I'd like us to talk to this Omar. You say he's one of Quigley's students?"

Burris had said no such thing, he was sure of it. "What for? He's just the messenger. Forget it, it was a dumb thought." Trying to make a joke of it, he added, "What, do you want to spirit him to a black site for an 'extraordinary rendition'?"

"Aren't we dramatic. In fact, since the border's a Constitution-free zone, we wouldn't have to go to such lengths. Plus, there's the Patriot Act. We don't need a warrant to interrogate him or search his phone or any of his stuff. Or anybody else's down there."

"Right. And ruin him as a go-between. Besides, how would coming down on him like that convince anybody Minerva doesn't have ties to us?"

"I concede your point. Smart man."

Was she patronizing him again? Well, this wasn't the time to bridle at it.

"Not that I'm saying we should sit around and wait for junior Gamboa to come around," he hastened to add. "Sandra, I've been thinking. Once we get her out of this, she's gonna make a great addition to our team. Just think about all she's seen from the inside about the collapse of a drug cartel!"

"All right, Doug." The condescension in her tone, with its little trip of a laugh, was now unmistakable. "I'll see what strings can be pulled. Bye, now."

The passive voice—*she* wouldn't pull any strings, though they *could be* pulled—allowed her to distance herself from possible failure. But the fact that she'd instructed him to call her from a secure line in the Bravo University library showed she took the situation seriously. That entire wing of the library housed the Global Security Studies and Leadership Databases and was controlled by Bravo's ICAP, which told Burris that the intelligence program had made greater inroads at the school than he'd previously known. It was still a work in progress, clearly. The little office into which the librarian had ushered him held only a metal desk and chair, a black phone and a photograph of the Pentagon on the wall. The large main room had only a scattering of tables and chairs and computer terminals. Not an attractive ambience for a culture studies scholar like Minerva, but she could liven it up. Put movie posters on the wall—not 007 movies or anything too corny or obvious, but… Well, she would know.

He meant what he said to Sandra. After Minerva's ordeal at the hands of those narcos, she was going to be gung-ho to join the US intelligence team. She'd want revenge. Any dismay she might feel upon learning that it was Burris' fault that she'd been taken for a spy would be quickly trumped by her having seen their cruelty first-hand. To Sandra, he was just going to have to admit he fucked up when he lied to Quigley about Minerva. But he would be able to spin it to Minerva herself as a blessing in disguise. Her eyes would be truly open now.

Chapter Thirty-Three

Eduardo snuck a diamond decanter of añejo tequila into the bedroom where he was pretending to be holding Minerva prisoner and poured shots for them both. They toasted their call to Burris. "¡Salud!"

"You're a good actor," Minerva said, knocking it back. "Sounded like a real hard-ass. Tipo duro."

"You sounded more angry than frightened," he said.

"Well, I *am* angry. He seriously thought he could groom me for his CIA program? Groom, like what pedophiles do. Or like brushing a horse, a racehorse being readied to make money for its owner."

"And the groom is the novio about to be married, no?"

"He presumes I'm going to want to marry into his family. The great family of spies. The 'intelligence community.'"

Eduardo poured them another, the amber liquid bright in the afternoon light.

"Here's to your father getting out of solitary," Minerva toasted.

He eyed her curiously as he raised his glass.

"It's a punishment not to be wished on anyone," she said, but did not add, "even on as ruthless an asshole as your father surely is."

Maybe Eduardo believed this empathy was Stockholm syndrome talking. Maybe he believed she had become the mouse so frightened it was going to the cat for love. Well, he could think what he pleased. They needed this hostage scheme to light a fire under him and pull him out of his lassitude, his paralysis.

Ah, the venerable female role, to inspire and energize men. She needed to tap into that now. The passivity he'd complained of in the La Sal kidnap victims and that he himself had displayed and seemed susceptible to falling back into when the scare was over and he realized she wasn't an enemy spy after all, that was the kiss of death. Another problem was that his men might keep believing she was an agent, an agent that had succeeded in catching him in—what did he call it?—a "honey trap." How much loyalty could the Gamboa *"hombres de confianza"* be expected to have then? But if they knew he was holding her captive to get his father, the boss, released and possibly back among them, it might keep them loyal for a while longer, buy her and Eduardo some time until they both could make their final escape.

"As for the second demand," he said, "I don't think the Americans will seek to extradite me. I don't think we needed to put that in. After the way the gringos violated Mexican sovereignty by snatching my father, there's no way Mexico's going to extradite me."

"It's still good to have that condition, just in case," Minerva said. She didn't have the heart to tell him that they needed that second demand purely as a negotiating tool, as something they could drop as a "concession."

"And if they don't go for any of it?" he wondered.

Was he weakening? Doubting himself again?

"Well, we tried, right? You're not going to have me chopped up and thrown out in the desert if they don't, are you? Another, what do they call it, femicide?"

"Don't offend me."

She told herself to go easy on the tequila. It brought out a flippant side of her that rubbed a lot of people the wrong way. She remembered that strong margarita she'd had with Quigley at that fateful lunch, their conversation about the movie in which a gringa disappeared into Mexico. Was it something she said then that had made him indifferent to her own disappearance? It must have been something pretty bad, if that's what had kept him from reporting her vanishing to the proper authorities. Or—now here was a novel thought— was Quigley himself involved in the spy school stuff and knew not to contact the police? Had he and Burris plotted to get Eduardo to release her by convincing him, through his "ear," that she was some kind of important agent he didn't want to mess with? Well, she and Eduardo had turned that around on them, hadn't they?

"Whether they meet our demands or not," Eduardo said, "the Marinas are going to come for you. As for me, I have a plan."

The plan was this: before the Marinas arrived to "rescue" her, Eduardo would escape down the tunnel and ultimately end up in a country yet to be determined, where he could live off "family money." Meanwhile, he'd bribe people in the office of the Mexican medical examiner to certify an unidentified body as his.

This gambit might not fool the Mexican authorities, but they'd go along with it so they could brag to their US counterparts that they'd closed the book on the Gamboas. And the end of the Gamboa organization would be a reason for the gringos to release his father from isolation and maybe even reduce his penalty.

"As for you," he said, "they'll be waiting for you with open arms at Bravo University."

She laughed. "Even if that were true, I don't want the job."

"Why not?"

"To be forever whispered about as the professor who got kidnapped during her campus visit? To have Quigley as a colleague? No, thanks."

"Screw that guy. You'll be a hero. You'll get to write your own ticket."

"No, no."

"And you'll be rid of Burris. I bet Bravo won't even care whether you finish your dissertation. No more asking that fucker for letters of recommendation because you'll have gotten the job."

"I *want* to finish the dissertation."

He did have a point, though, about the recommendations. Imagine having to keep kissing Burris' ass and humor him in his grooming until she landed another position.

"Es más, you won't have to participate in any of that spy shit to get funding for your research and stuff."

"What do you mean?"

Eduardo had another trick up his sleeve. Acting like a proper mañoso now, as narcos were called popularly in Mexico—crafty people, tricksters—he told her he was going to set up an educational foundation with monies from one or more of his offshore accounts. It would be a philanthropy tailor-made for academics seeking funding for disciplines such as, oh, border studies.

"That's insane," Minerva said.

"Why? I know all about philanthropy. I can even set it up so that the spy people will think it's coming from one of their own organizations. The CIA invents all kinds of fronts and foundations to funnel money to people. I remember this classmate of mine at Bravo, a Venezuelan guy in the petroleum engineering department, who bragged about being on full scholarship from something called the Oro Negro Society of Laredo. I looked it up. It didn't even have a website. I found out the guy's father had been an officer in the Venezuelan Army and this 'scholarship' was a part of the father's reward from the Americans for spying for them.

"And, speaking of oil money, did you know the Koch brothers subsidize like a thousand college professors all over your country to promote their politics and climate change denial? Look it up."

"It would still be blood money, your money," she said. "Drug money."

"But it's there," he said. "It's made. Why not put it to good use? John F. Kennedy's career was built on bootleg money, you know, and he's like a saint to you guys. Franklin Roosevelt's great-grandfather was an opium trader. So were the ancestors of this guy who ran for president a few years ago. Kerry. And Ford, Carnegie, those big foundation guys, they were no angels, either."

In words ringing of rote television commentary, he went on to blame the current problem on "America's insatiable demand for drugs" and the "failed war on drugs." She listened with half an ear until he added something she hadn't heard before: "Anyway, how else are our rural people supposed to survive? The free-trade agreements put Mexican corn farmers out of business, so now they have to cultivate the poppies that give sweet dreams to the Americans who are also out of work, thanks to those same trade agreements. The meth and the coke, the stimulants, are for those gringos who still have jobs, so they can work harder and longer."

"You're cynical."

"Not really. I think money can do good. Think about it. You could set up your own program. Make your own hires. Teach the raza what's really going on."

"Like how free-trade agreements fuel the drug war? Or how the CIA uses campuses to recruit spies?"

"For example."

"Offer some Eduardo Gamboa Fellowships?"

"Burris, who knows so much about grant-writing, will be able to give you some tips on how to apply."

"Touché."

They had another shot of tequila, and she could see the outline of his excitement in his jeans. He leaned into her, but she edged him back.

"It's not good anymore," she said.

He looked surprised. "¿Y eso?"

"I'm your hostage now, remember?"

"But that's just pretend."

"Yes, but even so. It interferes. The thought that—"

He backed off. "Yes, I understand," he said, relieving her of the need to bluntly tell him she couldn't stand the thought that Juanita and whoever else was downstairs might think he was up here abusing her.

"I'll go now. I've been here too long already."

"But make it seem to the people downstairs like we're still enemies."

"I'll yell at you something and stomp out."

"Yell it as if you mean it. But not the usual."

"What's that?"

"Puta. We're all so tired of that. Call me, I don't know. Cabrona."

She liked "cabrona." It meant bitch, but it also meant bad ass.

"Well, that… I sort of *will* mean that," he said, and they both laughed.

Chapter Thirty-Four

Omar sat in Quigley's office, feet on his professor's desk, regaling him with narco stories, as if their black humor would somehow make Quigley more comfortable with his chance involvement in that world.

"So, these Bravo students were down in La Reina," Omar said, "and they drive up behind a SUV that's stopped at a light...."

Quigley had heard this one before. It had become an urban legend, like the one about the narco boss who goes into the restaurant and doesn't let anyone enter or leave or use their phones until he's finished eating. Students had been using that one of late as an excuse for missing afternoon class, as if they were in the habit of having lunch on the other side of the border in fine restaurants frequented by narcos.

"The light turns green, and the SUV doesn't move. A big SUV, a Cheyenne, black with tinted windows. The students don't drive around it, don't honk, just sit there patiently. Finally, a guy gets out of the SUV and goes like this for the students to roll down their window. He tells them, 'My friend and I had a bet. He bet that you would honk or drive around, and we'd have to shoot you. I bet you wouldn't. I won, so here's your reward.' And he tosses them a fat stack."

"*Plomo o plata*," said Quigley. Lead or silver—Omar had taught him that narco motto.

"You remember that! Your Mexican is coming along, sir."

"Alliteration and assonance are powerful mnemonic devices."

"Whoa, yeah. Put that on the test, profe."

"Anyway, lovely story, Omar. So, what's the moral?"

"'Lovely.' That's so British. Or English. What's the difference, sir, between British and English?"

"No difference, Omar. And the moral?"

"The moral is: chill. Be patient."

"All good things come to those who wait."

"Even better. More poetical."

Omar took a sip of his Red Bull, and Quigley noticed his double-take at the candle to San Judas Tadeo on the bookshelf, flame guttering down deep in the glass.

"You don't think the situation is desperate, Omar?"

"A good luck candle just doesn't seem like you, sir."

"Desperate times call for desperate measures."

Omar had known Quigley to have a low tolerance for superstition. When at the beginning of this cold-ridden semester a chorus of bless yous had once again followed a student sneeze, Quigley mentioned a study demonstrating that patients who received "thoughts and prayers" actually got sicker. Everyone, including Omar, had looked at him nonplussed. Not a good start to the semester, and he made a note to keep the snark to himself. Bless you, yes. Now, let's move on.

"Sir, have you run out of chochos?"

"Chochos?"

"The yellow pills."

Quigley allowed that he was getting low, and Omar rummaged in his backpack. These were the same pills "they" gave their mules to calm them down when bringing product through Border Patrol checkpoints. When it came to smuggling, Omar always referred to "they" when pretty clearly he meant "we." Quigley had deduced that Omar and his relatives were what Norbert, the narcologist upstairs, called "brokers," the people who arranged, usually from a prudent distance, the transportation of the "merchandise," its warehousing, its loading and unloading. Sometimes they helped launder the ill-gotten gains, as when they lined up "smurfs" to open bank accounts with less than $10,000 in dirty cash— the bank was required to report any greater sum to the authorities—or sent them to casinos to buy chips which, after playing a couple of hands, they'd turn back in for a clean cashier's check. According to Norbert, it didn't matter to the brokers which cartels they got the dope from or which gangs helped them on the ground stateside. This made Quigley wonder how long Omar's loyalty to the Gamboas might last. When might he abandon the collapsing cartel and all interest in the Minerva affair, leaving Quigley and Burris to deal with it by themselves?

"Wash it down with Red Bull, sir. Red Bull and chochos, you're alert and relaxed at the same time. Can't beat that."

Quigley poured a slug of the lurid stuff into his plastic mug. "Omar, you haven't given up on convincing junior Gamboa that Minerva's not who he thinks she is, have you? He's still planning on letting her go, right?"

"I don't think he's gonna back down on his demands, whatever he thinks she is," Omar replied. "I mean, like you, when do you ever change a grade?"

"If I can be convinced there's been a mistake, of course I'll change it. What I don't understand is why he's being such a hard case all of a sudden. I mean, why hasn't he been holding her for ransom from the beginning?"

"I guess he thinks she makes a better hostage now. But I feel you, professor. The Gamboas don't kidnap. It's out of character, right? But remember, he's mad about the way DEA Special Ops went in and snatched his father. He doesn't want the same to happen to him."

Quigley groaned. It didn't make sense. If Eduardo Gamboa was afraid of the Americans coming to get him, why antagonize them by continuing to hold one of their citizens, especially one he believed to be an agent of some sort?

"What are his demands? What does he want in exchange for her?"

"You'll have to ask Burris that, sir."

But Burris was keeping a tight lid on the negotiations, as was reasonable. Omar might know and was just being coy, but come to think of it? Quigley didn't want to be in the loop. The less he knew about that, the better.

"The ball is in Burris' court now," he said.

"Exactly, sir. Stay calm, take *chochos* and carry on."

They walked together down the breezeway to rhet/comp class. Breezeway, what a nice word; and there was a breeze, mellow and moist, sighing in from the Gulf, swirling purple bougainvillea petals into corners, rustling the palm trees like a bustle skirt. That Omar didn't mind being seen with him was a good sign. Maybe Omar also felt off the hook now that the junior was in direct communication with Burris and the intelligence people.

Quigley's students greeted him cheerily. "Good evening, sir!"

He'd noticed a change in them recently. They still called him "sir" but were more at ease around him, as if they knew something was going on with him that called for their empathy. Did they, like Omar, know about the kidnapping and had they connected it to his nervousness in last Wednesday's class and his "hypothetical" about a woman disappearing in Mexico? It was difficult to know what they knew and didn't know. Their lives were a mystery to him, especially with regard to their ties to Mexico. Some, despite their Hispanic surnames, knew, or pretended to know, very little Spanish and claimed to never go across the border. Others could be heard speaking nothing but Spanish outside of class and seemed to spend half their lives south of the Rio Grande. Even the one blond kid in this English class, scion of the one of the pioneer Anglo citrus-growing families in the area, who had the annoying habit of sitting front and center and trying to co-teach the class, surprised Quigley when once he found him yakking in perfectly fluent Spanish with some of his classmates.

Maybe they knew nothing about the abduction and were just reacting to his chocho-induced laid-backness. Maybe his distraction endeared him to them, or maybe it was that he hadn't given them any assignments since his troubles began. Who didn't like a teacher that ignored the syllabus and just rambled on about weird stuff? It was said that teaching was the only profession in which the customers didn't want the goods.

In class, he began by speaking of the extreme youth of the universe. It was something he'd been thinking about a lot recently, and it gave him an odd kind of consolation in the midst of his troubles. If the universe was only 14 billion years old and the last proton wouldn't dissolve for another trillion trillion trillion years, didn't that put us a helluva lot closer to the beginning than the end? And then there was humanity's youth as a species. If the Earth's age were a twenty-four-hour clock, we'd have only been around for the last second! Or to put it spatially, we're the last coat of paint on the Eiffel tower! Or—his favorite analogy of all—if his outstretched arms represented the age of the Earth, one swipe of a nail file on this last finger would erase modern humanity! So take heart, people, we've only just begun!

The students regarded him with head-cocked curiosity, a couple of them smirking.

"Sorry, didn't mean to get carried away... standing up here pontificating like a sage on the stage. Have you guys heard that expression? A teacher has to decide whether he's going to be a sage on the stage or a guide on the side?"

A jocular voice from the back brought the house down. "You're more like a hippy on a trippy, sir!"

Omar had to get back home after class, so Quigley headed to his office alone. Too bad his newly discovered rapport with students had to come at the end of his teaching career. But now, now... it was all going to work out, was it not? It was in everybody's interest to have Minerva released/rescued as soon as possible. The Mexican authorities would avoid having an international hostage crisis on their hands. The junior narco would be unburdened of her. His narco rivals would have a better chance of getting the plazas they wanted. Omar and his family could resume smuggling as usual as soon as things settled down. And the intelligence community would evade any unwanted attention to its campus activities.

The halls were deserted, as they usually were after evening classes. Not that he dreaded encountering his search committee colleagues any longer. That morning, he had run into both Duarte and DeWitt, and neither had mentioned Ms. Mondragón. It was entirely possible they wouldn't mention her again until hiring revved back up in the fall when, in their grumbling about having to start a new search, they'd remind each other of that flake who'd stood them up in the spring, whatever her name was.

Nope, the halls were not quite empty. Here came Norbert, shouldering the burden of his book-laden bag.

"Scuttlebutt has it Gamboa junior's taken an American hostage," he said without preamble. "An agent of some kind."

Aghast, Quigley fell into step beside him. "How... Did you read it in the papers?"

"Just a rumor. Hard to believe. Little Eduardo Gamboa? Kidnapping an American agent? Female, at that."

"That's insane, right? Are you sure?"

"Nope. That's why they call it scuttlebutt. Matter of fact, I don't know why scuttlebutt's called scuttlebutt. Gotta look that up."

While Norbert clicked around on his phone to research the etymology of "scuttlebutt," Quigley dug discreetly in his satchel for his bottle of chochos.

"Aha, suspected something nautical," Norbert said. "It's the cask used to carry water on ships of yore. Gather round the scuttlebutt, swabs, I got gossip for ye. Now it's the office water cooler. How about that?"

Quigley had managed to knock out and palm a *chocho* without Norbert noticing. "Water, yes, be right back," he mumbled.

He swallowed the pill and let the icy fountain water bathe his face and jolt him into comprehending what he'd just heard. As soon as word got out that the son of a capo was holding an American spy, and a woman at that, it would spread like wildfire. Would it not? Why hadn't it already? Who knew where Norbert got his information?

"She's not in actual danger, though, right?" Quigley asked Norbert. That's what Omar had said, and Quigley wanted it confirmed.

"Why wouldn't she be?"

"Because the US will rain holy hell on them if they harm her, like we did to that cartel on the *Narcos* TV series."

"Ah, you mean the Enrique Camarena case. Yes, I think you're right that Eduardo Gamba won't harm her, for that very reason. Of course, he could always panic, do something stupid."

"But you said he was just a Fredo!"

"That's where the stupid comes in. Actually, I'd be more afraid of sicarios from a Gamboa splinter group getting at her, like that rogue outfit running the kidnapping operation in La Sal."

"I thought you said Gamboa's men took care of that bunch!"

"Sure. But recall that key term, 'fragmented criminal landscape.' There are bound to be other splinters. And to make an impression and scare everybody else, they can perform some spectacularly loco acts."

From what Norbert had told him previously about the decentralized narco world, crazies abounded who would love nothing better than to make their mark as top psycho by attacking and performing who-knows-what atrocious acts on an American agent. Fucking Omar hadn't mentioned that possibility.

Norbert, so seldom attentive to others' feelings, noticed how worked up Quigley had gotten.

"If you want to know more, you could talk to the people at ICAP," Norbert said solicitously. "You've heard of ICAP, haven't you? Intelligence Center for Academic Practice. Our little spy program has commandeered the whole west wing of the library's 3rd floor."

Quigley staggered to his office, thoughts racing ahead of the chocho. For a moment, he'd once again been tempted to spill the beans to Norbert. But what would that accomplish? The man would only have his scuttlebutt confirmed. And then what? No, Quigley could do better than that. Before something terrible happened to Ms. Mondragón and Burris fled and the spooks denied any knowledge of her, before Quigley became the fall guy, was left holding the bag, got thrown under the bus, or suffered any such cliché of downfall (unacceptable from his native-speaker students though laudable in his ESLers) he could get ahead of the curve by going full public. Launch the nuclear option. And by full public he meant not just the newspapers, but his congressman and senators, and the conspiracy-hungry talk jocks on AM radio. Plaster it all over the internet. He could go to that busybody OWLS group, the Objective Watchers of the Legal System, AKA Old White Ladies, who would no doubt be eager to believe his tale of an abducted American in Mexico. As would those fat militia fucks plunged in lawn chairs along the Rio, Gravy Seals cradling their AR-15s and watching for "wetbacks" but mostly for their waddling wives to bring them supper, semper pie!

Quigley would paint himself as the hapless victim of a bungled US attempt to insert a spy into a drug cartel, another example of government ineptitude, like that Fast and Furious operation in which the Bureau of Alcohol, Tobacco and Firearms allowed guns purchased in the US to get into narco hands, supposedly so they could track them. The media would eat it up.

Chapter Thirty-Five

Quigley squatted in the dry dirt of his carport, feeding antlions and trying to figure out how to avoid implicating Omar while still getting the press to believe his story. Burris obviously wasn't going to corroborate anything that would jeopardize his negotiations. And Norbert's "scuttlebutt" was just that: hearsay. Everybody would want to know who this mysterious student was, the one Quigley said had a hotline to the woman's abductors and possibly knew where she was being held. But Quigley remembered Omar's warning about ratting him out. And you never knew to what lengths Burris' spooks might go to silence him. Going public did not confer the protection it seemed to when the idea first struck him. Without any supporting evidence or witnesses, he was just some nutty professor with a CIA conspiracy story.

The ants he was feeding his lions were leaf-cutter ants. He'd listened to the ants the night before as they denuded his hackberry tree of its fresh spring growth. In their thousands, their activity made a steady hissing, like sand being blown across dunes. He'd given up trying to control them. He'd tried drowning them, feeding them toxic baits and sprinkling them with diatomaceous earth, a diabolic product dredged from the sea floor that was supposed to cut them up like microscopic shards of glass. None of it worked. According to a biology professor he had chatted with at a graduation ceremony, they lived by the millions in colonies as deep as twenty feet below the surface, where they cultivated a fungus from the chewed-up leaves. You had to admire their industriousness. If they hollowed out the ground beneath his house and he were to plunge some night into its sinkhole, okay, fine. Swallow me, earth, I had it coming.

The ants carried their bits of leaf aloft like parasols and clung to them tenaciously, legs flailing in the air, as he lifted them off the ground and carried them to his lions. After a few taps of his fingers, they fell into the sandy funnels. They tried clambering up the treacherous sides, but as soon as the lion, its long jaws visible in the hole below, sensed them nearing the top, it would kick up a spray of dirt, and the ants tumbled back down. Sooner or later they slid into the vertex, where jaws would snatch them and pull them under. The insatiable antlion in this particular cone had already consumed three ants.

Quigley sensed someone behind him, watching. "What the fuck!"

Burris beamed at him, arms crossed over his big belly.

"How'd you find me?" Quigley demanded.

It took Burris a moment. "You live here."

Quigley stood up and looked out at the squat grapefruit tree loaded with fat fruit, the green anole lizard puffing out its bright-pink dewlap, the prehistoric-looking chachalacas chasing each other raucously around the droopy-leaved tree cactus, and it was all very familiar. Yes, he supposed he did live in this weird place.

"I've got great news," Burris said. "The BOP was planning to release Robustiano Gamboa from solitary all along. His lawyers are calling his kid with the news as we speak. And DOJ's never even issued an extradition request for Eduardo, the kid. So, conditions have been met, just like that."

BOP? DOJ? Solitary? Huh?

Burris kept going, relishing his knowledge of the inside baseball. He seemed oblivious to the fact that Quigley didn't know what the conditions for Minerva's release were.

"Seems old man Robustiano Gamboa's arrest and quick extradition was done in a rush to meet DOJ drug-war certification, which in turn was required to wrap up the new international trade deal. But the Gamboas are local heroes down in that part of Mexico. Junior's grandfather even has a street named after him in La Reina, you know. There's pressure from the Mexicans to not treat Robustiano harshly. And the American authorities have concluded the Gamboa organization is done for, anyway. Minerva's kidnapping is proof enough of that. Gamboa plazas are falling into Zeta hands, or maybe to the Juárez cartel—nobody really knows. If anybody has a clue, it would be Robustiano, so he's probably collaborating with US intelligence on that, which would be another reason to get him out of solitary and to go easy on his son as well."

Quigley waved the words away. "So, the kid's gonna let her go now is what you're saying."

"Why wouldn't he? The old man's lawyers are already arranging which border bridge he's going to drop her off at."

The thought of the press now coming to grill him about his role in the whole thing, rather than he going to them, curdled Quigley's relief.

"I'm not going to be the fall guy, Burris, the guy responsible for it all. I'm going to tell them how I got caught up in a bungled spy caper. That you guys used me, and used Bravo, as pawns in your game to infiltrate a Mexican drug cartel, and you screwed it up."

Burris smiled. "So, the street kids that kidnapped her initially were working with us too? All part of an elaborate plot to get her close to the feckless heir to a failing local drug cartel? And for some inexplicable reason I blew her cover? Pretty wild."

"Okay, so maybe she just used me and the job interview as cover to scout out La Reina and Las Brasas, a known narco hangout, and it went wrong. In fact, it was she who urged me to take her down there, you know."

"William, you do know her rescue is going to be handled on the Q.T., right?"

It was to no one's advantage for any of it to go public, Burris assured him. Keeping it quiet would spare Bravo University the embarrassment of everyone knowing one of their job candidates had been kidnapped; the intelligence community wouldn't have to invent a cover for its involvement in her rescue; and the Mexican government would be saved from having to admit an American had been snatched by bad guys on the La Reina central square, literally within view of the border.

"And, of course, it's to your advantage to keep it on the downlow, William."

"No shit. But what about Minerva? Why wouldn't she tell it like it happened?"

"Why? She has a fascinating story to tell, obviously. But who's going to believe her? Who's going to corroborate it? No. I'll let her know right off that the only person this side of the border to know what happened to her besides you, Omar and me and my people is someone whose secret knowledge of it is very much to her advantage. Hers and yours both."

"And that is?"

"Dean Garza."

"That's two people."

"I'm sorry?"

"The chair and the dean. Those two guys look like twins, haven't you noticed? They think alike, they share everything, they're both named Garza. We call them the chean."

"Well, they're going to treat you with kid gloves."

"How's that?"

"You're associated with us now. You and Minerva both."

"By 'us' you mean these campus intelligence programs or centers or whatever the fuck?"

"That's correct. The source of much external funding for resource-starved schools, my friend, courtesy of Homeland Security."

"And how exactly am I associated with you? By the accident of having your girl snatched from under me?"

"Most of the details are classified. That means not available to your, what did you call them, chean? Very useful term, 'classified,' you know. Prettier than redacted. Which any written report on the matter would have to be, heavily, should it ever come to that. Lots of ugly black strikeouts."

"I'm assuming my own role in the matter is classified."

"You'll be known to have assisted in ways unspecified."

"And Omar, I trust, gets redacted completely."

"Omar? Who be Omar?"

Burris was having a good time. The woman hadn't even been released yet, and here he was acting as if he had the whole thing wrapped up and all was fine and dandy.

"What are you doing, by the way?" Burris asked, half-amused.

"Feeding the antlions."

"Aha."

An ant had made it to the top of a cone when the lion below gave three quick flicks of sand, unsettling the angle of repose. The ant slid down into its serrated jaws.

"I've been wondering," said Quigley, "how does all this spy stuff jibe with academic freedom? You know, the idea that our funding shouldn't come with strings attached?"

"Oh, there's always some faculty who are going to ask that very question," Burris said. "But what matters is administrators' lack of attachment to that lofty concept."

Burris was as full of himself now as he'd been the day he'd first appeared in Quigley's office. And he was surely right that the chean—and the provost and president, for that matter—were less concerned with the provenance of monies than getting it. Plus, the War on Terror, the War on Drugs, the War on Whatever gave cover and justification for programs whose lack of transparency would have made them unwelcome on college campuses not long ago.

All righty, then. As long as the chean believed Quigley was in with the spy bunch and chugging along with that gravy train, he could ask them to take him off committees—notably, search committees. No more service until he got tenure. Just leave him alone and let him publish his three required articles. If the articles got accepted for publication before his years on tenure track were up, he'd insist that they consider him for early promotion and tenure. Then, maybe, he could put all his courses online and go live on the beach somewhere. Or apply at his leisure for a position at another institution, one far from the border. Of course, making even a lateral move to another school would be more difficult once he got tenure at Bravo, unless he became a star scholar, which he had to admit seemed unlikely, or got administrative experience. Surely the chean could concoct something for him along administrative lines. Assistant dean or program director of something. Maybe something within the ICAP or another spook program, for which he could have Burris write him a letter of recommendation.

Silver linings in all this.

Meanwhile, he'd write up (sans redactions!) a full report about this whole affair, to be released by someone he could trust, in the event something unpleasant happened to him. Or that he would release in the event they did something to Omar. He owed the kid that much, didn't he? But he couldn't threaten that yet, not until he wrote it up. For now, he had to make it seem like he was only concerned with his career.

"No more service," Quigley said, "until I get tenure. Also, I'm going to want to teach some upper-division classes in my field, not just core courses like they make me do now. I guess that's what happens when they hire you as a 'generalist' like they did me. They flatter you by telling you that means someone with a great breadth of knowledge, but what they're looking for is someone they can bitch down to teach freshman comp and sophomore lit year in and year out. I wanna teach in my field, do my research, and come home and feed my lions. That's it."

"Why, of course," said Burris. "I'm sure they'll understand."

Chapter Thirty-Six

Eduardo burst into Minerva's room the next morning with the news. His father's lawyers had called to confirm that his father was getting out of solitary. Not only that, after Eduardo escaped and faked his death, they were going to argue for a reduction in his father's sentence, because with both his sons dead, the plazas fallen to his enemies, the oh fuck money and businesses forfeited, what more did the gringos want?

"Slow down! The *what* money?"

"OFAC. That's your Treasury Department's Office of Foreign Assets Control. They seized everything of ours they could. So yeah: oh, fuck. But it's not everything, okay? There's still money for what we talked about!"

"You told the lawyers about your disappearing scheme?"

"Yes, so they can warn my father. Reports of my death are going to get to him, and I can't have him believe them. And the lawyers are bound by confidentiality, no? Also, well paid."

Of course they were. As would be the persons who helped him escape, fake his death and get him to that mysterious third country. Presumably, Juanita and whoever else had remained with him here at the end would get generous severance pay, their families taken care of as well, in an ongoing gesture of Gamboa charity.

Minerva didn't have time to ask him about those things. Events were happening too fast. His radio crackled, one word clear to her: *listo*. Ready.

He gave her a hurried kiss and told her to hang tight there in the bedroom. The Marinas, the real Marinas this time, would be there any minute and knew exactly where to find her. They'd take her to the bridge, where she'd be met.

"By whom?"

"Burris. I don't know who he'll have with him, that's up to him. Play it cool with him, my advice. Use him like he's used you."

He handed her a wad of dollars.

"What's this for?" she asked. "Pain and suffering?"

"You need a new cell phone."

"I could buy ten with this."

"Buy ten."

And he was gone, tunneling toward his new life.

Within minutes, the Marinas were in the garden, baby-faced kids in full battle gear peeking around the orange spikes of the bird of paradise plants. The door behind her flew open, and there stood an older soldier, round pocked face under a round, netted helmet.

"*Señorita Minerva Mondragón,*" he announced, rather formally.

"*Presente.*" It sounded both appropriate and ridiculous.

He held the door open for her. She walked past the tarnished knight, who was still facing the wall, and down the stairs and into the solid sun. Marinas draped a Kevlar vest over her shoulders and placed a too-big helmet on her head, gently adjusting its chin strap. The older one held out his rough hand to help her up into an armored vehicle, sitting her protectively between himself and another soldier.

They bounced in a heavily armed convoy along the same roads those others had brought her in on, and it was possible to believe these were the same guys, moonlighting for the narcos then and back at their day jobs today, the only difference being that now they weren't wearing balaclavas. The morning was bright and cloudless, the air perfumed with a grapey sweetness, the landscape dotted cheerfully with green-barked little trees sprinkled with yellow flowers. On the slope of a rocky hill people were dismantling a big letter of whitewashed stone that she could swear had been a "G"—for Gamboa, no doubt.

She could tell they were getting closer to a city by the proliferation of plastic bags caught on the thorns of the mesquites. They paraded down the streets of La Reina, its pedestrians jumping onto the sidewalks to give them a wide berth, cooking and cloacal smells penetrating the armored car.

The pock-faced soldier placed a balaclava on her lap.

"*¿Y esto?*" she said.

"*Para que no la vean.*"

"*¿Quiénes?*"

He spun his finger in a circle to indicate everybody around. But what did she care if people saw her face, snapped pictures of her? She had nothing to hide or fear. She gave the mask back.

They came to a stop next to the little military tank at the foot of the bridge. Across the river billowed the stars-and-stripes whose enormousness had astonished her when she and Quigley had crossed—what, five, six days ago? Going innocently to lunch, guacamole on their minds. She flashed on the episode in *Pulp Fiction* where Bruce Willis returns to the danger zone to fetch his father's watch, promising his girlfriend he'll be right back and they'll get pancakes; a whole lifetime of horrific things happen to him in the couple of hours he's gone and then he's back to, where were we, honey? Ah, yes, pancakes.

No press to accost her, but they were being watched from across the street by a gaggle of official-looking men, some of them in suits. A few had their cell phones raised, recording the scene. A muscular man in a tight black t-shirt and wrap-around sunglasses got out of a black SUV with tinted windows and ushered her into the back, next to Burris.

"Minnie, oh my god." He reached over to hug her, but she put her hands up, warded him off.

"I understand," he said, drawing back. He kept staring at her, astonished.

Minerva supposed that what he "understood" was that, despite her assurances to the contrary over the phone, she'd been so traumatized that she couldn't stand to be touched right now by a man, any man. Or something like that. Because why the shocked expression? Compunction was the proper response. Or was he truly unaware that he had almost gotten her killed, or worse? That he'd been the sole source of the rumor that she was an American agent, and that if this "ear" Eduardo had at Bravo hadn't convinced Eduardo of her innocence, he might have disappeared into his tunnel sooner, leaving her to his rivals and who knew what horrible fate?

If he didn't know this, she wasn't about to show her hand by telling him. *Toréale,* Eduardo had advised. Burris was the toro, and she the matador.

US border agents waved them through without the driver even having to roll down his window. She could smell Burris' sweat even through the gushing conditioned air.

"I know you told us you haven't been… mistreated," he said at last, "but if you need to see—"

"No."

"Even if it's just to talk to someone—"

"No. I'm fine, Doug, honestly. All I need right now is some sleep." She could explain that those scratches he was eyeing on her arms were only from the thorny roadside plants she'd hidden in the night of her escape, but why give him the relief?

"Okay. Okay, then. I'll take you to the Mission. Best hotel in town. You'll be perfectly safe. I'm staying at a place called the Capri, not far from there. Call me at the Capri for anything. This university puts job candidates up at the Super 8, can you believe it? It seems strange to just leave you alone, but if that's what you need…"

Minerva let him babble. She'd never been more repelled by his bearish, bearded face, pink tongue working in the mouth hole. When he said, "Tomorrow, or whenever you're ready, we'll drive back to Albuquerque," she said nothing. Like hell we will. But she let it go, for now.

She reached for the carry-on he'd rescued from Quigley and lugged it to the front desk. See, fool? Strong and not visibly injured. You'll just have to imagine the invisible injuries and hope they haven't done too much damage to your promising little spy girl.

She gazed into the lobby as he got her a room, stone-fountain courtyard exploding with exuberant tropical foliage. He handed her the key card, and as she turned to the elevator, he cleared his throat.

"You know, Minnie, we'd like to keep this whole, ah, incident on the Q.T. It's US policy not to negotiate with terrorists. Fortunately, I was able to get an exception made, in your case. But we need to hold up our end and be discreet. I'm sure you understand."

So he'd done her a big favor, had he? So she owed him one for engineering her rescue from the notorious terrorist Eduardo Gamboa? She tightened the fingers of her spear hand around the grip of her carry-on and did her best to smile.

"The college dean knows about it, and since he's as one with the department chair, the chair too. Quigley, of course. But that's it. It's in no one's interest at Bravo for the story to get out. As far as the search committee is concerned, you were sidetracked by an unspecified family emergency."

"I won't say a word," Minerva said, trying to quell any note of sarcasm. "We'll just put it behind us. Move forward."

Minerva went up to her room and unpacked. At the top of her carry-on lay the pumps she'd changed out of before crossing the bridge with Quigley, the ones that went with her Jackie Browns. Tucked into her clothing was her laptop, but she didn't power up the computer just yet. First, she needed to calm down, center her *chi*. She stood beside the bed and brought her hands down in front of her chest to *gassho*. She pressed her palms together, and then her fingertips, as hard as she could. She performed the action over and over until she felt calm, her nerves balanced. And then she fell onto the bed and didn't wake up till the next day.

Chapter Thirty-Seven

Quigley sipped his latte and felt himself float above the imitation Frida Kahlo paintings in the student gallery below his office window. What a great new morning. Punching the "call end" button after getting off the phone with Burris last evening had popped him out of the nightmare. Minerva Mondragón had been delivered unharmed to Burris at the international bridge and was now resting up at the Mission Hotel on this side of the border. Burris had assured him that as soon as she got her bearings, she'd be heading back with him to New Mexico, where she could put the ordeal behind her.

If it felt too good to be true, it was. Because here was Charles DeWitt, standing at Quigley's office door and telling him to saddle up because they were going to interview Ms. Mondragón in a couple of hours.

"Oh, come on," said DeWitt. "It's not that shocking. You look like you've seen the *chupacabras*. You know how things work around here. The chean says jump, so we jump, right?"

"But how—"

"Who knows. Wires crossed everywhere. I guess her family emergency, or whatever, got resolved, and she called to say she could come down now. Chean is blaming the office work-studies for not passing on the message. Welcome to the Bravocracy; when in doubt, blame the work-studies."

"She's here? On campus?"

"Yep. She called this morning to see about rescheduling her campus visit, and the chean asked her to come right on over. They're interviewing her as we speak, and we're next. I know, it breaks protocol, but that's our Bravo. See you in the meeting room at 3:00?"

As soon as DeWitt's footsteps receded down the hall, Quigley called Burris.

"I don't know what to tell you," said Burris. "I'm as surprised as you are. I had understood she would be going back with me. I was just waiting for her call to say she was ready. I see she has her own plans."

"The chean—you know, the chair and the dean—you say they know I've been collaborating with you, but they don't know the details of her disappearance. Anyone else know the whole story? I gotta know, Burris. This can't come back to bite me. I thought it was a done deal!"

"People in the intelligence community know. Some of them. But so what? They're on our team. Go interview her for the job, William! Play the hand you've been dealt."

"What cards am I holding? How much does *she* know? Does she think I've been on the 'team' all along? That I knew exactly what to do the moment she disappeared, which was to contact you so we could mobilize her, her, her what does the team call it, 'extraction'?"

"That sounds like a fine account to me," said Burris. "The term we need to avoid, I'll remind you again, is 'negotiation.' There is no negotiating with terrorists, never has been. Minnie and I didn't get to talk much, but that much she understands. And we haven't talked about you at all."

Quigley slipped his cell into his satchel and stared at the cold foam in his cup. Goddammit, he should have called her at the hotel last night to ask her how she was, express heartfelt sympathy and, most importantly, feel her out, ascertain how much she really knew about his role in the debacle. But he'd thought, he'd hoped, he'd never see her again. He had believed Burris when the man said he would be spiriting her off to New Mexico for a debriefing, believed him when he said she'd want nothing more than to put the nightmare behind her. Now, what if Burris were to tell her that Quigley had never been on the team, had abandoned her in La Reina, and that he, Burris, had to come down here to rescue her? What if he tried to make himself look good at Quigley's expense?

But instead of calling her, he'd downed several shots of bourbon, danced to a couple of chill-out jams, and flopped into bed for his first dead sleep in a week, confident that by the time he was back in his Bravo office the two of them, former job candidate and her faculty mentor, would be on the road, this ill-fated place in their rearview mirror.

Now here she was, on campus, coming after the fucking job. Fucking unbelievable. He hoped to hell that Burris was right, and she didn't know Quigley's real role in her ordeal and would believe the narrative in which he'd notified Burris and the "team" right away of her disappearance. But Burris and certain unspecified team members knew the real story. How long were they going to cover for Quigley, and why would they, really? Very trustworthy people, these CIA types, never known for treachery, right? As if he hadn't read all of Graham Greene's work. As if he didn't live in Greeneland, a hellish place where nobody trusts anybody.

Burris had assured Quigley that the chean had been briefed. Now that Minerva had returned, was it too late to call in one of the chits that Burris' narrative provided, which was to ask to do less service? Specifically, was it too late to be released from search committees, starting with this one? Why of all things would he want to be taken off this hiring committee, they would want to know, and just a couple of hours before the committee was to interview her? Were he and Ms. Mondragón not "teammates," wink wink?

Where were those chochos? Then he remembered that, as part of his private little celebration last night, he'd flushed the last of the yellow things down the toilet. He had told himself that he no longer needed to be cloaked in their fuzziness. Now he had to go interview her naked, as it were, the nightmare having returned as an anxiety dream.

Quigley dropped to the floor to do push-ups. Exercise would clear his head, dissipate the stress. He did jumping jacks—let his office neighbors think what they pleased about the thumping. He reminded himself that he had one over on Burris, namely, that it was Burris' fault that her captor had come to believe she was a spy. If Burris told her Quigley hadn't raised the alarm about her disappearance, Quigley could counter and say Burris had put her in danger by coming down and yelling about her being a valuable member of the intelligence team, blowing her cover. Omar could back him up on that, if it came down to it— but where the hell was Omar now? Burris had better stick by the narrative that they'd both done everything by the book and that her being held hostage as an enemy agent was perhaps inevitable, given the narcos' own intelligence.

After all, Ms. Mondragón was, however marginally, on the team, was she not? Therefore, she should also go along with that narrative, should she not? Maybe not on the team in the way Burris had portrayed her initially, maybe she was deep on the back bench, but she was still a player, or wannabe player. With a wink and a nod, Quigley would give her to understand that he had known they were teammates all along and had conducted himself accordingly. He had known not to go to the cops, either Mexican or American, but straight to Burris and report that one of their own, one of their team members, had run into trouble. How her captors had discovered her ties to the team, tenuous as they were, was anybody's guess. (Because surely she didn't already know about Omar; why would the narco boss reveal to her, his hostage and a presumed spy, the identity of his own counterspy?) What mattered was that in the end it had worked out. They had freed her. Tragedy averted. Here she was. Welcome, Ms. Mondragón, most welcome.

Five sets of twenty push-ups, three hundred jumping jacks, two hard slaps to his face and a fresh application of deodorant later, he found himself in the windowless meeting room across from Cindy Wheeler and Charles DeWitt, and next to the EEOC rep, the old guy from engineering. Esmeralda was still trying to round up Diosdado Duarte.

"Hope he shows," a visibly annoyed Cindy Wheeler said, "because I don't think it's exactly kosher to conduct the interview without our committee chair."

"Not sure it matters," said DeWitt. "I get the feeling the chean already considers her hired."

"How so?"

"Just by the fact that they've been so eager to accommodate her and that they've already interviewed her. Big smiles on their twin faces."

"Well, that's just great. Yay for faculty governance."

She looked around for support. Quigley shook his head in agreeable disgust, but the EEOC rep maintained his stone face. What did this rep, a STEM professor, care about politics in the lowly College of Humanities?

"At least we kept the line," DeWitt said. "Remember, last week they were going to sweep up the funds allocated to this appointment?"

"What about her teaching demo?" Cindy said.

"I think we're going to have to dispense with that, as it would involve keeping her over until next week. Ah, here he be, the chair of the chopped liver committee!"

"What's that?" said Diosdado in bashful confusion as he settled into the high-backed chair they normally reserved for the candidates.

"Why is she here now and how did she even get here?" Cindy persisted. "Or are we to believe the work-studies rescheduled her visit and forgot to tell everybody else?"

"Stranger glitches have happened around here," DeWitt said.

The rep cleared his throat. "I don't think we need to get into that with her."

"Why not?" Cindy said.

"We'd be circling around her family emergency then, and we need to avoid getting personal."

"Not to mention how stupid it makes us look to have our work-study students handling travel arrangements," said De-Witt.

Esmeralda opened the door. "Professors, I present to you Ms. Minerva Mondragón," she announced, with exaggerated formality.

To Quigley's amazement, Minerva came in wearing the same black suit with the sharp-collared white blouse she'd been wearing when she got off the plane. She made the same entrance, smiling and relaxed, she would have made had she and Quigley gotten to campus without incident from Las Brasas. The only difference was that now she shook Quigley's hand with the same nice-to-meet-you as she gave the others, nothing in her demeanor betraying that they had already met.

"So sorry about the mix-up—"

"These things happen," DeWitt assured her.

"I hope nobody's in trouble." She gave a barely perceptible flick of a glance in Quigley's direction, gutting him.

"Not at all," said DeWitt. "The important thing is that you made it!"

What might the chean have promised DeWitt in exchange for being so uncharacteristically accommodating? Quigley wondered.

Since Diosdado had unthinkingly taken the chair which was normally the candidate hot seat, DeWitt motioned her to the empty chair next to Quigley. Well, at least Quigley wasn't across from her now. He didn't think he could face her. He could smell her, though, the citrusy scent of the soaps and shampoos all the hotels in the area carried, as if to remind guests they were in the land of the lemon and the grapefruit. On the floor next to her she placed a Bravo tote bag, her laptop gleaming within.

Cindy started in brutally. "Will you be able to take the job if it's offered to you?"

The EEOC rep cleared his phlegmy throat. "Let's not get into 'able.'"

"Let's not get into 'able,'" DeWitt repeated with a laugh. "Spoken with a true engineer's eloquence. Okay, strike that question."

"No, no, I can answer that," said Minerva. "I most certainly am able to take the job, and, if offered, most certainly will."

"Now there's your eloquence," Diosdado chortled.

Everyone seemed to relax then, even the engineer, because what did he care about English faculty gibes? He earned twice as much as they and taught a lighter load. He'd invented some sort of sensor that Homeland Security had adopted for the border wall and that Bravo, which held the patent, had profited handsomely from. Wait a minute... was he, too, on the spy team? That would make a lot of sense, given his field of expertise. But his stone face gave no sign of knowing about Quigley, Minerva, any of it.

The hot seat turned out to be the catbird seat as Minerva parlayed the predictable questions with scary self-possession. What contribution does your research make to the discipline? Would you be interested in helping develop a cross-disciplinary program in border studies, and if so, how would you go about it? Quigley tried desperately to remember what questions he'd had for her, listening to the others with only half an ear. Where would you seek funding for this program? someone asked. Her answer to that one, or what he heard of it, mystified him a little. No mention of grants and such from the intelligence services, as might be expected. But what exactly were those international foundations she was alluding to for external funding? No one pressed her. Cindy was sulking, Diosdado hopelessly shy and DeWitt laid-back as he obviously considered her hiring a fait accompli. Maybe the chean had promised him a perk if he expedited it. My god, was *De-Witt* on the team?

DeWitt lobbed her a softball. "So, tell us about your poetry."
Who doesn't like to talk about their creative work? But her swing at this one was awkward. "It speaks for itself, I guess?"

"Perfect," said DeWitt.

And then it was Quigley's turn. All he could think of was the question meant to bring things to a close, and which properly was Diosdado's: "Are there any questions you have for us?"

She looked at him with a butter-wouldn't-melt-in-her-mouth expression and asked, "Is it safe to go to Mexico? Like to La Reina for lunch, say?"

Chapter Thirty-Eight

Her interviews, the dinner with faculty, and the au revoirs finally over, Minerva sat in the Mission Hotel courtyard, sipping a nightcap margarita. It was not as good as the tart and slightly smoky one she'd had at that interrupted lunch with Quigley in La Reina, but good enough to celebrate the end of such a long, strange day.

Poor Quigley. He'd looked so terrified from the outset of the search committee interview, and then she'd blanched him out with her wicked question to his question. He had not shown for the dinner. *Ay, qué mala eres, Minerva.*

That morning, she had woken up feeling far from wicked. She had awakened weeping—actually sobbing—worried about Eduardo and his escape, but also grieving about her lost relationship with Burris, the man who had most believed in her, had stuck with her and been a good mentor to her throughout her graduate years. What a disappointment to discover that he had tried to influence her hiring by touting her as a good prospect for campus spy programs, just to further *his* interests. As if she were his creature, sprung from his Jovian head like the Minerva of mythology. It was unforgivable. And then to have put her in actual, mortal danger by telling Quigley that she was a spy! How stupid could he be? Imagine if it had been Eduardo's brother, or any narco other than Eduardo, whom she had ended up with. She'd be just another femicide right now, her bloated body tossed into the huizaches and pecked by zopilotes.

Eduardo... He had given her no method of contacting him, and unless he contacted her, or was captured, she would not know his fate. Reports of his death would be either the best of news, or the worst; they would mean his ruse had worked, or it hadn't.

Halfway through her first cup of dull hotel-room tea, she'd decided to call Bravo to see what credibility she had left there. In her mind, she could hear Eduardo's encouragement. He'd like the idea of her leaving Burris hanging, waiting with growing worry for her call to say she was ready to go back with him to Albuquerque. "Move on," Burris had advised, saying exactly what you're not supposed say to someone traumatized. But okay, Doug, my mentor, will do.

She picked up the bedside phone and had the front desk connect her to Bravo University's Languages and Literatures Department.

Nope, no credibility at all left at Bravo University, to judge from administrative assistant Esmeralda García's hostile tone. "*Ay, sí, no. Now* you call." But then someone had interrupted her, and she put Minerva on hold. She returned with a tone so comically honeyed that Minerva was sure they had either concocted some humiliating trick to play on her or, more likely, the person who had called Esmeralda aside knew what had happened to her and was desperate for damage control. Esmeralda asked her melodiously if she would be able to come in that morning to talk to the dean and the chair. Ten o'clock?

Her Jackie Brown suit could use a touch of ironing, but other than that it was good to go. The little tears that Juanita had so meticulously repaired had not reopened. After ironing the jacket, she had tucked two of the $50 bills Eduardo had given her into its breast pocket. It apparently had not occurred to idiot Douglas that her abductors might have relieved her of her cash. She descended to the lobby and had the doorman hail a cab.

Middle-aged and round-faced, and with identical trim moustaches, rumpled white shirts and murky ties, the college dean and the department chair looked so much alike that faculty called them collectively the "chean," or so Dr. DeWitt would tell her at the dinner; and she might have deemed it racist if it weren't so true. They regarded her with a kind of wary marvel, observing her scratched hands and, without mentioning the kidnapping directly, asked how she was "holding up."

"I'm okay," she said. "Okay," pronounced neutrally like that, could mean just about anything, and she needed to play this by ear. No doubt the possibility of a lawsuit weighed on their minds, and there was no point in disabusing them of that until she heard what they had to offer.

"Okay, then. Okay, well." They glanced at each other, then looked down and flipped through the pages of her CV.

"Your teaching evaluations are excellent," Dean Garza murmured. "Three semesters as a T.A.?"

"Yes. And I'm looking forward to my teaching demonstration here."

"You were scheduled to teach one of Dr. Quigley's Introduction to Literature classes?"

"I was."

They studied her to see what effect the invocation of Quigley had on her, and again she tried to keep her expression neutral. They offered no apology for his having put her in harm's way by taking her to La Reina. Maybe doing so would be to admit liability on the university's part. Or maybe, it occurred to her suddenly, they believed she and Quigley both worked for intelligence and had known very well what they were getting into. Could Dr. Burris have possibly spun it that way to them? She wouldn't put it past him.

"Well, it's Friday, and Dr. Quigley's class doesn't meet on Fridays," said the dean, "so we can skip that. We know you need to get back home. Would you be able to meet with the search committee today? Assuming we can round up its members, or at least a couple of them."

They didn't ask her about her research or request any assurance that she'd have her dissertation finished and defended by the hiring date. Their tone was so solicitous and they made the committee meeting sound so pro forma that she knew the job was hers if she simply kept mum about her abduction. Just as Sensei advised "grabbing the enemy by the belt," they figured keeping her close meant less chance she'd blab, and they were right. She'd be part of the Bravo "family" and protective of it. Besides, she wouldn't want to be known for being the professor who got kidnapped, would she? Another thing guaranteeing her silence, and which they couldn't have known, was that she wouldn't want any attention drawn to Eduardo in the event he made good his escape.

On the other hand, if they believed she and Burris and Quigley were in intelligence, they'd know that the three of them were bound by oaths of nondisclosure and that none of them would talk anyway. If the dean and chair believed that, and had any balls, they'd tell the lot of them to take a hike, so as to keep their school from being turned into—what was Eduardo's term?—a "spy school." But they couldn't do that, Eduardo would say in his cynical way, since there was good money attached to becoming such a school and since Bravo, like many institutions on the highly militarized US side of the border, was "captured" by Homeland Security.

"We'll get someone to show you around campus," her new captors offered. (Or were they *her* captives?)

Minerva said she'd be fine exploring on her own. She'd go to the student union for a bite, visit the library.

"You sure? All right." They shook her hand. *"Bueno, pues. Bienvenida."*

That "bienvenida" sealed it, in her mind. It was the "welcome aboard" pronounced to the just hired.

The warm spring air smelled vaguely of onion, and she realized how hungry she was. A campus map in a kiosk showed the student union to her north, and she wandered in that direction, pausing to admire a baobab-like tree, its elephant-leg trunk studded with fearsome thorns. (Did *every* plant down here come with thorns?) At its roots hopped a bird with a lemon-yellow breast and eyeliner as pronounced as that of some of the students eddying around her. "Kiskadee!" one of those students pointed out brightly and kept walking. Other birds strutted on the grass, raucous blue-black ones, squawking and chasing one another.

The food court was already getting crowded with students lined up at the *taquería* and the Subway. What had Quigley said was the favored meat in these parts? The dish he was going to order at Las Brasas? Cabrito. She ordered cabrito tacos.

They were a little gamey, but the green sauce was great, as were the deckle-edged hand-made tortillas, flipped on an enormous comal by a laughing girl in tight jeans. Was there any other student center in the country that offered goat tacos on homemade tortillas? She believed she could come to like Bravo University very much.

She surveyed the crowd. Yep, student body at least 90% Hispanic, just as advertised. One young man, standing by the taquería, would have blended into the crowd if not for the way he was eyeing her. He approached.

The bucking bronco on his t-shirt, bringing to mind the rampant horses on the ni-nis' Ferrari shirts, gave her a start. Then she realized it was only the Bravo mascot.

Barely pausing, he said, "He's okay. He made it," and disappeared into the crowd of students.

It took her a moment to comprehend what he'd said and to realize this person must be the go-between, the student who had acted as a contact between Eduardo and Quigley. The famous "ear." She had seen him so fleetingly, she wondered if she'd even recognize him if she saw him again. Not that it mattered. He had given her the message she was waiting for. She was elated.

She strode into the committee meeting on the air of that elation, feeling almost obscenely self-confident but trying not to seem too full of herself. They must have thought that the family emergency that had delayed her had come to a happy resolution, though the portly, courtly chair, Diosdado Duarte, kept glancing worriedly at her hands, perhaps wondering what those scratches might have to do with it. Except for the question about poetry—damn Dr. Burris for making her list her attempts at verse on her CV!—she'd fielded their questions with aplomb. She'd even charmed the crusty old guy, Dr. DeWitt, though the linguist, Wheeler, remained taciturn. It had been reckless to mention that she hoped to get money from "international foundations" without being able to name one, but fortunately they hadn't pressed it. Her question to Quigley's question had been cruel, perhaps, paralyzing him as it did in front of everyone. Downright uncollegial—almost like abandoning a job candidate in Mexico, or something like that.

Duarte drove her back to the Mission Hotel, stuttering through his shyness in an effort to make small talk about the area, lauding the Gulf coast beaches and avoiding—studiously, it seemed to her—any mention of Mexico. She had many questions about life on the border, but she spared him a grilling. She would learn it all in due time.

The bedside phone in her room blinked red: a message from Burris, offering her congratulations. In a bemused voice, he said Professor Quigley had informed him of the interviews. They were buds now, he and Quigley, it would seem. He praised her for her "brio" and for having seen "the advantages of forging forward" and not letting "the obstacles in life, no matter how great, impede her," yadda, yadda. He understood they had gotten her a plane ticket, so he'd just drive by his lonesome (ironic self-pity here) back to Albuquerque—see her there when she returned!

She didn't call him back. She didn't have to. He was going to sign off on her dissertation no matter how she scorned him. Even if he didn't, she knew Bravo would hire her without it finished.

The restaurant the committee had taken her to, Pancho's Villa, sans Quigley and Wheeler but with a couple of other faculty members, was so noisy that they mostly gave up on conversation and succumbed to an ear-splitting mariachi. The committee sensed her contentment, and their apologetic good-byes in the parking lot—yeah, sorry about that, forgot Friday was mariachi night at Pancho's—were jocular and collegial.

Now she was finally alone, savoring her margarita amid the cycads and crotons of the Mission Hotel courtyard. As the tequila bloomed pleasantly in her stomach and she thought back on the campus visit and the dinner, it seemed pretty clear that what Doug had told her was true: none of the Bravo faculty, except of course Quigley, knew about her abduction. The committee valued her for her scholarship and teaching and would recommend her on her merits and not just as a consolation prize for her ordeal, or as a way of buying her silence about it. In other words, they appeared to believe they had captured the best, or at least a very good, candidate.

Captured. That sounded like Eduardo again. After all, *todo es un secuestradero, ¿no?* Everyone was a captive in some way or another. He'd been captured by his family's business, Quigley by his job and career and fear of losing them, Burris by his grants and the intelligence agencies that funded them. Eduardo would have appreciated Dr. Burris having once referred to the "golden handcuffs" of tenure, meaning it was hard for your institution to get rid of you once you had it, but also then harder for you to get a position in another. Captured, yes.

So why, then, would she not also be captured by this "foundation" Eduardo had promised to set up? Good question, but a bridge she'd cross when she came to it, so to speak. For now, it was delicious to think of using that money to set up her own program, with its own curriculum and conferences designed to expose and undermine, in one way or another, the very ones Burris wanted to involve her in.

Chapter Thirty-Nine

Burris piled mega-calories onto his plate at the Capri breakfast buffet, squares of overcooked scrambled eggs and soggy hash browns and curls of cold bacon, fuel to get him through as much of the no-country-for-old-men badlands as possible without having to stop. Spring break was over for his school, classes were resuming on Monday and his work here in Texas was done. His bags were in the trunk, and he had his driving sandals on, the flesh of his pudgy red feet bulging between the straps.

Yesterday afternoon, as he was awaiting—hoping for—a call from Minerva to tell him how the interviews had gone, he had instead received a second one from Quigley. Minerva, Quigley informed him dolefully, had indeed interviewed with both the chean and the search committee, and Quigley had observed the secretary, Esmeralda, drawing up a Memorandum of Employment for her.

A contract already? Burris tried to tamp down his astonishment. "What can I say, William? That I'm not glad that my most promising student seems to have secured a tenure-track position?"

"What if she tells everyone what happened?"

"She won't. She wouldn't want people to think she was hired as a consolation for her ordeal. Nor would Bravo want it known that one of their job candidates was abducted, and I have no doubt they've told her as much."

239

"But what *if.*"

"Well, what if she does, William? All you have to say is that as soon as she disappeared, you contacted me immediately and I took care of it—without alluding to any negotiation for her release, of course. We both acted as expeditiously as possible. Win-win. Hell, you'll be a hero for helping bring down a drug cartel!"

"Yeah, right."

"No need for you to mention Omar, or that you knew what had happened to her and sat on it for days until I squeezed it out of you. Right?"

"Uh-huh."

"You sound uncertain."

"She might already know all that."

"How? You think her captors gave her a play-by-play? In any case, I'll be sussing her out about it on our drive back to Albuquerque, see how much she does know. Okay?"

"I don't think she's driving back with you. Esmeralda's already booked a flight for her, leaving tomorrow."

As soon as he'd gotten rid of Quigley, Burris called the Mission Hotel and left a message for Minerva to tell her how impressed he was at her having gone forward. Impressed, but not surprised. If he knew anything about her, it was her—he searched for the word—"brio." He'd like to hear all about it: the campus, her future colleagues. Call me when you get the chance, Minnie, he'd said. And congratulations!

To his disappointment, she hadn't returned his call. No doubt too busy. She would've gone to her candidate dinner last night, and this morning she was probably hustling to get on her flight to Albuquerque. Still, it added to the letdown he'd felt on learning that she'd gone to her campus visit without calling him beforehand for a little coaching. He, her mentor, her advisor, patiently waiting in a motel to hear from her, after liberating her from her abductors! And no word.

He would give the girl her space. Let her find her center, get her head together, ha ha. If she needed to distance herself from him as part of her healing process, so be it. People like Minerva instinctively knew what they needed, and no doubt she sensed trauma counseling was not his bailiwick. If she needed someone to talk to, she had her mother, and the UNM counseling services.

He got up for more coffee. If he were to venture a lay opinion, he would say her anger was a healthy thing. He'd first detected it on the ransom call, which had been handled by a trained Homeland Security negotiator. Her indignation had been palpable even over the spotty connection—*just do what they say and get me out of here!* He'd thought, *that's my girl, spunky as always.* It was still very much there when they'd picked her up at the bridge, and it had flashed through his mind that perhaps she was annoyed that there wasn't a bigger contingent to meet her: press, government officials. Or maybe her irritation stemmed from something as trivial as the fact that he hadn't gotten out from behind the protection of the black SUV's tinted windows to greet her. Surely she understood that he hadn't wanted his likeness captured by those sinister-looking men across the street?

As for her continued coolness toward him, was it possible, as Quigley seemed to suggest, that she had some knowledge of the peril he'd placed her in by the bull-in-the- china-shop way he'd come looking for her? If so, she'd eventually come around to understand that he'd only been trying to save her, and that his threats had in fact succeeded in getting Quigley to reveal her whereabouts. Burris had then quickly mobilized his people and won her release, right? All's well that ends well. This was something he could easily explain to her if it came up. More likely, she was suffering from a kind of survivor's guilt and blamed herself for causing him such grief and obliging Homeland Security to negotiate for her. That they hadn't actually had to concede to any of her captors' demands was something else he hoped to explain to her.

Whatever it was, she'd soon pull out of it. Of that he was confident. She was one tough cookie. They made 'em resilient in the South Valley of Albuquerque. That was his Minnie!

A Lincoln Navigator as hulking as Homeland Security's drove into the parking space next to Burris' car. Two men heaved their great bodies to the ground and lumbered into the restaurant. They left the SUV's engine running with the air conditioner on—he could hear its panting. They heaped their plates and sat down at the table next to his, where they could guard their laboring vehicle, keeping itself cool so they would have only ten steps of humid discomfort between two climate-controlled bubbles.

They were sitting too close for him to be able to talk to Sandra privately. He took his phone and coffee to a back table.

"I guess you can come in from the cold now, Doug," Sandra said after Burris had told her about Minerva and the job.

"Cold? It's sweltering as hell down here."

"Wait. You don't know the expression, Mr. Spycraft?"

"Ha! Of course I do."

"You had me there, Douglas."

"I'm feeling chipper."

"Well, I have news that'll buck you up even more. Unconfirmed reports have it that your junior narco's been killed."

"Ha! In a confrontation with the Marinas, I presume?"

"Resisting apprehension. Isn't that what they always say? But don't tell her till we get an affirmative from Center, okay?"

"That's gonna be hard to resist, speaking of. But sure, I'll wait. You know, this whole experience is going to make her a great fit for ICAP. Like I said before, her eyes are really gonna be open now to the narco threat and the need for robust intelligence on the border here. Maybe she can turn this kid Omar, bring him aboard too."

"Turn him into some kind of double agent, huh." That mocking tone again. "Getting a little ahead of yourself again, aren't you, Doug?"

Well, maybe so. But as he headed west, the sun rising in his rearview mirror, a white heron flapping languidly in the growing blueness ahead, a faint citrus-bloom fragrance wafting in through the cracked window, he felt great about what he'd done. At the end of the day, this whole affair was going to redound handsomely to his performance metrics with the Center. When Minerva came around, he'd entertain her with some of the Cormac McCarthy parodies he was already spinning as he *ingressed into that no country for old men, world's burning perimeter of unshadowed ground naked beneath the faultless sky....* He'd get a good laugh out of her for sure.